The Blessed Touch

The Blessed Touch

Aqib Farid Al-Qadri

Suffah Foundation

Typesetting by Beacon Books
www.beaconbooks.net

ISBN: 978-1-910051-00-9

First Edition   3,000 Copies   June 2014

Published by Suffah Foundation.
PO Box 1625
Huddersfield
HD1 9QW

www.suffahfoundation.com
email: info@suffahfoundation.com

Printed in Turkey by Mega Printing
export@mega.com.tr

Available from:
Markazi Jamia Masjid Ghausia, 73 Victoria Road,
Huddersfield, HD1 3RT, UK

Suffah Institute for Education, Block No.2 Islami Colony,
Airport Road, Bahawalpur, Pakistan.

Contents

Introduction to Suffah Foundation

Islam came as a religion of peace and tranquillity spreading a canopy of mercy over the entire world. By implementing its teachings, the Muslims presented a civilised society before the world; one which raised the status of humanity and strengthened their ties with their spirituality. By spreading the message of equality and the deliverance of rights, they were able to eradicate all types of racial, territorial and all other types of prejudices.

Unfortunately all that remains of this golden era of peace and tranquillity are its memories. However, the golden rules, based upon which the early Muslims were able to conquer the hearts of the people of the world, are still with us in the form of the Qur'an and the teachings of our beloved Prophet Muhammad ﷺ. The brilliant Islamic teachings of high moral conduct, outstanding character, fairness, compassion and mercy, if adopted, can once again bring contentment to our lives and allow us to spread happiness into the lives of others.

This message of peace has always been delivered and passed on from generation to generation by our scholars and spiritual leaders (Sufi's). Through their teachings and practices they were able to nurture the souls of their students and present them before the world as ambassadors of peace, striving to strengthen such values as tolerance and dignity and respect for all human beings.

In today's ever more troubled society, where humanity weeps and that impeccable moral conduct is long forgotten, there is a dire need for us to once again take up the teachings of the holy Prophet ﷺ and in light of these teachings, work to further this noble cause on all fronts; academic, religious, spiritual, social, missionary and humanitarian fronts.

The establishment of *Suffah Foundation* is an important link in this very chain, through which we hope to propagate this message of peace and mutual respect in a more organised and effective manner. By doing this, we hope to propagate a better understanding of Islam and strengthen the beliefs and practices of the Muslim Ummah, in effect helping people to better their practices and awaken sentiments of compassion for humanity within them. Whilst also trying to bridge the gap between Muslims and non-Muslims through mutual understanding, peace and cooperation.

This is a unique opportunity for you to also become part of this global movement for peace and mutual respect by implementing the teachings of the Qur'an and Sunnah within your lives.

We pray to Almighty Allah, through the mediation of his beloved Messenger ﷺ to keep us all under his guardianship- always.

Ameen!

Umar Hayat Qadri
Chairman, Suffah Foundation

Foreword

The Blessed Touch – the very name of this book speaks volumes of the bounties and blessings that Allah Almighty showers upon His chosen people. A glance at the contents reveals that while compiling this unique book, an endeavour has been made to make it a comprehensive compendium of verses from the Holy Quran, unanimously accepted ahadees and references from other authentic sources that encompass various themes and topics concerning the blessings associated with Allah's special bondsmen. We often confront misguided people who believe in the false notion that all are equal in Allah's sight and that you cannot have any benefit from those who are dead irrespective of their exalted position in their lives. Now I feel greatly relieved because this book gives an ample evidence to nullify the claims of those who are doing nothing but groping in the dark.

Imbibed with the love of the Holy Prophet ﷺ, Mr. Aqib Qadri, the author, is ever intent upon removing all misconceptions regarding the exalted position that Allah has bestowed upon our beloved Prophet ﷺ. His English translation of the Holy Qur'an adapted from *"Kanz ul Iman" (The Treasure of faith)* stands as a testimony to the fact that he is vehemently striving to disseminate the cause of Imam Ahmad Raza Khan Barelvi (RA), who throughout his life waged a war of words against those who blasphemously try to undermine the glorious status of Muhammad Mustafa ﷺ. The care with which he chooses English expressions to convey the real meanings is enormously amazing. Even his other books and articles are deceptively simple in style. In a very qualitative language, he easily communicates even highly sophisticated facts and ideas.

3

Dwelling again upon *"The Blessed Touch"*, I must say that the way this book has been arranged is undoubtedly marvellous. There are nineteen sections and each section has a number of chapters, logically and chronologically developing the themes and topics from general to the specific. This makes it quite easy to build up arguments against those who have gone astray by Khawarij cult.

Particularly from Section 5 to the concluding one, corporeal miracles and the blessings of Allah's selected people and their relics have been highlighted. To establish the conspicuousness of the Holy Prophet Muhammad ﷺ, the instances of his blood and urine put forward a solid proof that he ﷺ stands aloof from the entire creation. Full credit goes to Mr. Aqib Qadri for this exquisite effort to put all the relevant material at one place. As this has to serve as a reference, the long list of topics and sub-topics is justified in view of the sensitivity of the matter.

In the concluding remarks, I would recommend that every Sunni Muslim must read this book, not only to kindle his own faith but also to counter the ignominious propaganda launched by those cursed people who take delight in undermining the elevated souls. May Allah shower His unbound bounties and blessings on Mr. Aqib Qadri and his family.

Prof. Muhammad Iqbal Siddiqui

(College of Engineering, Majmah University)

Preface

All Praise to Allah, the Supreme, and countless blessings & peace upon our master Mohammed, the leader of the creation.

The miracles of our dear Prophet Mohammed ﷺ have been enumerated and studied all along the centuries since his blessed arrival. Billions of man-hours have been spent wondering at the marvelous qualities and traits of the "Leader of the Creation". It is my firm belief that Allah the Supreme has granted these extra-ordinary & miraculous qualities to His special bondmen, in order that they become signs for people of intellect. For those who do not agree to accept the existence of the Supreme Being, or do not agree to accept the truthfulness of Islam, these miracles are the overwhelming proofs for them to bow their heads in submission.

On many occasions Allah, the Supreme, has showed the disbelievers great signs in order for them to accept faith or to the believers in order to strengthen their faith. Miracles could be in the form of a great blessing for the creation or a punishment for the wicked, or a sign for those who encountered the holy Prophets (Peace be upon them all).

A miracle is an extra-ordinary event – unachievable through material means by normal human beings. It defies accepted norms of science, bewilders the spectator. The witness accepts defeat, acknowledging his inability to achieve what has been shown. It is this trait - of making the witness accept defeat - that gives this event its name. In Arabic it is therefore called "Mu'jizah" – one that causes the witness to acknowledge inability to achieve the same.

Many such events and miraculous powers of Allah's closest bondmen are listed in the Qur'an itself – and many more in the sacred sayings of the Holy Prophet ﷺ.

May Allah shower His choicest blessings on the great scholars of Islam who painstakingly memorized and wrote down these gems in huge voluminous books of Exegesis (Tafseer), Traditions (Hadeeth) & Noble Character (Seerah). Some authors narrowed down their choice of miracles to the physical miracles – especially in the books of Seerah. I had the good fortune of reading some of them. Whilst there is a huge treasure of such books readily available in Arabic, Persian and Urdu, a very limited amount is available in English, which prompted me to take up this work.

Furthermore, we hear from various sources that all human beings are created equal and that all the beloved bondmen are also humans, so it is incorrect to accord any special status to them. This book will attempt to dispel the notion that all are equal in Allah's sight, for indeed Allah states in the Holy Qur'an:

"Indeed the more honourable among you, in the sight of Allah, is one who is more pious amongst you." [Surah Hujurat 49:13]

This book is an attempt to compile the various evidences of miracles in the following categories:-

1.   Allah's special favours upon His closest bondmen.

2. Miracles of the pious bondmen through their physical characteristics which prove that, although human, they have superior physical traits and spiritual status.
3. The evidence of blessings in the things built, used or touched by such noble souls.

The compilation attempts to provide proofs only from the Holy Qur'an and well known Hadeeth sources. It excludes the miracles that occurred due to the prayers of Allah's close bondmen and also excludes those that came as a punishment for the disbelievers. Although not very exhaustive, I trust the readers will find it a good reference to such topics.

I dedicate this book to all of Allah's beloved Apostles, beginning with our master the Holy Prophet Mohammed 🌿, to all of Allah's noble friends, and to my parents, my tutors, my spiritual guides, my family and friends.

The first release of this book is on 22 Zil-Hajj, which is the birth anniversary of the Ghawth of the Era, Mujaddid of the 15th Century Hijri, Hazrat Mufti-e-A'zam Hind, Maulana Mustafa Raza Khan Sahab (Alayhe Rehmah wa Ridhwan), and also the death anniversary of the Ambassador of Islam of the 14th century, Hazrat Muballigh-e-A'zam, Maulana Abdul Aleem Siddiki Sahab (Alayhe Rehmah wa Ridhwan), who now rests in the blessed graveyard of Baqie in Medina.

May Allah the Glorious, the Most Merciful accept this endeavor. I hope for its reward from Allah, the Most Gracious, as He may wish to grant. I also beg Him to make the blessed soil of Medina my resting place – the soil favored by the touch of the sandals of the Holy Prophet 🌿, and mixed with the sweat and saliva of His close bondmen.

All Praise is to Allah – and countless blessings & peace be upon his beloved apostle Mohammed – and peace be upon all the noble Prophets – and all his Companions and those who righteously follow him in faith, until the last day.

Aqib Qadri. (With hope in Allah's mercy and being forgiven)

Completed on: 19 November 2011 – 22 Zil-Hajj 1432.

Section 1: The Excellent Souls

An enemy of Allah's Friends is an enemy of Allah.

[Surah Baqarah 2:98] "Whoever is an enemy to Allah, and His angels and His Noble Messengers, and Jibreel and Mikaeel *(Michael)* -, then *(know that)*, Allah is an enemy of the disbelievers."

[Surah Yunus 10:62-64] Pay heed! Indeed upon the friends of Allah is neither any fear, nor any grief. Those who have accepted faith and practice piety. There are good tidings for them in the life of this world and in the Hereafter; the Words of Allah cannot change; this is the supreme success.

Narrated Abu Hurairah ﷺ: Allah's Apostle ﷺ said, "Allah said, 'I will declare war against him who shows hostility to a pious worshipper of Mine. And the most beloved things with which My slave comes nearer to Me, is what I have enjoined upon him; and *My slave keeps on coming closer to Me through performing Nawafil (praying or doing extra deeds besides what is obligatory) till I love him, so I become his sense of hearing with which he hears, and his sense of sight with which he sees, and his hand with which he grips, and his leg with which he walks; and if he asks Me, I will give him, and if he asks My protection, I will protect him*; and I do not hesitate to do anything as I hesitate to take the soul of the believer, for he hates death, and I hate to disappoint him." (Bukhari)

Whoever hurts any of My friends has waged war against Me. And nothing brings My slave closer to Me, like his performance of the obligations; and *he keeps coming closer to Me through performing Nawafil (praying or doing extra deeds besides what is obligatory) till I love him – so when I love him, I become his eye with which he sees, and his ear with which he hears, and his leg with which he walks, and his heart (or mind) with which he reflects and his tongue with which he speaks. If he asks Me, I give him, if he prays to Me, I accept his prayer. I do not hesitate about anything I do — (however) I hesitate to take away his life, for he hates death and I dislike harming him.* (Ahmad bin Hambal)

Nothing brings My slave closer to Me, as does his performance of the obligations I placed upon him; and *he keeps coming closer to Me through performing Nawafil (praying or doing extra deeds besides what is obligatory) till I love him — so when I love him, I become his leg with which he walks, and his hand with which he grips, and his tongue with which he speaks, and his heart (or mind) with which he reflects. If he asks Me, I give him, if he prays to Me, I accept his prayer.* (Ibn Al-Saniyy)

Allah Commands others to Love his friends.

Narrated Abu Hurairah ﷺ: Allah's Apostle ﷺ said, "If Allah loves a person, He calls Jibreel, saying, 'Allah loves so and so, O Jibreel love him' So Jibreel would love him and then would make an announcement in the Heavens: 'Allah has loved so and-so therefore you should love him also.' So all the dwellers of the Heavens would love him, and then he is granted the pleasure of the people on the earth." (Bukhari)

The Best in the Creation

Indeed My friends among My slaves and the most beloved among My creation are those who are remembered when I am remembered, and I am remembered when they are remembered. (Al-Hakim, Al-Tabarani)

Chapter 2: They are the Signs of Allah

[Surah Kahf 18:9-11] Did you know that the People of the Cave and People close to the Woods were Our exceptional signs? When the young men took refuge in the Cave, then said, "Our Lord! Give us mercy from Yourself, and arrange guidance for us in our affair." We then thumped upon their ears in the Cave for a number of years.

[Surah Nisa 4:171] O People given the Book(s)! Do not exaggerate in your religion nor say anything concerning Allah, but the truth; the Messiah, Eisa the son of Maryam, is purely a Noble Messenger of Allah, and His Word; which He sent towards Maryam, and a Spirit from Him; so believe in Allah and His Noble Messengers; and do not say "Three"; desist, for your own good; undoubtedly Allah is the only One God; Purity is to Him from begetting a child; to Him only belongs all whatever is in the heavens and all whatever is in the earth; and Allah is a Sufficient Trustee.

Allah's Mercy Due to his Beloved Friends.

Narrated Anas 🙶: Allah's Apostle 🙷 said, "How many (like this) are there - the person with disheveled hair, covered with dust, wearing two worn clothes, not paid heed to – were he to swear by Allah, Allah would certainly fulfill it! Bara'a bin Malek is one of them." (Tirmizi, Baihaqi)

Reported Abu Hurairah 🙶: Allah's Apostle 🙷 as saying: *Many a person with disheveled hair and covered with dust is turned away from the doors (whereas he is held in such a high esteem by Allah) that if he were to adjure in the name of Allah (about anything) Allah would fulfill that.* (Muslim)

Narrated Shuraih bin Obaid 🙶: The people of Shaam were mentioned in the presence of Syedena Ali 🙶, and it was said, "Curse them, O the leader of the faithful!" He said, "No! I have heard from Allah's Apostle 🙷 – 'There will be Abdaals in Shaam, and they will be forty men. Whenever one of them dies, Allah will replace him with another man. *It will rain because of them, and victory will be granted over the enemies because of them, and people will remain safe from the punishment because of them.'-*" (Ahmad, Mishkaat)

'Umar b. Khattab 🙶 reported: I heard Allah's Apostle 🙷 as saying: Worthy amongst the successors would be a person who would be called Uwais. He would have his mother (living with him) and he would have (a small) sign of leprosy. *Ask him to beg pardon for you (from Allah).* (Muslim, Mishkaat)

Usair b. Jabir 🕮 reported that when people from Yemen came to help (the Muslim army at the time of jihad) he asked them: Is there amongst you Uwais b. 'Amir? (He continued finding him out) until he met Uwais. He said: Are you Uwais b. Amir? He said: Yes. He said: Are you from the tribe of Qaran? He said: Yes. He (Hazrat) 'Umar 🕮 (again) said: Did you suffer from leprosy and then you were cured from it but for the space of a dirham? He said: Yes. He ('Umar 🕮) said: Is your mother (living)? He said: Yes. He ('Umar 🕮) said: I heard Allah's Apostle 🕮 say: There would come to you Uwais b. Amir with the reinforcement from the people of Yemen. (He would be) from Qaran, (the branch) of Murid. He had been suffering from leprosy from which he was cured but for a spot of a dirham. His treatment with his mother would have been excellent. *If he were to take an oath in the name of Allah, He would honour that. And if it is possible for you, then do ask him to beg forgiveness for you (from your Lord).* So he (Uwais) begged forgiveness for him. Umar 🕮 said: Where do you intend to go? He said: To Kufa. He ('Umar 🕮) said: Let me write a letter for you to its governor, whereupon he (Uwais) said: I love to live amongst the poor people. When it was the next year, a person from among the elite (of Kufa) performed Hajj and he met Umar 🕮. He asked him about Uwais. He said: I left him in a state with meager means of sustenance. (Thereupon) Umar 🕮 said: I heard Allah's Apostle 🕮 as saying: There would come to you Uwais b. 'Amir, of Qaran, a branch (of the tribe) of Murid, along with the reinforcement of the people of Yemen. He had been suffering from leprosy which would have been cured but for the space of a dirham. His treatment with his mother would have been very kind. If he would take an oath in the name of Allah (for something) He would honour it. Ask him to beg forgiveness for you (from Allah) in case it is possible for you. So he came to Uwais and said: Beg forgiveness (from Allah) for me. He (Uwais) said: You have just come from a sacred journey (Hajj); you, therefore, ask forgiveness for me. He (the person who had performed Hajj) said: Ask forgiveness for me (from Allah). He (Uwais again) said: You have just come from the sacred journey, so you ask forgiveness for me. (Uwais further) said: Did you meet Umar ﷺ? He said: Yes. He (Uwais) then begged forgiveness for him (from Allah). So the people came to know about (the status of religious piety) of Uwais. He went away (from that place). Usair said: *His clothing consisted of a mantle, and whosoever saw him said: From where did Uwais get this mantle?* (Muslim) *It is also reported that the Holy Prophet* ﷺ *had given his mantle to Syedena Umar* ﷺ *to hand it over to Syedena Uwais.* (Muslim)

The Special Status for Sham (Syria)

Narrated Zaid bin Sabet ﷺ: Allah's Apostle ﷺ said, "Happy (or fortunate) is Shaam." We asked, "O Allah's Apostle, upon what?' He said, *"Because the angels of the Most Merciful have their wings spread over it."* (Ahmad, Tirmizi, Mishkaat)

Narrated Ibn Hawalah ﷺ: The Prophet ﷺ said: It will turn out that you will be armed troops; one is Syria, one in the Yemen and one in Iraq. Ibn Hawalah said: Choose for me, Allah's Apostle ﷺ, if I reach that time. He replied: *Go to Syria, for it is Allah's chosen land, to which his best servants will be gathered*, but if you are unwilling, go to your Yemen, and draw water from your tanks, for Allah has on my account taken special charge of Syria and its people. (Abu Dawud)

Narrated Ibn `Umar ﷺ: The Holy Prophet ﷺ said, "O Allah! Bless our Sham and our Yemen." People said, "Our Najd as well." The Prophet ﷺ again said, "O Allah! Bless our Sham and Yemen." They said again, "Our Najd as well." On that the Prophet ﷺ said, "There will appear earthquakes and afflictions,

and from there will come out the side of the head of Satan."
(Bukhari, Muslim, Mishkaat)

Chapter 3: The Faces of Such People Remind of Allah

Narrated by Abu Malik al-Ash`ari 🙵: When the Prophet 🙵 finished his prayer he turned to face the people and said: "O people! Listen to this, understand it, and know it. Allah has servants who are neither Prophets nor martyrs and whom the Prophets and martyrs yearn to be like, due to their seat and proximity in relation to Allah." One of the bedouin Arabs who came from among the most isolated of people twisted his hand at the Prophet 🙵 and said: "O Allah's Apostle 🙵! People from humankind who are neither Prophets nor martyrs and yet the Prophets and the martyrs yearn to be like them due to their seat and proximity in relation to Allah?! Describe them for us!" The Prophet's 🙵 face showed delight at the bedouin's question and he said: "They are of the strangers from this and that place. They frequent this or that tribe without belonging to them. They do not have family connections among themselves. They love one another for Allah's sake. They are of pure intent towards one another. *On the Day of Resurrection* Allah will place for them pedestals of light upon which He will make them sit, and *He will turn their faces and clothes into light.* On the Day of Resurrection the people will be terrified but not those. They are Allah's Friends upon whom fear comes not, nor do they grieve." (Musnad Imam Ahmad)

Narrated by Syedena Ali 🙵: They are the fewest in number, but the greatest in rank before Allah. Through them Allah preserves His proofs until they bequeath it to those like them (before passing on) and plant it firmly in their hearts. By them knowledge has taken by assault the reality of things, so that they found easy what those given to comfort found hard, and found intimacy in what the ignorant found desolate. They accompanied the world with bodies whose spirits were attached to the highest station. *Ah, ah! how one yearns to see them!* (Ibn al-Jawzi in Sifat al-safwa)

Chapter 4: Allah's Mercy by the Presence of Such Persons

Narrated Abu Hurairah: Allah 's Apostle 🕊 said, "Allah has some angels who look for those who celebrate the Praises of Allah on the roads and paths. And when they find some people celebrating the Praises of Allah, they call each other, saying, "Come to the object of your pursuit.' " He added, "Then the angels encircle them with their wings up to the sky of the world." He added. "(after those people celebrated the Praises of Allah, and the angels go back), their Lord, asks them (those angels)---- though He knows better than them----'What do My slaves say?' The angels reply, 'They say: Subhan Allah, Allahu Akbar, and Alham-du-lillah". Allah then says 'Did they see Me?' The angels reply, 'No! By Allah, they didn't see You.' Allah says, How it would have been if they saw Me?' The angels reply, 'If they saw You, they would worship You more devoutly and celebrate Your Glory more deeply, and declare Your freedom from any resemblance to anything more often.' Allah says (to the angels), 'What do they ask Me for?' The angels reply, 'They ask You for Paradise.' Allah says (to the angels), 'Did they see it?' The angels say, 'No! By Allah, O Lord! They did not see it.' Allah says, How it would have been if they saw it?' The angels say, 'If they saw it, they would have greater covetousness for it and would seek it with greater zeal and would have greater desire for it.' Allah says, 'From what do they seek refuge?' The angels reply, 'They seek refuge from the (Hell) Fire.' Allah says, 'Did they see it?' The angels say, 'No By Allah, O Lord! They did not see it.' Allah says, How it would have been if they saw it?' The angels say, 'If they saw it they would flee from it with the extreme fleeing and would have extreme fear from it.' Then Allah says, 'I make you witnesses that I have forgiven them.'" Allah's Apostle 🕊 added, "One of the angels would say, 'There was so-and-so amongst them, and he was not one of them, but he had just come for

16

some need.' Allah would say, *'These are those people whose companions will not be reduced to misery.'* (Bukhari. Other versions in Muslim, Tirmizi)

My love is due for those who meet each other because of Me, those who sit together because of Me, those who spend on each other because of Me and those who visit each other because of Me. (Ahmad)

Narrated Abu Sa`id Al-Khudri ﷺ: "Allah's Apostle ﷺ said, "A time will come upon the people, when a group of people will wage a holy war and it will be said, *'Is there amongst you anyone who has accompanied Allah's Apostle?'* They will say, 'Yes.' And so victory will be bestowed on them. Then a time will come upon the people when a group of people will wage a holy war, and it will be said, "Is there amongst you anyone who has accompanied the companions of Allah's Apostle?' They will say, 'Yes.' And so victory will be bestowed on them. Then a time will come upon the people when a group of people will wage a holy war, and it will be said, "Is there amongst you anyone who has been in the company of the companions of the companions of Allah's Apostle ﷺ?' They will say, 'Yes.' And victory will be bestowed on them." (Bukhari, Muslim)

Narrated Anas ﷺ: Allah's Apostle ﷺ said: *The Hour shall not be established upon anyone who utters "Allah, Allah."* (Muslim)

Narrated Abu Sa`id Al-Khudri ﷺ: The Prophet ﷺ said, "Amongst the men of Bani Israel there was a man who had murdered ninety-nine persons. Then he set out asking (whether his repentance could be accepted or not). He came upon a monk and asked him if his repentance could be accepted. The monk replied in the negative and so the man killed him. He kept on asking till a man advised to go to such and such village. (So he left for it) but death overtook him on the way. *While dying, he turned his chest towards that village* (where he had hoped his repentance would be accepted), and so the angels of mercy and the angels of punishment quarreled amongst themselves regarding him. Allah ordered the village (towards which he was going) to come closer to him, and ordered the village (whence he had come), to go far away, and then He ordered the angels to measure the distances between his body and the two villages. *So he was found to be one span closer to the village (he was going to). So he was forgiven.*" (Bukhari)

Abu Burda 🌸 reported on the authority of his father: We offered the sunset (maghrib) prayer along with Allah's Apostle 🌸. We then said: If we sit (along with Allah's Apostle 🌸) and observe night prayer with him it would be very good, so we sat down and he came to us and said: You are still sitting here. I said: Allah's Apostle 🌸, we observed the evening prayer with you, then we said: Let us sit down and observe night prayer along with you, whereupon he said: You have done well or you have done right. He then lifted his head towards the sky and it often happened that as he lifted his head towards the sky, he said: The stars are a source of security for the sky and when the stars disappear there comes to the sky, i.e. (it meets the same fate) as it has been promised (it would plunge into darkness). *And I am a source of safety and security to my Companions and when I would go away there would fall to the lot (of my Companions) as they have been promised with and my Companions are a source of security for the Ummah and as they would go there would fall to the lot of my Ummah as (its people) have been promised.* (Muslim)

My love is due for those who meet each other because of Me. (Tabarani)

Those who are on the Straight Path & fear Allah

[Surah Fatihah 1:5-6] Guide us on the Straight Path. The path of those whom You have favoured.

[Surah Yunus 10:62-64] Pay heed! Indeed upon the friends of Allah is neither any fear, nor any grief. Those who have accepted faith and practice piety. There are good tidings for them in the life of this world and in the Hereafter; the Words of Allah cannot change; this is the supreme success.

Those who deserve Allah's proximity!

[Surah Nisa 4:69] And whoever obeys Allah and His Noble Messenger, will be with those upon whom Allah has bestowed grace - that is, the Prophets and the truthful and the martyrs and the virtuous; and what excellent companions they are! This is Allah's munificence; and Allah is Sufficient, the All Knowing.

[Surah Yusuf 12:101] "O my Lord! You have given me a kingdom and have taught me how to interpret some events; O Creator of the heavens and the earth - You are my Supporter in the world and in the Hereafter; cause me to die as a Muslim, and unite me with those who deserve Your proximity."

[Surah Qamar 54:54-55] Indeed the pious are amidst Gardens and springs. Seated in an assembly of the Truth, in the presence of Allah, the Omnipotent King.

The devil cannot misguide these chosen bondmen.

[Surah Hijr 15:39-40] He said, "My Lord! I swear by the fact that You sent me astray, I shall distract them in the earth, and I shall lead all of them astray. Except those among them who are Your chosen bondmen."

[Nahl 16:99] Indeed he has no power over the believers and who rely only upon their Lord. Satan's power is only over those who make friendship with him and ascribe him as a partner *(in worship).*

[Surah b/Israel 17:65] "Indeed My bondmen - you *(Satan)* do not have any power over them"; and your Lord is Sufficient as a Trustee.

[Surah Saad 38:82-83] He said, "Therefore, by oath of Your honour, I will surely mislead all of them. Except Your chosen bondmen among them."

Chapter 6: Allah Asking – Why Did You Not Feed Me?

Abu Huraira 🕮 reported Allah's Apostle 🕮 saying: Verily, Allah, the Exalted and Glorious, would say on the Day of Resurrection: O son of Adam, I was sick but you did not visit Me. He would say: "O my Lord; how could I visit You whereas You are the Lord of the worlds? Thereupon He would say: Didn't you know that such and such servant of Mine was sick but you did not visit him and were you not aware of this that if you had visited him, you would have found Me by him? O son of Adam, I asked food from you but you did not feed Me. He would say: My Lord, how could I feed You whereas You are the Lord of the worlds? He said: Didn't you know that such and such servant of Mine asked food from you but you did not feed him, and were you not aware that if you had fed him you would have found him by My side? (The Lord would again say:) O son of Adam, I asked drink from you but you did not provide Me. He would say: My Lord, how could I provide You whereas You are the Lord of the worlds? Thereupon He would say: Such and such servant of Mine asked you for a drink but you did not provide him, and had you provided him drink you would have found him near Me. (Muslim)

Section 2: The Exalted Position Of The Holy Prophet Mohammed ﷺ.

Chapter 1: Allah Sends Greetings of Peace to the Holy Prophet

[Surah Ahzab 33:56] Indeed Allah and His angels send blessings on the Prophet; O People who Believe! Send blessings and abundant salutations upon him.

(Everlasting peace and unlimited blessings be upon the Holy Prophet Mohammed ﷺ)

Chapter 2: The Holy Prophet is the Leader of All Prophets

[Surah A/I'mran 3:81] And Remember When Allah Took A Covenant From The Prophets; "If I Give You The Book And Knowledge And The *(Promised)* Noble Messenger *(Prophet Mohammed ﷺ)* Comes To You, Confirming The Books You Possess, You Shall Positively, Definitely Believe In Him And You Shall Positively, Definitely Help Him"; He Said, "Do You Agree, And Accept My Binding Responsibility In This Matter?" They All Answered, "We Agree"; He Said, "Then Bear Witness Amongst Yourselves, And I Myself Am A Witness With You."

[Surah Baqarah 2:253] These are the Noble Messengers, to whom We gave excellence over each other; of them are some with whom Allah spoke, and some whom He exalted high above all others; and We gave Eisa *(Jesus)*, the son of Maryam, clear signs and We aided him with the Holy Spirit; and if Allah willed, those after them would not have fought each other after the clear evidences had come to them, but they differed - some remained on faith and some turned disbelievers; and had Allah willed, they would not have fought each other; but Allah may do as He wills.

Narrated Hazrat Ubai Ibn Ka'ab: The Holy Prophet ﷺ the Intercessor of the Sinners, said, "On the day of judgement, I shall be the Leader of the Prophets, and their orator and the owner of their intercession – and I do not say this with any pride." (Ibn Abi Shaibah, Tirmizi, Ibn Majah and Hakim)

Chapter 3: The Holy Prophet is the Closest to Allah

Narrated Salman al Farsi ﷺ said that Jibreel descended on the Prophet ﷺ and said, "O Muhammad, Allah subhanahu wa ta'ala says, 'If I had taken Ibrahim as my Friend, I took you as my Beloved One (Habeeb). And I did not create a creation dearer to Me than you. And I have created the whole world (dunya) and its people to show them [and] so they might acknowledge your dearness to Me and your station of closeness to Me and if it was not for you I would not have created this dunya.'" (Ibn Asakir)

Chapter 4: Allah Seeks to Please the Holy Prophet

[Surah Baqarah 2:144] We observe you turning your face, several times towards heaven *(O dear Prophet Mohammed - peace and blessings be upon him)*; so We will definitely make you turn *(for prayer)* towards a qiblah which pleases you; therefore now turn your face towards the Sacred Mosque *(in Mecca)*; and O Muslims, wherever you may be, turn your faces *(for prayer)* towards it only; and those who have received the Book surely know that this is the truth from their Lord; and Allah is not unaware of their deeds.

[Surah Duha 93:5] And indeed your Lord will soon give you so much that you will be pleased.

Chapter 5: The Holy Prophet is Allah's Mercy and Greatest Gift

[Surah Ambiya 21:107] And We did not send you except as a mercy for the entire world.

[Surah A/I`mran 3:164] Allah has indeed bestowed a great favour upon the Muslims, in that He sent to them a Noble Messenger from among them, who recites to them His verses, and purifies them, and teaches them the Book and wisdom; and before it, they were definitely in open error.

[Surah Taubah 9:128] Indeed there has come to you a Noble Messenger from among you - your falling into hardship aggrieves him, most concerned for your well-being, for the Muslims most compassionate, most merciful.

Chapter 6: The Holy Prophet is the Leader of All Mankind

[Surah Baqarah 2:124] And *(remember)* when Ibrahim's Lord tested him in some matters and he fulfilled them; He said, "I am going to appoint you as a leader for mankind"; invoked Ibrahim, "And of my offspring"; He said, "My covenant does not include the unjust."

Abu Hurairah 🕮 reported: Meat was one day brought to Allah's Apostle 🕮 and a foreleg was offered to him, a part which he liked. He sliced with his teeth a piece out of it and said: I shall be the leader of mankind on the Day of Resurrection. Do you know why? Allah would gather in one plane the earlier and the latter (of the human race) on the Day of Resurrection. (Bukhari – part of a longer Hadeeth)

Chapter 7: The Holy Prophet is Mentioned in Earlier Books

[Surah Baqarah 2:89] And when the Book from Allah *(the Holy Qur'an)* came to them, which confirms the Book in their possession *(the Torah)* - and before that they used to seek victory through the medium of this very Prophet *(Mohammed - peace and blessings be upon him)* over the disbelievers; so when the one whom they fully recognised *(the Holy Prophet* 🕮 *)* came to them, they turned disbelievers - therefore Allah's curse is upon the disbelievers.

[Surah A/I`mran 3:81] And remember when Allah took a covenant from the Prophets; "If I give you the Book and knowledge and the *(promised)* Noble Messenger *(Prophet Mohammed - peace and blessings be upon him)* comes to you, confirming the Books you possess, you shall positively, definitely believe in him and you shall positively, definitely help him"; He said, "Do you agree, and accept My binding responsibility in this matter?" They all answered, "We agree"; He said, "Then bear witness amongst yourselves, and I Myself am a witness with you."

[Surah Aa`raf 7:157] "Those who will obey this Noble Messenger *(Prophet Mohammed* 🕮 *)*, the Herald of the Hidden who is untutored* *(except by Allah)*, whom they will find mentioned in the Taurat and the Injeel with them; he will command them to do good and forbid them from wrong, and he will make lawful for them the good clean things and prohibit the foul for them, and he will unburden the loads and the neck chains which were upon them; so those who believe in him, and revere him, and help him, and follow the light which came down with him - it is they who have succeeded. (*Not taught by any human in the world.)

[Surah Fath 48:29] Mohammed *(peace and blessings be upon him)* is the Noble Messenger of Allah; and his companions are stern with the disbelievers and merciful among themselves - you will see them bowing and falling in prostration, seeking Allah's munificence and His pleasure; their signs are on their faces, from the effects of their prostration; this trait of theirs is mentioned in the Taurat; and their trait is mentioned in the Injeel; like a cultivation that sprouted its shoot, then strengthened it, then thickened and then stood firm upon its stem, pleasing the farmer - in order to enrage the disbelievers with them; Allah has promised forgiveness and a great reward to those among them who have faith and do good deeds.

[Surah Saff 61:6] And remember when Eisa the son of Maryam said, "O Descendants of Israel! Indeed I am Allah's Noble Messenger towards you, confirming the Book Torah which was before me, and heralding glad tidings of the Noble Messenger who will come after me – his name is Ahmad *(the Praised One)*"; so when Ahmad came to them with clear proofs, they said, "This is an obvious magic."

Chapter 8: It is Obligatory to Respect the Holy Prophet

[Surah Aa`raf 7:157] "Those who will obey this Noble Messenger *(Prophet Mohammed* ﷺ *)*, the Herald of the Hidden who is untutored* *(except by Allah)*, whom they will find mentioned in the Taurat and the Injeel with them; he will command them to do good and forbid them from wrong, and he will make lawful for them the good clean things and prohibit the foul for them, and he will unburden the loads and the neck chains which were upon them; so those who believe in him, and revere him, and help him, and follow the light which came down with him - it is they who have succeeded. (*Not taught by any human in the world.)

[Surah Fath 48:9] In order that you, O people, may accept faith in Allah and His Noble Messenger, and honour and revere the Noble Messenger; and may say the Purity of Allah, morning and evening.

[Surah Hujurat 49:2] O People who Believe! Do not raise your voices higher than the voice of the Prophet, nor speak to him loudly the way you shout to one another, lest your deeds go to waste whilst you are unaware.

Faith will go to waste due to the slightest disrespect towards the Holy Prophet ﷺ. To honour him is a requirement of faith. To disrespect him is blasphemy.

Chapter 9: Allah Swears by His Life & Era.

[Surah Hijr 15:72] *By your life O dear Prophet (Mohammed ﷺ) -* they are indeed straying in their intoxication.

[Surah A`sr 103:1] *By oath of this era of yours (O dear Prophet Mohammed ﷺ).*

[Surah Balad 90:1-3] I swear by this city *(Mecca) - For you (O dear Prophet Mohammed ﷺ) are in this city.* And by oath of your forefather Ibrahim, and by you - his illustrious son!

[Surah Naml 27:91] "I *(Prophet Mohammed ﷺ)* have been commanded to worship the Lord of this city, *Who has deemed it sacred,* and everything belongs to Him; and I have been commanded to be among the obedient."

[Surah Teen 95:1-3] By oath of the fig and of the olive. And by oath of Mount Sinai. And by oath of this secure land.

Chapter 10: Allah, The Supreme, Observes The Holy Prophet

[Surah Baqarah 2:144] *We observe you turning your face, several times towards heaven (O dear Prophet Mohammed ﷺ);* so We will definitely make you turn *(for prayer)* towards a qiblah which pleases you; therefore now turn your face towards the Sacred Mosque *(in Mecca)*; and O Muslims, wherever you may be, turn your faces *(for prayer)* towards it only; and those who have received the Book surely know that this is the truth from their Lord; and Allah is not unaware of their deeds

[Surah Shua`ra 26:217-219] And rely upon *(Allah)* the Almighty, the Most Merciful. *Who watches you when you stand up. And watches your movements among those who prostrate in prayer.*

Chapter 11: The Holy Prophet Said – I Am Not Like You!!

Say I Am a Human Being Like You (But Not Equal to You)

[Surah Kahf 18:110] Proclaim, "Physically I am a human like you - my Lord sends divine revelations to me - that your God is only One God; so whoever expects to meet his Lord must perform good deeds and not ascribe anyone as a partner in the worship of his Lord."

(Human but not equal to you, in fact the greatest in spiritual status.)

I am not like you!

Ibn 'Umar ☙ said that Allah's Apostle ☙ forbade uninterrupted fasting. They *(some of the Companions)* said: You yourself fast uninterruptedly, whereupon he said: *I am not like you. I am fed and supplied drink (by Allah).* (Muslim)

Anas ☙ reported that Allah's Apostle ☙ observed Saum Wisal *(continuous fast)* during the early part of the month of Ramadan. The people among Muslims also observed uninterrupted fast. This *(news)* reached him *(the Holy Prophet ☙)* and he said: Had the month been lengthened for me I would have continued observing Saum Wisal, so that those who act with forced hardness would *(have been obliged)* to abandon it. *You are not like me (or he said): I am not like you. I continue to do so (in a state) that my Lord feeds me and provides me drink.* (Muslim, Malik's Muwatta)

Narrated Abu Hurairah ﷺ: Allah's Apostle ﷺ forbade Al-Wisal. The people said *(to him)*, "But you fast Al-`Wisal," He said, "*Who among you is like me? When I sleep (at night), my Lord makes me eat and drink.*" But when the people refused to give up Al-Wisal, he fasted Al-Wisal along with them for two days and then they saw the crescent whereupon the Prophet ﷺ said, "If the crescent had not appeared I would have fasted for a longer period," as if he intended to punish them herewith. (Bukhari)

Narrated Abdullah bin Amr ﷺ: I was informed that Allah's Apostle ﷺ has said, "Prayer of a man sitting is half the prayer. He said, 'Then I came to him and found him praying sitting, so I placed my hand upon his head.' He said, "What is the matter with you, O Abdullah bin Amr?" And I said, "O Allah's Apostle ﷺ! I have been informed that you said that the prayer of a man sitting is half the prayer, whilst you are offering prayer sitting!" *He said, "Yes, but I am not like you!"* (Muslim, Mishkaat).

Ascribing false things to the Holy Prophet.

Narrated Al-Mughira ﷺ: I heard the Prophet ﷺ saying, "*Ascribing false things to me is not like ascribing false things to anyone else.* Whosoever tells a lie against me intentionally then surely let him occupy his seat in Hell-Fire." I heard the Prophet ﷺ saying, "The deceased who is wailed over is tortured for that wailing." (Bukhari)

The Prophet's Resting Place

It is the consensus of all the scholars that the portion of earth upon which rests the body of the Holy Prophet ﷺ, is the most superior of all places — better that any place on earth, in the skies or in heaven. (Khasais Kubra)

For more on this subject, see chapter on the Holy Places.

No One Can Achieve This by Any Act of Worship

Narrated Jaber 🌸: The Holy Prophet 🌸 said, *"Fire will not touch the Muslim who saw me, and the Muslim who saw the Muslim who saw me."* (Tirmizi, Mishkaat).

Chapter 13: All Muslims are the Slaves of the Holy Prophet

[Surah Noor 24:32] And enjoin in marriage those among you who are not married, and your deserving slaves and bondwomen; if they are poor, Allah will make them wealthy by His munificence; and Allah is Most Capable, All Knowing.

[Surah Shua`ra 26:215] And spread your wing of mercy for the believers following you.

[Surah Zumar 39:10] Proclaim *(O dear Prophet Mohammed 🌸)*, "O my slaves who have accepted faith! Fear your Lord; for those who do good deeds in this world, is goodness *(in return)*; and Allah's earth is spacious; it is the steadfast who will be paid their full reward, without account."

[Surah Zumar 39:53] Proclaim *(O dear Prophet Mohammed 🌸)*, "O my slaves, who have wronged themselves, do not lose hope in Allah's mercy; indeed Allah forgives all sins; indeed He only is the Oft Forgiving, the Most Merciful."

[Surah Ahzab 33:6] The Prophet 🌸 is closer to the Muslims than their own lives, and his wives are their mothers; and the relatives are closer to each other in the Book of Allah, than other Muslims and immigrants, except that you may be kind towards your friends; this is written in the Book.

[Surah Najm 53:2] Your master did not err, nor did he go astray.

[Surah Anfal 8:24] O People who Believe! Present yourselves upon the command of Allah and His Noble Messenger, when the Noble Messenger calls you towards the matter that will bestow you life; and know that the command of Allah becomes a barrier between a man and his heart's intentions, and that you will all be raised towards Him.

Narrated Anas ﷺ: The Prophet ﷺ said "None of you will have faith till he loves me more than his father, his children and all mankind." (Bukhari)

Section 3: The Exalted Position Of The Sahaba

[Surah Baqarah 2:274] Those who spend their wealth by night and day, secretly and openly - their reward is with their Lord; and there shall be no fear upon them nor shall they grieve.

[Surah Nisa 4:69] And whoever obeys Allah and His Noble Messenger, will be with those upon whom Allah has bestowed grace - that is, the Prophets and the truthful and the martyrs and the virtuous; and what excellent companions they are!

[Surah Taubah 9:40] If you do not help him *(Prophet Mohammed* 🌼*)*, Allah has helped him - when he had to go forth due to the mischief of the disbelievers, just as two men - when they were in the cave, when he was saying to his companion "Do not grieve; indeed Allah is with us"; then Allah caused His calm to descend upon him and helped him with armies you did not see, and disgraced the word of the disbelievers; and Allah's Word is supreme; and Allah is the Almighty, the Wise.

The Holy Prophet migrated only with Syedena Abu Bakr -who later became the first caliph as his sole companion.

[Surah Fath 48:29] Mohammed 🌼 is the Messenger of Allah; and his companions are stern with the disbelievers and merciful among themselves - you will see them bowing and falling in prostration, seeking Allah's munificence and His pleasure; their signs are on their faces, from the effects of their prostration; this trait of theirs is mentioned in the Taurat; and their trait is mentioned in the Injeel; like a cultivation that sprouted its shoot, then strengthened it, then thickened and then stood firm upon its stem, pleasing the farmer - in order to enrage the disbelievers with them; Allah has promised forgiveness and a great reward to those among them who have faith and do good deeds.

[Surah A`adiyat 100:3-5] And by oath of those who raid at dawn. So thereupon raising dust. Then penetrate to the centre of the enemy army.

The Sahaba have been mentioned with praise, in the Holy Qur'an, on numerous occasions. I hope the above will suffice for the readers.

Chapter 2: All the Companions are Successful & Saved from Hell.

[Surah Taubah 9:100] And leading everyone, the first are the Muhajirs and the Ansaar, and those who followed them with virtue - Allah is pleased with them and they are pleased with Him, and He has kept ready for them Gardens beneath which rivers flow, to abide in it for ever and ever; this is the greatest success.

Narrated Jaber ﷺ: The Holy Prophet ﷺ said, *"Fire will not touch the Muslim who saw me, and the Muslim who saw the Muslim who saw me."* (Tirmizi, Mishkaat).

Chapter 3: Abusing the Companions is Forbidden

Narrated Abu Sa`id ﷺ: The Holy Prophet ﷺ said, *"Do not abuse my companions* for if any one of you spent gold equal to (Mount) Uhud (in Allah's Cause) it would not be equal to a Mud or even half a Mud spent by one of them." (Muslim)

Narrated Sa'id ibn Zayd ibn Amr ibn Nufayl ﷺ: The company of one of those man whose face has been covered with dust by Allah's Apostle ﷺ is better than the actions of one of you for a whole life time even if he is granted the life-span of Noah. (Sunan Abu Dawud – part of a longer hadeeth)

Narrated ibn Masud ﷺ: The Holy Prophet ﷺ said, "Indeed Allah has chosen for me my companions, whom He made my friends, and my relative and my aides. *So soon after them will come some people who will try to degrade them and speak evil regarding them.* So if you find them, do not marry amongst them, do not make relations with them, do not have food or drink with them, do not pray along with them nor offer the funeral prayers for them. (Dar Qutni)

Narrated Syedena Ali 🕮: The Holy Prophet 🕮 said, "Soon after me will come a group of people who will have an evil name – they will be called "Rafidhis". So (O Ali), if you find them, wage war against them for they are polytheists". I said, "O Allah's Apostle, what is their sign?" He said, *"They will say excessive matters regarding you which you do not have, and they will speak evil regarding the predecessors".* (Dar Qutni)

Narrated Ibn Jabir 🕮: The Holy Prophet said, "When the latter ones among this nation curse the former ones of this nation – when this time comes, whoever suppresses just a single truth will be as if he has hidden what Allah has sent down." (Sunan Ibn Majah)

Chapter 4: The Companions are a Guiding Light for the Ummah

Narrated Abdullah bin Buraidah 🕮, from his father: Allah's Apostle 🕮 said, *"No companion (Sahabi) will die in a land without being raised up as a guide and a light for them on the Day of Resurrection."* (Tirmizi, Mishkaat)

Abu Burda 🕮 reported on the authority of his father: We offered the sunset (maghrib) prayer along with Allah's Apostle 🕮. We then said: If we sit (along with Allah's Apostle 🕮) and observe night prayer with him it would be very good, so we sat down and he came to us and said: You are still sitting here. I said: Allah's Apostle 🕮, we observed the evening prayer with you, then we said: Let us sit down and observe night prayer along with you, whereupon he said: You have done well or you have done right. He then lifted his head towards the sky and it often happened that as he lifted his head towards the sky, he said: The stars are a source of security for the sky and when the stars disappear there comes to the sky, i.e. (it meets the same fate) as it has been promised (it would plunge into darkness). *And I am a source of safety and security to my Companions and when I would go away there would fall to the lot (of my Companions) as they have been promised with and my Companions are a source of security for the Ummah and as they would go there would fall to the lot of my Ummah as (its people) have been promised.* (Muslim)

The Holy Prophet ﷺ said, "The best of people are those living in my time. Then come those who follow them, and then come those who follow them. Those will be followed by a generation whose witness is sometimes true, sometimes false. (Bukhari, Muslim.)

The Holy Prophet ﷺ said "My Companions are like the stars; whoever among them you use for guidance, you will be rightly guided." (Dar Qutni & others)

Chapter 5: The Excellence of the Four Caliphs

[Surah Fath 48:29] Mohammed (ﷺ) is the Noble Messenger of Allah; and his companions are stern with the disbelievers and merciful among themselves - you will see them bowing and falling in prostration, seeking Allah's munificence and His pleasure; their signs are on their faces, from the effects of their prostration.

Narrated Muhammad bin Al-Hanafiya ؓ: I asked my father (`Ali bin Abi Talib), "Who are the best people after Allah's Apostle ﷺ?" He said, "Abu Bakr." I asked, "Who then?" He said, "Then `Umar. " I was afraid he would say "Uthman, so I said, "Then you?" He said, "I am only an ordinary person. (Bukhari)

Narrated Ibn `Umar ﷺ: During the lifetime of the Prophet we considered Abu Bakr as peerless and then `Umar and then `Uthman (coming next to him in superiority) and then we used not to differentiate between the companions of the Prophet. (Bukhari)

Narrated Syedah `Aisha ﷺ: When Allah's Apostle ﷺ became seriously ill, Bilal came to him for the prayer. He said, "Tell Abu Bakr to lead the people in the prayer." I said, "O Allah's Apostle! Abu Bakr is a softhearted man and if he stands in your place, he would not be able to make the people hear him. Will you order `Umar (to lead the prayer)?" The Prophet ﷺ said ﷺ, "Tell Abu Bakr to lead the people in the prayer." Then I said to Hafsa, "Tell him, Abu Bakr is a softhearted man and if he stands in his place, he would not be able to make the people hear him. Would you order `Umar to lead the prayer?'" Hafsa did so. The Prophet ﷺ said, "Verily you are the companions of Joseph. Tell Abu Bakr to lead the people in the prayer." So Abu Bakr stood for the prayer. In the meantime Allah's Apostle ﷺ felt better and came out with the help of two persons and both of his legs were dragging on the ground till he entered the mosque. When Abu Bakr heard him coming, he tried to retreat but Allah's Apostle ﷺ beckoned him to carry on. The Prophet ﷺ sat on his left side. Abu Bakr was praying while standing and Allah's Apostle ﷺ was leading the prayer while sitting. Abu Bakr was following the Prophet and the people were following Abu Bakr (in the prayer). (Muslim)

'Abdullah b. Mas'ud reported Allah's Apostle ﷺ as saying: If I were to choose a bosom friend I would have definitely chosen Abu Bakr as my bosom friend, but he is my brother and my companion and Allah, the Exalted and Glorious has taken your brother and companion (meaning Prophet himself) as a friend. (Muslim).

Reported Ibn Abu Mulaika 🌼: I heard Ibn 'Abbas as saying: When 'Umar b. Khatab was placed in the coffin the people gathered around him. They praised him and supplicated for him before the bier was lifted up, and I was one amongst them. Nothing attracted my attention but a person who gripped my shoulder from behind. I saw towards him and found that he was 'Ali. He invoked Allah's mercy upon 'Umar and said: You have left none behind you (whose) deeds (are so enviable) that I love to meet Allah with them. By Allah, I hoped that Allah would keep you and your two associates together. I had often heard Allah's Apostle 🌼 as saying: I came and there came too Abu Bakr and 'Umar; I entered and there entered too Abu Bakr and 'Umar; I went out and there went out too Abu Bakr and 'Umar, and I hope and think that Allah will keep you along with them. (Muslim).

Reported Abu Musa al-Ash'ari 🌼: While Allah's Apostle 🌼 was in one of the gardens of Medina, reclining against a pillow and fixing a stick in a mud, a person came asking for the gate to be opened, whereupon he said: Open it for him and give him glad tidings of Paradise and, lo, it was Abu Bakr. I opened (the gate) for him and gave him the glad tidings of Paradise. Then another person asked for the door to be opened, whereupon he said: Open it and give him the glad tidings of Paradise. He said: I went away and, lo, it was 'Umar. I opened it for him and gave him the glad tidings of Paradise. Then still another man asked for the door to be opened, and thereupon Allah's Apostle 🌼 said: Open it and give him the glad tidings of Paradise after a trial would afflict him. I went and, lo, it was 'Uthman b. 'Affan. I opened the door and gave him the glad tidings of Paradise and informed him (what the Holy Prophet 🌼 had said). Thereupon he said: O Allah, grant me steadfastness. Allah is one Whose help is to be sought (Muslim).

Narrated Ibn Omar 🌼: Allah's Apostle 🌸 said, "*Allah has indeed placed the truth upon the tongue of Umar, and upon his heart.*" (Tirmizi, Abu Dawud)

Narrated 'Umar (bin Al-Khattab) 🌼: *My Lord agreed with me in three things*: (1). I said, "O Allah's Apostle 🌸, I wish we took the station of Abraham as our praying place (for some of our prayers). So came the Divine revelation: And take the place where Ibrahim stood, as your place of prayer; (2.125) (2). And as regards the (verse of) the veiling of the women, I said, 'O Allah's Apostle! I wish you ordered your wives to cover themselves from the men because good and bad ones talk to them.' So the verse of the veiling of the women was revealed. (3). Once the wives of the Prophet 🌸 made a united front against the Prophet 🌸 and I said to them, "It is likely that, if he divorces you, his Lord will give him wives better than you in your place": (66.5).So this verse (the same as I had said) was revealed." (Bukhari, Muslim)

Narrated Ubaida 🌼: 'Ali said (to the people of 'Iraq), "Judge as you used to judge, for I hate differences (and I do my best) till the people unite as one group, or I die as my companions have died." And narrated Sa`d that the Prophet 🌸 said to 'Ali, "Will you not be pleased from this that you are to me like Harun was to Moses?" (Bukhari)

Narrated Salama bin Al-Akwa` 🌼: 'Ali remained behind the Prophet 🌸 during the battle of Khaibar as he was suffering from some eye trouble but then he said, "How should I stay behind Allah's Apostle?" So, he set out till he joined the Prophet 🌸. On the eve of the day of the conquest of Khaibar, Allah's Apostle 🌸 said, "(No doubt) I will give the flag, tomorrow, to a man whom Allah and His Apostle love or who loves Allah and His Apostle will take the flag. Allah will bestow victory upon him." Suddenly 'Ali joined us though we were not expecting him. The people said, "Here is `Ali. "So, Allah's Apostle ﷺ gave the flag to him and Allah bestowed victory upon him. (Bukhari).

Narrated Al-Bara bin `Azib ﵁: When Allah's Apostle ﷺ concluded a peace treaty with the people of Hudaibiya, `Ali bin Abu Talib wrote the document and he mentioned in it, "Muhammad, Allah's Apostle" The pagans said, "Don't write: 'Muhammad, Allah's Apostle', for if you were an Apostle we would not fight with you." Allah's Apostle ﷺ asked `Ali to rub it out, but `Ali said, "I will not be the person to rub it out." Allah's Apostle ﷺ rubbed it out and made peace with them on the condition that the Prophet ﷺ and his companions would enter Mecca and stay there for three days, and that they would enter with their weapons in cases. (Bukhari)

Chapter 6: The Unique Position of Some Sahabah

Abdul Rahman bin `Awf said ﵁: The Holy Prophet ﷺ said: Abu Bakr in Paradise, Omar in Paradise, 'Uthman in Paradise, Ali in Paradise, Talha in Paradise, al- Zubair (bin al-'Awwam) in Paradise, AbdulRahman bin `Awf in Paradise, Saad (bin Abi Waqqass) in Paradise, Saeed (bin Zaid), and abu 'Ubaida bin al- Jarrah in Paradise." (Tirmizi)

Syedah 'A'ishah ﵂ reported that Allah's Apostle ﷺ went out one morning wearing a striped cloak of the black camel's hair –so there came Hasan b. 'Ali ﵁. He wrapped him under it, then came Husain and he wrapped him under it along with the other one (Hasan). Then came Fatima ﵂ and he took her under it, then came 'Ali ﵁ and he also took him under it and then said: Allah only wills to remove all impurity from you, O the People of the Household, and by cleansing you make you utterly pure. (Muslim)

Narrated Syedena `Ali ﷺ: I never saw the Holy Prophet ﷺ saying, "Let my parents sacrifice their lives for you," to any man after Sa`d. I heard him saying (to him), "Throw (the arrows)! Let my parents sacrifice their lives for you." (Bukhari)

Jabir b. 'Abdullah ﷺ reported Allah's Apostle ﷺ as saying while the bier of Sa'd b. Mu'adh ﷺ was placed before them: The Throne of the most Gracious shook at the death of Sa'd b. Mu'adh. (Muslim, Bukhari)

Section 4: The Best Companions

[Surah Taubah 9:40] If you do not help him *(Prophet Mohammed* 🌸 *)*, Allah has helped him - when he had to go forth due to the mischief of the disbelievers, just as two men - when they were in the cave, when he was saying to his companion "Do not grieve; indeed *Allah is with us*"; then Allah caused His calm to descend upon him and helped him with armies you did not see, and disgraced the word of the disbelievers; and Allah's Word is supreme; and Allah is the Almighty, the Wise.

[Surah Nahl 16:128] Indeed Allah is with the pious and the virtuous.

[Surah Shua`ra 26:62] Said Moosa, "Never! Indeed *my Lord is with me*, He will now show me the way."

[Surah Qamar 54:54-55] Indeed the pious are amidst Gardens and springs. Seated in an assembly of the Truth, *in the presence of Allah*, the Omnipotent King.

Narrated Syedah `Aisha 🌸: I heard Allah's Apostle 🌸 saying, "No prophet gets sick but he is given the choice to select either this world or the Hereafter." `Aisha added: During his fatal illness, his voice became very husky and I heard him saying: "With those upon whom Allah has bestowed grace - that is, the Prophets and the truthful and the martyrs and the virtuous.' (4.69) And from this I came to know that he has been given the option. (Bukhari, Muslim)

Narrated Syedah Aisha 🌸: When Allah 's Apostle 🌸 was in good health, he used to say, "Never does a prophet die unless he is shown his place in Paradise (before his death), and then he is made alive or given option." When the Prophet 🌸 became ill and his last moments came while his head was on my thigh, he became unconscious, and when he came to his senses, he looked towards the roof of the house and then said, *"O Allah! With the highest companion."* Thereupon I said, "So he is not going to stay with us?" Then I came to know that his state was the confirmation of the narration he used to mention to us while he was in good health. (Bukhari).

Chapter 2: Allah's Command - Stay with the Pious!

[Surah Taubah 9:119] O People who Believe! Fear Allah, and be with the truthful.

[Surah Kahf 18:28] And restrain yourself along with those who pray to their Lord morning and evening, seeking His pleasure; and may not your sight fall on anything besides them; would you desire the adornment of the life of this world? And do not follow him whose heart We have made neglectful of Our remembrance – the one who has followed his own desires and his matter has crossed the limits.

Chapter 3: The Pious are the Best Companions

[Surah Nisa 4:69-70] And whoever obeys Allah and His Noble Messenger, will be with those upon whom Allah has bestowed grace - that is, the Prophets and the truthful and the martyrs and the virtuous; *and what excellent companions they are!* This is Allah's munificence; and Allah is Sufficient, the All Knowing.

[Surah Yusuf 12:101] "O my Lord! You have given me a kingdom and have taught me how to interpret some events; O Creator of the heavens and the earth - you are my Supporter in the world and in the Hereafter; cause me to die as a Muslim, and *unite me with those who deserve Your proximity."*

[Surah Maidah 5:84] "And what is the matter with us, that we should not believe in Allah and this truth which has come to us? *And we hope that our Lord will admit us along with the righteous.*"

Chapter 4: Allah Rescues those who are with the Pious.

[Surah Taubah 9:119] O People who believe! Fear Allah, and be with the truthful.

[Surah Aa`raf 7:64] In response they denied him, so We rescued him (Nooh) and those with him in the ship, and We drowned those who denied Our signs; indeed they were a blind group.

[Surah Aa`raf 7:72] We therefore rescued him (Hud) and those with him by a great mercy from Us, and We cut off the lineage of those who denied Our signs - and they were not believers.

[Surah Aa`raf 7:83] And We rescued him (Lut) and his family, except his wife - she became of those who stayed behind.

[Surah Hud 11:58] And when Our command came, We rescued Hud and the Muslims who were with him, by Our mercy; and We saved them from a severe punishment.

[Surah Hud 11:66] Therefore when Our command came, We rescued Saleh and the Muslims who were with him by Our mercy, and from the disgrace of that day; indeed your Lord is the Strong, the Almighty.

[Surah Hud 11:94] And when Our command came, We rescued Shuaib and the Muslims who were with him by Our mercy; and the terrible scream seized the unjust - so at morning they remained lying flattened in their homes.

Chapter 5: And on the Day of Judgement!!

[Surah Zumar 39:61] And Allah will rescue the pious, to their place of salvation; neither will the punishment touch them, nor shall they grieve.

Narrated `Abdullah bin `Umar 🕮: The Prophet 🕮 said, "A man keeps on asking others for something till he comes on the Day of Resurrection without any piece of flesh on his face." The Prophet 🕮 added, "On the Day of Resurrection, the Sun will come near (to, the people) to such an extent that the sweat will reach up to the middle of the ears, so, when all the people are in that state, they will ask Adam for help, and then Moses, and then Muhammad." The sub-narrator added "Muhammad 🕮 will intercede with Allah to judge amongst the people. He will proceed on till he will hold the ring of the door (of Paradise) and then Allah will exalt him to Maqam Mahmud (the privilege of intercession, etc.). And all the people of the gathering will send their praises to Allah. (Bukhari)

Narrated Abu Hurairah 🕮: We were in the company of the Prophet 🕮 at a banquet and a cooked (mutton) forearm was set before him, and he used to like it. He ate a morsel of it and said, "I will be the chief of all the people on the Day of Resurrection. Do you know how Allah will gather all, the first and the last (people) in one level place where an observer will be able to see (all) of them and they will be able to hear the announcer, and the sun will come near to them? Some People will say: Don't you see, in what condition you are and the state to which you have reached? Why don't you look for a person who can intercede for you with your Lord? Some people will say: Appeal to your father, Adam.' They will go to him and say: 'O Adam! You are the father of all mankind, and Allah created you with His Own Hands, and ordered the angels to prostrate for you, and made you live in Paradise. Will you not intercede for us with your Lord? Don't

49

you see in what (miserable) state we are, and to what condition we have reached?' On that Adam will reply, 'My Lord is so angry as He has never been before and will never be in the future; (besides), He forbade me (to eat from) the tree, but I disobeyed (Him), (I am worried about) myself! Myself! Go to somebody else; go to Noah.' They will go to Noah and say; 'O Noah! You are the first amongst the messengers of Allah to the people of the earth, and Allah named you a thankful slave. Don't you see in what a (miserable) state we are and to what condition we have reached? Will you not intercede for us with your Lord? Noah will reply: 'Today my Lord has become so angry as he had never been before and will never be in the future Myself! Myself! Go to the Prophet (Muhammad). The people will come to me, and I will prostrate myself underneath Allah's Throne. Then I will be addressed: 'O Muhammad! Raise your head; intercede, for your intercession will be accepted, and ask (for anything), for you will be given." (Bukhari)

Chapter 6: Other Things That Benefit from the Company of the Pious

Fish became alive in the company of Syedena Khizr

[Aurah Kahf 18:61] And when they reached the place where the two seas meet, *they forgot about their fish, and it took its way into the sea*, making a tunnel.

The Pet Birds were raised again

[Surah Baqarah 2:260] And when Ibrahim said, "My Lord! Show me how You will give life to the dead"; He said, "Are you not certain *(of it)*?" Ibrahim said, "Surely yes, why not? But because I wish to put my heart at ease"; He said, "Therefore take four birds *(as pets)* and cause them to become familiar to you, then place a part of each of them on separate hills, then call them - *they will come running towards you*; and know well that Allah is Almighty, Wise."

The birds & walls praise Allah

[Surah Ambiya 21:79] And We explained the case to Sulaiman; and to both We gave the kingdom and knowledge; *and subjected the hills to proclaim the Purity along with Dawud, and (also subjected) the birds*; and these were Our works.

Section 5: The Light Of Imaan And The Light Of The Bodies

Chapter 1: The Light of the Holy Prophet.

[Surah Noor 24:35] Allah is the Light of the heavens and the earth; the example of His light is like a niche in which is a lamp; the lamp is in a glass; the glass is as if it were a star shining like a pearl, kindled by the blessed olive tree, neither of the east nor of the west – it is close that the oil itself get ablaze although the fire does not touch it; light upon light; Allah guides towards His light whomever He wills; and Allah illustrates examples for mankind; and Allah knows everything.

Says Hazrat Kaab ibn Ahbaar ﷺ:- Here, in the words of Allah, the second "Noor" means the Holy Prophet ﷺ. (Kitaab ul-Shifa). Says Hazrat Abdullah bin Umar ﷺ: The niche means the chest of the Holy Prophet ﷺ, the glass lamp means the heart of the Holy Prophet ﷺ, and the lamp means the light that Allah placed in it. The light is neither of the east nor of the west, neither Jewish nor Christian. The blessed tree is illuminated – i.e. there is light upon the light of Ibrahim ﷺ – i.e. the light of Mohammed's ﷺ heart is upon the light of Ibrahim's ﷺ heart. (Tafseer Khazin)

Jābir ibn 'Abd Allāh ﷺ said to the Prophet ﷺ, "O Messenger of Allāh, may my father and mother be sacrificed for you, tell me of the first thing Allāh created before all things." He said: O Jābir, the first thing Allāh created was the light of your Prophet from His light, and that light remained in the midst of His Power for as long as He wished, and there was not, at that time, a Tablet or a Pen or a Paradise or a Fire or an angel or a heaven or an earth. And when Allāh wished to create creation, he divided that Light into four parts and from the first made the Pen, from the second the Tablet, from the third the Throne, then He divided the fourth into four parts [and from them created everything else]. (Musannaf Abd al-Razzāq, Baihaqi)

Chapter 2: The Holy Prophet is a Light from Allah

[Surah Ahzab 33:45 - 46] O Herald of the Hidden! We have indeed sent you as an observing present witness and a Herald of glad tidings and warning. And as a caller towards Allah, by His command, and as a sun that enlightens.

[Surah Maidah 5:15] O People given the Book(s)! Indeed this Noble Messenger *(Prophet Mohammed 	)* of Ours has come to you, revealing to you a lot of the things which you had hidden in the Book, and forgiving a lot of them; indeed towards you has come a light from Allah, and a clear Book.

Chapter 3: Light of the Holy Prophet's Body.

The Holy Prophet's Prayer for Light (Noor).

Ibn 'Abbas 	 said: I spent the night in the house of my mother's sister, Maimuna, and observed how Allah's Apostle 	 prayed (at night). He got up and relieved himself. He then washed his face and hands and then went to sleep. He again got up and went near the water-skin and loosened its straps and then poured some water in a bowl and inclined it with his hands (towards himself). He then performed a good ablution between the two extremes and then stood up to pray. I also came and stood by his left side. He took hold of me and made me stand on his right side. It was in thirteen rak'ahs that the (night) prayer of Allah's Apostle 	 was completed. He then slept till he began to snore, and we knew that he had gone to sleep by his snoring. He then went out (for the dawn prayer) and then again slept, and said while praying or prostrating himself:" *O Allah! place light in my heart, light in my hearing, light in my sight, light on my right, light on my left, light in front of me, light behind me, light above me, light below me, make light for me,"* or *he said:" Make me light."* (Muslim)

55

The Light of His Face, Body, Teeth.

Narrated Ibn Saba' 🌸:- Among the special attributes of the Holy Prophet 🌸 is that he had no shadow, and he was pure light. So whenever he walked in the sunlight or moonlight, his body never cast a shadow. (Zarkani, Khasais Kubra).

The body of the Holy Prophet 🌸 did not cast a shadow either in the light of the sun or in the light of the moon. (Hakim, Tirmizi)

Narrated Syedah Aisha 🌸: I was sewing (something in the dark room) when the needle slipped out of my hand. I searched for it but was unable to find it. Thereupon the Holy Prophet 🌸 entered (the room) and by the bright light rays emanating from his face, the needle shone and I came to know where it is. (Ibn Asakir, Khasais Kubra)

Narrated Hazrat Jaber 🌸: "I once saw Allah's Apostle 🌸 on the night of a full moon. On that night he wore red clothing. At times I looked at the full moon and at times at Allah's Apostle 🌸. Ultimately I came to the conclusion that Allah's Apostle 🌸 was more handsome, beautiful and more radiant than the full moon." (Tirmizi)

Narrated Abu Ishaq 🌸: Al-Bara' was asked, "Was the face of the Holy Prophet (as bright) as a sword?" He said, "No, but (as bright) as a moon." (Bukhari)

Holy Prophet Travelled Faster Than Light Itself.

[Surah b/Israel 17:1] Purity is to Him Who took His bondman in a part of the night from the Sacred Mosque to the Aqsa Mosque around which We have placed blessings, in order that We may show him Our great signs; indeed he is the listener, the beholder.

(This verse refers to the physical journey of Prophet Mohammed ﷺ - to Al Aqsa Mosque and from there to the heavens and beyond. The entire journey back to Mecca was completed within a small part of the night.)

Light in the Things Touched by the Holy Prophet.

Narrated Anas bin Malik ﷺ: Two of the companions of the Holy Prophet ﷺ departed from him on a dark night and were led by two lights like lamps (going in front of them from Allah as a miracle) lighting the way in front of them, and when they parted, each of them was accompanied by one of these lights till they reached their (respective) houses. (Bukhari)

Narrated Abu Said Khudri ﷺ: Hazrat Qatadah bin Noman ﷺ once remained in the company of the Holy Prophet ﷺ, while it was a dark and stormy night. When he was about to leave, the Holy Prophet ﷺ gave him a stick of date palm, and said, "Take this with you – it shall illuminate the space around you by ten yards in front and ten yards behind. When you reach home, you will see a dark object there – so beat it with this stick until it goes away from there, for that dark object is the Satan." So when Hazrat Qatadah left, the stick turned bright and he reached home. Entering his home, he found the dark object and he beat it so much that it ran away. (Shifa Shareef, Zarqani)

Light in the Hereafter

[Surah A/I`mran 3:107] And those whose faces will be shining, are in the mercy of Allah; they will abide in it forever.

[Surah Hadeed 57:12-13] The day when you will see the believing men and believing women, that their light runs before them and on their right - it being said to them, "This day, the best tidings for you are the Gardens beneath which rivers flow - abide in it forever; this is the greatest success." The day when hypocrite men and hypocrite women will say to the Muslims, "Look mercifully towards us, so that we may gain some of your light!"; it will be said to them, "Turn back, search light over there!"; so they will turn around, whereupon a wall will be erected between them, in which is a gate; inside the gate is mercy, and on the outer side is the punishment.

Narrated Abdullah bin Buraidah ☙, from his father:- Allah's Apostle ☙ said, *"No companion (Sahabi) will die in a land without being raised up as a guide and a light for them on the Day of Resurrection."* (Tirmizi, Mishkaat)

Narrated by Abu Malik al-Ash`ari ☙: When the Holy Prophet ☙ finished his prayer he turned to face the people and said: "O people! Listen to this, understand it, and know it. Allah has servants who are neither Prophets nor martyrs and whom the Holy Prophets and martyrs yearn to be like, due to their seat and proximity in relation to Allah." One of the Bedouin Arabs who came from among the most isolated of people twisted his hand at the Holy Prophet ☙ and said: "O Allah's Apostle! People from humankind who are neither Prophets nor martyrs and yet the Holy Prophets and the martyrs yearn to be like them due to their seat and proximity in relation to Allah?! Describe them for us!" The Holy Prophet's ☙ face showed delight at the Bedouin's question and he said: "They are of the strangers from this and that place. They frequent this or that tribe without belonging to them. They do not have family connections among themselves. They love one another for Allah's sake. They are of pure intent towards one another. On the Day of Resurrection Allah will place for them pedestals of light upon which He will make them sit, and *He will turn their faces and clothes into light*. On the Day of Resurrection the people will be terrified but not those. They are Allah's Friends upon whom fear comes not, nor do they grieve." (Musnad Imam Ahmad)

Narrated Abu Hurairah ﷺ: Allah's Apostle ﷺ said, "*The first group (of people) who will enter Paradise will be (glittering) like the moon when it is full*. They will not spit or blow their noses or relieve nature. Their utensils will be of gold and their combs of gold and silver; in their centers the aloe wood will be used, and their sweat will smell like musk. Every one of them will have two wives; the marrow of the bones of the wives' legs will be seen through the flesh out of excessive beauty. They (the people of Paradise) will neither have differences nor hatred amongst themselves; their hearts will be as if one heart and they will be glorifying Allah in the morning and in the evening." (Bukhari)

Syedena Abu Hurayra ﷺ said, "I heard the Messenger of Allah ﷺ say 'On the Day of Resurrection, my community will be called 'those with white blazes on their foreheads and limbs from the effects of ablution (wudu)'. So whoever of you can increase the extent of the whiteness, should do so.'" (Bukhari, Muslim)

Light in this world

Narrated Abdullah ibn Amr ibn al-'As: Allah's Apostle ﷺ said: Do not pluck out grey hair. *If any believer grows a grey hair in Islam, he will have light on the Day of Resurrection.* (Abu Dawud)

Narrated Syedah Aisha ﷺ: When Najashi died, we started talking of the *light which continued to be seen over his grave.* (Abu Dawud, Mishkaat)

Section 6: The Bodies & Souls, In This World & In The Hereafter

Alive As Souls in the Heavens

[Surah A/I`mran 3:81] And remember when Allah took a covenant from the Prophets; "If I give you the Book and knowledge and the *(promised)* Noble Messenger *(Prophet Mohammed* 🌸 *)* comes to you, confirming the Books you possess, you shall positively, definitely believe in him and you shall positively, definitely help him"; He said, "Do you agree, and accept My binding responsibility in this matter?" They all answered, "We agree"; He said, "Then bear witness amongst yourselves, and I Myself am a witness with you."

"I was a prophet while Adam was between the spirit and body" (Haakim, Tirmizi – with words variation)

Alive with Bodies in the Heavens

[Surah Baqarah 2:35-36] And We said, "O Adam! You and your wife dwell in this Garden, and eat freely from it wherever you please - but do not approach this tree for you will become of those who transgress." We said, "*Go down from Paradise, all of you*; then if a guidance comes to you from Me - so whoever follows My guidance, for such is neither fear nor any grief."

[Surah Nisa 4:157-158] And because they said, "We have killed the Messiah, Eisa the son of Maryam, the Messenger of Allah"; they did not slay him nor did they crucify him, but a look-alike was created for them; and those who disagree concerning it are in doubt about it; they know nothing of it, except the following of assumptions; and without doubt, they did not kill him. *In fact Allah raised him towards Himself*; and Allah is Almighty, Wise.

[Surah b/Israel 17:1] Purity is to Him Who took His bondman in a part of the night from the Sacred Mosque to the Aqsa Mosque around which We have placed blessings, in order that We may show him Our great signs; indeed he is the listener, the beholder. *(This verse refers to the physical journey of Prophet Mohammed* 🌼 *- to Al Aqsa Mosque and from there to the heavens and beyond. The entire journey back to Mecca was completed within a small part of the night.)*

[Surah Najm 53:9-10] So *the distance between the Spectacle and the beloved was only two arms' length, or even less.* So Allah divinely revealed to His bondman, whatever He divinely revealed. *(The Heavenly Journey of Prophet Mohammed* 🌼 *was with body and soul.)*

It is narrated on the authority of Abu Hurairah🌼 that Allah's Apostle 🌼 said: When I was taken for the night journey I met Moses🌼. Allah's Apostle 🌼 gave his description thus: He was a man, I suppose-and he (the narrator) was somewhat doubtful (that the Holy Prophet 🌼 observed): (Moses) was a man erect in stature with straight hair on his head as it he was one of the men of the Shanu'a; and I met Jesus 🌼 and Allah's Apostle 🌼 described him as one having a medium stature and a red complexion as if he had (just) come out of the bath He observed: I saw Ibrahim 🌼 and amongst his children I have the greatest resemblance with him. He said: There were brought to me two vessels. In one of them was milk and in the other one there was wine. And it was said to me: Select any one you like. So I selected the vessel containing milk and drank it. He (the angel) said: You have been guided on al-fitra or you have attained al-fitra. Had you selected wine, your Ummah would have been misled. (Muslim)

Alive on the Earth

[Surah Furqan 25:20] And all the Noble Messengers We sent before you were like this – eating food and walking in the markets; and We have made some of you a test for others; so will you, O people, patiently endure? And O dear Prophet, your Lord is All Seeing.

[Surah Kahf 18:9-11] Did you know that the People of the Cave and People close to the Woods, were Our exceptional signs? When the young men took refuge in the Cave, then said, "Our Lord! Give us mercy from Yourself, and arrange guidance for us in our affair." We then thumped upon their ears in the Cave for a number of years.

[Surah Baqarah 2:259] Or like him* who passed by a dwelling and it had fallen flat on its roofs; he said, "How will Allah bring it to life, after its death?"; so Allah kept him dead for a hundred years, then brought him back to life; He said, "How long have you stayed here?"; he replied, "I may have stayed for a day or little less"; He said, "In fact, you have spent a hundred years - so look at your food and drink which do not even smell stale; and look at your donkey whose bones even are not intact - in order that We may make you a sign for mankind - and look at the bones how We assemble them and then cover them with flesh"; so when the matter became clear to him, he said, "I know well that Allah is Able to do all things." (* Prophet Uzair - peace be upon him.)

Alive Inside the Fire

[Surah Ambiya 21:68-69] They said, "Burn him and help your Gods, if you want to." *We said, "O fire, become cool and peaceful upon Ibrahim."*

[Surah Saffat 37:97-98] They said, "Construct a building *(furnace)* for him, and then cast him in the blazing fire!" *So they tried to execute their evil scheme upon him – We therefore degraded them.*

Allah saved Syedena Ibrahim ﷺ by commanding the fire to turn cool.

Alive Inside the Fish Belly

[Surah Qalam 68:48-49] Therefore wait for your Lord's command, and do not be *like the one of the fish; who cried out when he was distraught.* Were it not for his Lord's favour that reached him, he would have surely been cast onto the desolate land, reproached.

It is reported that *Prophet Yunus ﷺ stayed inside the fish belly for 40 days, all the while glorifying Allah, and seeking His favour.*

Alive Inside the Grave

[Surah Baqarah 2:154] And do not utter regarding those who are slain in Allah's cause as "dead"; *in fact they are alive, but it is you who are unaware.*

[Surah A/I`mran 3:169] And do not ever assume that those who are slain in Allah's cause, are dead; *in fact they are alive with their Lord, receiving sustenance.*

[Surah A/I`mran 3:170-171] *Happy over what Allah has bestowed upon them from His grace, and rejoicing for those who will succeed them,* and have not yet joined them; for on them is no fear nor any grief. *They rejoice because of the favours from Allah and (His) munificence,* and because Allah does not waste the reward of the believers.

[Surah Nisa 4:69-70] And whoever obeys Allah and His Noble Messenger, will be with those upon whom Allah has bestowed grace - that is, the Holy Prophet ﷺ and the truthful and the martyrs and the virtuous; *and what excellent companions they are!* This is Allah's munificence; and Allah is Sufficient, the All Knowing.

[Surah Saba 34:13-14] They made for him whatever he wished - synagogues and statues, basins like ponds, and large pots built into the ground; "Be thankful, O the people of Dawud!" And few among My bondmen are grateful. *So when We sent the command of death towards him, no one revealed his death to the jinns except the termite of the earth which ate his staff;* and when he came to the ground, the truth about the jinns was exposed - if they had known the hidden, they would not have remained in the disgraceful toil.

It is reported that Syedena Sulaiman 🕊️ *stood in that position for one year, but the slaves and Jinns could not come to know about his demise, as his body did not decay, nor did his eyes close.*

Narrated Fazal bin Abbas 🕊️: When the Holy Prophet 🕊️ was laid in his noble grave, I took a last glimpse at his face. *I noticed that his lips were moving, so I put my ear close to his lips to listen. He was saying, "O Allah, forgive my Ummah."* I related this to all those present, upon which they were all shocked at the compassion of the Holy Prophet 🕊️ for his Ummah. (Kazul-Ummaal, Hujjatullah Alalalameen, Madarij alNubuwaah)

Narrated Abu al-Darda' 🕊️: Make abundant invocations of blessings upon me the day of Jum'a, for that day is witnessed by the angels. Verily, no one invokes blessings upon me except his invocation is shown to me until he finishes it." Abu al-Darda' said: "Even after death?" The Holy Prophet 🕊️ replied: "*Even after death! Truly Allah Most High forbade the earth to consume the bodies of Prophets. Therefore the Holy Prophet* 🕊️ *of Allah is alive and sustained!*" (Ibn Majah).

Narrated Abu Hurairah 🕊️: The Holy Prophet 🕊️ said: "*Whoever invokes blessings upon me at my grave I hear him,* and whoever invokes blessings on me from afar, I am informed about it." (Baihaqi)

Narrated Aws ibn Aws 🕊️: The Holy Prophet 🕊️ said: Among the most excellent of your days is Friday; on it Adam was created, on it he died, on it the last trumpet will be blown, and on it the shout will be made, so invoke more blessings on me that day, for your blessings will be submitted to me. The people asked: Allah's Apostle, how can it be that our blessings will be submitted to you while your body is decayed? *He replied: Allah, the Exalted, has prohibited the earth from consuming the bodies of Prophets.* (Abu Dawod)

Narrated Hazrat Ibn Umar ﷺ The Holy Prophet Muhammad ﷺ said: "The one who after Hajj *visits me after my death (i.e. the Holy Raudah) is like one who has visited me while I was alive.*" (Baihaqi, Mishkaat).

Narrated Syedah `Aisha ﷺ: Abu Bakr ﷺ came riding his horse from his dwelling place in As-Sunh. He got down from it, entered the Mosque and did not speak with anybody till he came to me and went direct to the Holy Prophet ﷺ, who was covered with a marked blanket. Abu Bakr ﷺ uncovered his face. He knelt down and kissed him and then started weeping and said, "*My father and my mother be sacrificed for you, O Allah's Prophet ﷺ! Allah will not combine two deaths on you. You have died the death which was written for you.*" (Bukhari – part of a longer hadeeth)

"*The Prophets are alive in their graves. They perform salaat.*" (Baihaqi, Ibn 'Asakir, Ibn Hajar)

Anas b. Malik reported Allah's Apostle ﷺ as saying: I came. And in the narration transmitted on the authority of Haddib (the words are): I happened to pass by Moses ﷺ on the occasion of the Night journey near the red mound (and found him) *saying his prayer in his grave.* (Muslim)

Narrated Syedah 'Aisha ﷺ: "When I used to go in my room after my husband and father were buried there, I would take off my overcoat. *I never took it off after Hazrat 'Umar ﷺ was buried. Because, he was not my near kin.* I was restrained by my sense of modesty because he was there." (Imam Ahmad and Hakim)

Said 'Abdullah ibn 'Abbas 🕮 "Some Sahabis set up a tent at a place where there was a grave that could not be noticed. *They heard Surah al-Mulk being recited inside the tent.* Allah's Apostle 🕮 came in the tent after the recitation ended. When they told him what they had heard, he said, 'This honorable surah protects men from the punishment in the grave.'" (At-Tirmizi, Hakim and Baihaqi)

Dawud ibn Salih 🕮 says: "Marwan [ibn al-Hakam] one day saw a man placing his face on top of the grave of the Holy Prophet 🕮. He said: "Do you know what you are doing?" When he came near him, he realized it was Abu Ayyub al-Ansari 🕮. The latter said: *"Yes; I came to the Holy Prophet 🕮, not to a stone."* (Ibn Hibban, Ahmad, Tabarani, Haythami, al-Hakim)

It is narrated on the authority of Anas b. Malik 🕮 that Allah's Apostle 🕮 said: I was brought al-Buraq Who is an animal white and long, larger than a donkey but smaller than a mule, who would place his hoof a distance equal to the range of version. I mounted it and came to the Temple (Bait-ul-Maqdis in Jerusalem), then tethered it to the ring used by the Holy Prophet 🕮. I entered the mosque and prayed two rak'ahs in it, and then came out and Gabriel brought me a vessel of wine and a vessel of milk. I chose the milk, and Gabriel 🕮 said: You have chosen the natural thing. Then he took me to heaven. Gabriel 🕮 then asked the (gate of heaven) to be opened and he was asked who he was. He replied: Gabriel (🕮). He was again asked: Who is with you? He (Gabriel 🕮) said: Muhammad (🕮). It was said: Has he been sent for? Gabriel 🕮 replied: He has indeed been sent for. And (the door of the heaven) was opened for us and lo! we saw Adam 🕮. He welcomed me and prayed for my good. Then we ascended to the second heaven. Gabriel 🕮 (asked the door of heaven to be opened), and he was asked who he was. He answered: Gabriel (🕮); and was again asked: Who is with you?

He replied: Muhammad (ﷺ). It was said: Has he been sent for? He replied: He has indeed been sent for. The gate was opened. When I entered 'Isa b. Maryam ﷺ and Yahya b. Zakariya ﷺ, cousins from the maternal side, welcomed me and prayed for my good Then I was taken to the third heaven and Gabriel ﷺ asked for the opening (of the door). He was asked: Who are you? He replied: Gabriel (ﷺ). He was (again) asked: Who is with you? He replied Muhammad (ﷺ). It was said: Has he been sent for? He replied He has indeed been sent for. (The gate) was opened for us and I saw Yusuf ﷺ who had been given half of (world) beauty. He welcomed me prayed for my well-being. Then he ascended with us to the fourth heaven. Gabriel ﷺ asked for the (gate) to be opened, and it was said: Who is he? He replied: Gabriel (ﷺ). It was (again) said: Who is with you? He said: Muhammad (ﷺ). It was said: Has he been sent for? He replied: He has indeed been sent for. The (gate) was opened for us, and lo! Idris ﷺ was there. He welcomed me and prayed for my well-being (About him) Allah, the Exalted and the Glorious, has said:" We elevated him (Idris ﷺ) to the exalted position" (Qur'an xix. 57). Then he ascended with us to the fifth heaven and Gabriel ﷺ asked for the (gate) to be opened. It was said: Who is he? He replied Gabriel ﷺ. It was (again) said: Who is with you? He replied: Muhammad ﷺ. It was said Has he been sent for? He replied: He has indeed been sent for. (The gate) was opened for us and then I was with Harun (Aaron ﷺ). He welcomed me prayed for my well-being. Then I was taken to the sixth heaven. Gabriel ﷺ asked for the door to be opened. It was said: Who is he? He replied: Gabriel (ﷺ). It was said: Who is with you? He replied: Muhammad ﷺ. It was said: Has he been sent for? He replied: He has indeed been sent for. (The gate) was opened for us and there I was with Musa (Moses ﷺ) He welcomed me and prayed for my well-being. Then I was taken up to the seventh heaven. Gabriel ﷺ asked the (gate) to be opened. It was said: Who is he? He said: Gabriel (ﷺ). It was said. Who is with you?

He replied: Muhammad (ﷺ). It was said: Has he been sent for? He replied: He has indeed been sent for. (The gate) was opened for us and there I found Ibrahim (Abraham ﷺ) reclining against the Bait-ul-Ma'mur and there enter into it seventy thousand angels every day, never to visit (this place) again. Then I was taken to Sidrat-ul-Muntaha whose leaves were like elephant ears and its fruit like big earthenware vessels. And when it was covered by the Command of Allah, it underwent such a change that none amongst the creation has the power to praise its beauty.

Then Allah revealed to me a revelation and He made obligatory for me fifty prayers every day and night. Then I went down to Moses (ﷺ) and he said: What has your Lord enjoined upon your Ummah? I said: Fifty prayers. He said: Return to thy Lord and beg for reduction (in the number of prayers), for your community shall not be able to bear this burden. As I have put to test the children of Isra'il and tried them (and found them too weak to bear such a heavy burden). He (the Holy Prophet ﷺ) said: I went back to my Lord and said: My Lord, make things lighter for my Ummah. (The Lord) reduced five prayers for me. I went down to Moses (ﷺ) and said. (The Lord) reduced five (prayers) for me, He said: Verily thy Ummah shall not be able to bear this burden; return to thy Lord and ask Him to make things lighter. I then kept going back and forth between my Lord Blessed and Exalted and Moses, till He said: There are five prayers every day and night. O Muhammad, each being credited as ten, so that makes fifty prayers. He who intends to do a good deed and does not do it will have a good deed recorded for him; and if he does it, it will be recorded for him as ten; whereas he who intends to do an evil deed and does not do, it will not be recorded for him; and if he does it, only one evil deed will be recorded. I then came down and when I came to Moses (ﷺ) and informed him, he said: Go back to your Lord and ask Him to make things lighter. Upon this Allah's Apostle ﷺ remarked: I returned to my Lord until I felt ashamed before Him. (Muslim)

Narrated Abu Hurairah ؓ: The Holy Prophet ﷺ said while standing near the graves of the martyrs of Uhud, "I bear witness that you are alive in the sight of Allah." Then turning towards those present he said, *"So visit them, and greet them – I swear by the One in whose power lies my life, they will answer back to whoever greets them until the Last Day."* (Hakim, Baihaqi)

Narrated Jabir ؓ: When the time of the Battle of Uhud approached, my father called me at night and said, "I think that I will be the first amongst the companions of the Holy Prophet ﷺ to be martyred. I do not leave anyone after me dearer to me than you, except Allah's Apostle's soul and I owe some debt and you should repay it and treat your sisters favorably (nicely and politely)." So in the morning he was the first to be martyred and was buried along with another (martyr). *I did not like to leave him with the other (martyr) so I took him out of the grave after six months of his burial and he was in the same condition as he was on the day of burial, except a slight change near his ear.* (Bukhari)

Alive As Souls in Barzakh

[Surah Nisa 4:69-70] And whoever obeys Allah and His Noble Messenger, will be with those upon whom Allah has bestowed grace - that is, the Holy Prophet (ﷺ) and the truthful and the martyrs and the virtuous; *and what excellent companions they are!* This is Allah's munificence; and Allah is Sufficient, the All Knowing.

Narrated 'Abdullah ibn 'Abbas ؓ: He was sitting by Allah's Apostle ﷺ, when suddenly Allah's Apostle ﷺ, raised his head and said "Wa alaykum as-salaamo wa rahmatu-Allah". Those present asked in surprise, "O Allah's Apostle! What is this?" He said, *"Jafar bin Abi Talib greeted me while passing by along with a group of angels, so I greeted him back."* (Khasais Kubra, Mustadrak)

Narrated Masruq 🙛: We asked Abdullah (i.e. Ibn Masud) about this verse: And do not ever assume that those who are slain in Allah's cause, are dead; *in fact they are alive with their Lord, receiving sustenance* (Quran Chapter 3 Verse 169). He said: We asked about that and the Holy Prophet 🙛 said: Their souls are in the insides of green birds having lanterns suspended from the Throne, roaming freely in Paradise where they please, then taking shelter in those lanterns. So their Lord cast a glance at them (the martyrs) and said: Do you wish for anything? They said: What shall we wish for when we roam freely in Paradise where we please? And thus did He do to them three times. When they saw that they would not be spared from being asked [again], they said: O Lord, we would like for You to put back our souls into our bodies so that we might fight for Your sake once again. And when He saw that they were not in need of anything they were let be. (Muslim, Tirmizi, Nasa'i and Ibn Majah).

Narrated 'Abdullah ibn 'Abbas 🙛: He was sitting by Allah's Apostle 🙛, and Asma' bint 'Umais was also present; Allah's Apostle 🙛, after saying "Alaikum salaam," declared: *'Oh Asma! Your husband Jafar came to me with [Archangels] Jibreel and Mikaeel just a moment ago. They greeted me. I answered their greeting.* He said, "I fought with disbelievers in the Battle of Muta for a few days. I got wounded on seventy-three points all over my body. I held the flag with my right hand. Then my right arm was cutoff. I held the flag with my left hand, them my left arm was cut off. *Allah ta'ala gave me two wings instead of my two arms: I fly with Jibreel (🙛) and Mikaeel (🙛). I fly out from Paradise whenever I wish. And I go in and eat its fruits whenever I wish."* ' Upon this, Asma' said, 'May Allah ta'ala's favours do good to Jafar! But I am afraid people will not believe it when they hear it. Oh Allah's Apostle 🙛! Would you tell them on the minbar! They will believe you.' Allah's Apostle 🙛

honored the masjid and ascended the minbar. After praising and glorifying Allah ta'ala, he said, *'Jafar ibn Abi Talib (؏) came to me with Jibreel (؏) and Mikaeel (؏). Allah ta'ala has granted him two wings. He greeted me.'* Then he repeated what he had told Asma' about her husband." (Hakim)

Chapter 2: The Holy Prophet is a Witness over the Ummah's Deeds

[Surah Muzzammil 73:15] We have indeed sent a Noble Messenger towards you, *a present witness over you* – the way We had sent a Noble Messenger towards Firaun.

Sa`id ibn al-Musayyib said ؏: "*Not one day passes except the Holy Prophet's ؏ Community is shown to him morning and evening. He knows them by their marks [or names] and their actions, thereby giving witness concerning them.* (Ibn Kathir, Qurtubi, Ibn Hajar)

The Holy Prophet ؏ said: "Allah Most High has an angel to whom he has given the names of all creatures, and he shall stand at my grave, after I die, so that none shall invoke blessings upon me except he (the angel) shall say: `*O Muhammad, So-and-so son of So-and-so has just invoked blessings upon you.*' Thereupon the Almighty Lord shall send a blessing upon that person, tenfold for each blessing he invoked upon me." (al-Bazzar Musnad, Daylami. Also in Al-Tareekh by Bukhari –shorter version)

Narrated Ibn Masud ؏: The Holy Prophet ؏ said: "My life is a great good for you, you will relate about me and it will be related to you, *and my death is a great good for you, your actions will be exhibited to me, and if I see goodness I will praise Allah, and if I see evil I will ask forgiveness of Him for you.*" (al-Bazzar, al-Khasa'is al-Kubra)

Al-`Utbi ؏, a Sahabi, said: "As I was sitting by the grave of the Holy Prophet ؏, a Bedouin Arab came and said: "Peace be upon you, O Allah's Apostle! I have heard Allah saying: "and if they, when they have wronged their own souls, come humbly to you *(O dear Prophet Mohammed - peace and blessings be upon him)* and seek forgiveness from Allah, and the Noble Messenger intercedes for them, they will certainly find Allah as the Most Acceptor Of Repentance, the Most Merciful. (4:64)", SO I HAVE COME TO YOU ASKING FORGIVENESS FOR MY SIN, SEEKING YOUR INTERCESSION with my Lord." Then he began to recite poetry: *'O best of those whose bones are buried in the deep earth, And from whose fragrance the depth and the height have become sweet, May I be the ransom for a grave which you inhabit, And in which are found purity, bounty and munificence!'* Then he left, and *I dozed and saw the Holy Prophet* ﷺ *in my sleep.* He said to me: "O `Utbi, run after the Bedouin and give him glad tidings that Allah has forgiven him."" (Nawawi, al-Qurtubi, Ibn Kathir, Ibn al-Jawzi)

Chapter 3: Given the Choice between Life & Death

Narrated Syedah `Aisha ﷺ: I heard Allah's Apostle ﷺ saying, "No prophet gets sick but he is given the choice to select either this world or the Hereafter." `Aisha ﷺ added: During his fatal illness, his voice became very husky and I heard him saying: *"In the company of those whom is the Grace of Allah, of the prophets, the Siddiqin (those followers of the prophets who were first and foremost to believe in them), the martyrs and the pious.'* (4:69) And from this I came to know that he has been given the option. (Bukhari, Muslim)

Narrated Syedah Aisha ﷺ: When Allah 's Apostle ﷺ was in good health, he used to say, "Never does a prophet die unless he is shown his place in Paradise (i.e. before his death), and then he is made alive or given option." When the Prophet ﷺ became ill and his last moments came while his head was on my thigh, he became unconscious, and when he came to his senses, he looked towards the roof of the house and then said, *"O Allah! With the highest companion."* Thereupon I said, "Hence he is not going to stay with us?" Then I came to know that his state was the confirmation of the narration he used to mention to us while he was in good health. (Bukhari)

Chapter 4: Seeing the Holy Prophet in a Dream

Narrated Abu Hurairah ﷺ: I heard the Prophet ﷺ saying, "*Whoever sees me in a dream will see me in his wakefulness,* and Satan cannot imitate me in shape." Abu `Abdullah said, "Ibn Seereen said, 'Only if he sees the Prophet ﷺ in his (real) shape.'" (Bukhari)

Narrated Abu Sa'id Al-Khudri ﷺ: The Prophet ﷺ said, "*Whoever sees me (in a dream) then he indeed has seen the truth,* as Satan cannot appear in my shape." (Bukhari)

Chapter 5: The Holy Prophet – Present in the Momin's Grave!

Narrated Anas bin Malik ﷺ: Allah's Apostle ﷺ said, "When (Allah's) slave is put in his grave and his companions return and he even hears their footsteps, two angels come to him and make him sit and ask, '*What did you use to say about this man* (i.e. Muhammad ﷺ)?' The faithful Believer will say, 'I testify that he is Allah's slave and His Apostle.' Then they will say to him, 'Look at your place in the Hell Fire; Allah has given you a place in Paradise instead of it.' So he will see both his places." (Qatada said, "We were informed that his grave would be made spacious." Then Qatada went back to the narration of Anas ﷺ who said;) Whereas a hypocrite or a non-believer will be asked, "What did you use to say about this man." He will reply, "I do not know; but I used to say what the people used to say." So they will say to him, "Neither did you know nor did you take the guidance (by reciting the Qur'an)." Then he will be hit with iron hammers once, that he will send such a cry as everything near to him will hear, except Jinns and human beings. (Bukhari, Muslim)

Section 7: The Excellent Faces

Chapter 1: The Best Sight for Allah

[Surah Baqarah 2:144] *We observe you turning your face, several times towards heaven (O dear Prophet Mohammed ﷺ)*; so We will definitely make you turn *(for prayer)* towards a qiblah which pleases you; therefore now turn your face towards the Sacred Mosque *(in Mecca)*; and O Muslims, wherever you may be, turn your faces *(for prayer)* towards it only; and those who have received the Book surely know that this is the truth from their Lord; and Allah is not unaware of their deeds.

[Surah Shua`ra 26:217-219] And rely upon *(Allah)* the Almighty, the Most Merciful. *Who watches you when you stand up. And watches your movements among those who prostrate in prayer.*

Chapter 2: The Faces of Such People Remind of Allah

Narrated by Abu Malik al-Ash`ari ﷺ: When the Holy Prophet ﷺ finished his prayer he turned to face the people and said: "O people! Listen to this, understand it, and know it. Allah has servants who are neither Prophets nor martyrs and whom the Holy Prophets and martyrs yearn to be like, due to their seat and proximity in relation to Allah." One of the beduin Arabs who came from among the most isolated of people twisted his hand at the Holy Prophet ﷺ and said: "O Allah's Apostle ﷺ! People from humankind who are neither Prophets nor martyrs and yet the Holy Prophets and the martyrs yearn to be like them due to their seat and proximity in relation to Allah?! Describe them for us!" The Holy Prophet's ﷺ face showed delight at the Bedouin's question and he said: "They are of the strangers from this and that place. They frequent this or that tribe without belonging to them. They do not have family connections among themselves. They love one another for Allah's sake. They are of pure intent towards one another. *On the Day of Resurrection* Allah will place for them pedestals of light upon which He will make them sit, and *He will turn their faces and clothes into light.* On the Day of

Resurrection the people will be terrified but not those. They are Allah's Friends upon whom fear comes not, nor do they grieve." (Musnad Imam Ahmad)

Narrated Syedena Ali ﷺ: They are the fewest in number, but the greatest in rank before Allah. Through them Allah preserves His proofs until they bequeath it to those like them (before passing on) and plant it firmly in their hearts. By them knowledge has taken by assault the reality of things, so that they found easy what those given to comfort found hard, and found intimacy in what the ignorant found desolate. They accompanied the world with bodies whose spirits were attached to the highest station. *Ah, ah! how one yearns to see them*! (Ibn al-Jawzi in Sifat al-safwa)

Chapter 3: The Face of the Holy Prophet

Narrated Hazrat Jaber ﷺ: "I once saw Allah's Apostle ﷺ on the night of a full moon. On that night he wore red clothing. At times I looked at the full moon and at times at Allah's Apostle ﷺ. *Ultimately I came to the conclusion that Allah's Apostle ﷺ was more handsome, beautiful and more radiant than the full moon*." (Tirmizi)

Narrated Abu Ishaq ﷺ: Al-Bara' was asked, "Was the face of the Holy Prophet ﷺ (as bright) as a sword?" He said, "*No, but (as bright) as a moon*." [Bukhari]

Narrated Syedah Aisha ﷺ: I was sewing (something in the dark room) when the needle slipped out of my hand. I searched for it but was unable to find it. *Thereupon the Holy Prophet ﷺ entered (the room) and by the bright light rays emanating from his face, the needle shone and I came to know where it is*. (Ibn Asakir, Khasais Kubra)

Narrated Yazid ibn Sa'id al-Kindi ﷺ: When the Holy Prophet ﷺ made supplication (to Allah) he would raise his hands and wipe his face with his hands. (Abu Dawud)

Narrated on the authority of Ibn Shamasa Mahri 🕮: He said: We went to Amr b. al-As and he was about to die. He wept for a long time and turned his face towards the wall. His son said: Did Allah's Apostle 🕮 not give you tidings of this? Did Allah's Apostle 🕮 not give you tidings of this? He (the narrator) said: He turned his face (towards the audience) and said: The best thing which we can count upon is the testimony that there is no god but Allah and that Muhammad is Allah's Apostle. Verily I have passed through three phases. (The first one) in which I found myself averse to none else more than I was averse to Allah's Apostle 🕮 and there was no other desire stronger in me than the one that I should overpower him and kill him. Had I died in this state, I would have been definitely one of the denizens of Fire. When Allah instilled the love of Islam in my heart, I came to the Apostle 🕮 and said: Stretch out your right hand so that I may pledge my allegiance to you. He stretched out his right hand, I withdrew my hand, He (the Holy Prophet) said: What has happened to you, O 'Amr? replied: I intend to lay down some condition. He asked: What condition do you intend to put forward? I said: should be granted pardon. He (the Holy Prophet) observed: Are you not aware of the fact that Islam wipes out all the previous (misdeeds)? Verily migration wipes out all the previous (misdeeds), and verily the pilgrimage wipes out all the (previous) misdeeds. And then no one was more dear to me than Allah's Apostle 🕮 and none was more sublime in my eyes than he. *Never could I, pluck courage to catch a full glimpse of his face due to its splendor.* So if I am asked to describe his features, I cannot do that for I have not eyed him fully. Had I died in this state I had every reason to hope that I would have been among the dwellers of Paradise. Then we were responsible for certain things (in the light of which) I am unable to know what is in store for me. When I die, let neither female mourner nor fire accompany me. When you bury me, fill my grave well with earth, then stand around it for the time within which a camel is slaughtered and its meat is distributed so that I may enjoy your intimacy and (in your company) ascertain what answer I can give to the messengers (angels) of Allah. (Muslim)

Abu Hurairah ﷺ reported Allah's Apostle ﷺ as saying: The people most loved by me from amongst my Ummah would be those who would come after me but everyone amongst them would have the keenest desire to catch a glimpse of me even at the cost of his family and wealth. (Muslim)

Chapter 4: The Shining Faces on the Last Day

[Surah A/I`mran 3:106] On the Day *(of Resurrection)* when some faces will be shining and some faces black; so, *(to)* those whose faces are blackened, "What! You disbelieved after you had accepted faith! Therefore now taste the punishment, the result of your disbelief."

[Surah A/I`mran 3:107] And *those whose faces will be shining*, are in the mercy of Allah; they will abide in it forever.

Chapter 5: The Handkerchief of the Holy Prophet

Narrated Ibaad bin Abdul Samad ﷺ: We once went to the house of Anas bin Malik ﷺ. He ordered his maid-servant, "Serve food, we shall eat." She brought the food. He then said, "Bring the handkerchief too." She brought the handkerchief which was soiled. He then said, "Put it in the oven." She inserted the handkerchief into the oven, that was burning fiercely. After a while when it was removed, the handkerchief was white like milk. Astonished, we asked him what was the secret of this. He answered, "*This was the handkerchief of the Holy* Prophet ﷺ *, which he used for cleaning his holy face. Whenever it gets soiled, we clean it by inserting it into the burning oven, like we did now — because fire does not destroy any thing that has touched the face of any prophet.*" (Abu Nuaim, Khasais Kubra).

Narrated Hazrat Abu Zaid bin Amr bin Akhtab 🕮: The Holy Prophet 🕮 once passed his hands over my head and beard, and supplicated thus, "O Allah, grant him beauty." The sub-narrator adds that Abu Zaid lived for more than a hundred years but there was not a single white hair on his head nor in his beard. *All his hair remained black, his face kept shining and there was not a single wrinkle on his face until he died.* (Tirmizi, Baihaqi, Khasais Kubra).

Chapter 6: Water and Saliva, Applied by Sahaba on their Faces

Reported Abu Musa 🕮: I was in the company of Allah's Apostle 🕮 as he had been sitting in Ji'ranah (a place) between Mecca and Medina and Bilal was also there, that there came to Allah's Apostle 🕮 a desert Arab, and he said: Muhammad 🕮, fulfill your promise that you made with me. Allah's Apostle 🕮 said to him: Accept glad tidings. Thereupon the desert Arab said: You shower glad tidings upon me very much; then Allah's Apostle 🕮 turned towards Abu Musa and Bilal seemingly in a state of annoyance and said: Verily he has rejected glad tidings but you two should accept them. We said: Allah's Apostle 🕮, we have readily accepted them. *Then Allah's* Apostle 🕮 *called for a cup of water and washed his hands in that, and face too, and put the saliva in it and then said: Drink out of it and pour it over your faces and over your chest and gladden yourselves. They took hold of the cup and did as Allah's* Apostle 🕮 *had commanded them to do. Thereupon Umm Salamah called from behind the veil: Spare some water in your vessel for your mother also, and they also gave some water which had been spared for her.* (Muslim)

Hajjaj ibn Hassan 🕮 said: "We were at Anas's house and he brought up the Holy Prophet's 🕮 cup from a black pouch. *He ordered that it be filled with water and we drank from it and poured some of it on our heads and faces and sent blessings on the Holy* Prophet 🕮 ". (Ahmad, Ibn Kathir)

Narrated Abu Juhaifa 🕮: Allah's Apostle 🕮 came to us at noon and water for ablution was brought to him. After he had performed ablution, the remaining water was taken by the people and they started smearing their bodies with it (as a blessed thing). The Holy Prophet 🕮 offered two rak`at of the Zuhr prayer and then two rak`at of the `Asr prayer while a short spear (or stick) was there (as a Sutra) in front of him. Abu Musa said: *The Holy Prophet 🕮 asked for a tumbler containing water and washed both his hands and face in it and then threw a mouthful of water in the tumbler and said to both of us (Abu Musa and Bilal), "Drink from the tumbler and pour some of its water on your faces and chests."* (Bukhari)

Narrated Al-Miswar bin Makhrama 🕮 and Marwan 🕮 (part of a longer hadeeth): Before embracing Islam Al-Mughira was in the company of some people. He killed them and took their property and came (to Medina) to embrace Islam. The Holy Prophet 🕮 said (to him, "As regards your Islam, I accept it, but as for the property I do not take anything of it. (As it was taken through treason). `Urwa then started looking at the Companions of the Holy Prophet 🕮. *By Allah, whenever Allah's Apostle 🕮 spat, the spittle would fall in the hand of one of them (i.e. the Holy Prophet's🕮 companions) who would rub it on his face and skin*; if he ordered them they would carry his orders immediately; *if he performed ablution, they would struggle to take the remaining water*; and when they spoke to him, they would lower their voices and would not look at his face constantly out of respect. `Urwa returned to his people and said, "O people! By Allah, I have been to the kings and to Caesar, Khosrau and An-Najashi, yet I have never seen any of them respected by his courtiers as much as Muhammad 🕮 is respected by his companions. By Allah, if he spat, the spittle would fall in the hand of one of them (i.e. the Holy Prophet's 🕮 companions) who would rub it on his face and skin; if he ordered them, they would carry out his order immediately; if he performed ablution, they would struggle to take the remaining water; and when they spoke, they would lower their voices and would not look at his face constantly out of respect." `Urwa added, "No doubt, he has presented to you a good reasonable offer, so please accept it." (Bukhari)

Chapter 7: Sahabah Wiped their Faces with Things Used by the Holy Prophet

Narrated Abu Abdullah 🕮: My grandfather had the blanket of the Holy Prophet 🕮. When Hazrat Umar bin Abdul Azeez became the Khalifah, he summoned my grandfather. My grandfather went to him with the blanket, wrapped in leather. *Hazrat Umar bin Abdul Azeez rubbed the blanket over his face.* (Bukhari in Tareekh)

Chapter 8: The Holy Prophet's Minbar

Hazrat Abdullah Ibn `Umar 🕮 used to touch the seat of the Holy Prophet's 🕮 minbar and then wipe his hands on his face for blessing. (al-Mughni, Shifa', Tabaqat Ibn Saad, and others)

Section 8: The Excellent Eyes & Vision

Chapter 1: Says Allah, "I Become His Sight"......

Narrated Abu Hurairah ﷺ: Allah's Apostle ﷺ said, "Allah said, 'I will declare war against him who shows hostility to a pious worshipper of Mine. And the most beloved things with which My slave comes nearer to Me, is what I have enjoined upon him; and *My slave keeps on coming closer to Me through performing Nawafil (praying or doing extra deeds besides what is obligatory) till I love him, so I become his sense of hearing with which he hears, and his sense of sight with which he sees, and his hand with which he grips, and his leg with which he walks; and if he asks Me, I will give him, and if he asks My protection (Refuge), I will protect him*; (i.e. give him My Refuge) and I do not hesitate to do anything as I hesitate to take the soul of the believer, for he hates death, and I hate to disappoint him." (Bukhari)

Chapter 2: Worship Allah As Though You See Him

Narrated Omar bin Khattab ﷺ: One day while we were sitting with Allah's Apostle ﷺ there appeared before us a man whose clothes were exceedingly white and whose hair was exceedingly black; no signs of journeying were to be seen on him and none of us knew him. He walked up and sat down by the Holy Prophet ﷺ. Resting his knees against his and placing the palms of his hands on his thighs, he said: "O Muhammad, tell me about Islam". Allah's Apostle ﷺ said: "Islam is to testify that there is no god but Allah and Muhammad is the Messenger of Allah, to perform the prayers, to pay the Zakat, to fast in Ramadan, and to make the pilgrimage to the House if you are able to do so." He said: "You have spoken rightly", and we were amazed at him asking him and saying that he had spoken rightly. He said: "Then tell me about Eeman. "He said: "It is to believe in Allah, His angels, His books, His messengers, and the Last Day, and to believe in divine destiny, both the good and the evil thereof." He said: "You have spoken rightly". *He said: "Then tell me about Ehsan." He said: "It is to worship Allah as though you are seeing Him, and while you see Him not yet truly He sees you*". He said: "Then tell me about the Hour". He said: "The one questioned about it knows no better than the questioner." He said: "Then tell me about its signs." He said: "That the slave-girl will give birth to her mistress and that you will see the barefooted, naked, destitute herdsman competing in constructing lofty buildings." Then he took himself off and I stayed for a time. Then he said: "O Omar, do you know who the questioner was?" I said: "Allah and His messenger ﷺ know best". He said: "He was Jibreel (Gabriel), who came to you to teach you your religion." (Muslim)

Chapter 3: The Holy Prophet Saw His Lord, Allah

Narrated Hazrat Abdul Rehman bin Aaesh ﷺ: The Holy Prophet ﷺ said, "I saw my Lord in the best shape. He said, 'In what matter are the close angels disputing?' I said, 'It is You who know!' " The Holy Prophet ﷺ then said, "*He then placed His Hand of mercy between my shoulders and I felt its coolness at the centre of my chest – and I came to know all that is in the skies and in the earth.*" The Holy Prophet ﷺ then recited the following verse of the Holy Qur'an – "[Ana`am 6:75] And likewise We showed Ibrahim the entire kingdom of the heavens and the earth and so that he be of those who believe as eyewitnesses." (Mishkaat, Tirmizi, Ahmad)

Said Abdullah ibn Abbas ﷺ: "Undoubtedly, the *Holy Prophet* ﷺ *saw his Lord (Allah) twice – once with the eyes of his head and once with the eyes of the heart.*" (Tibrani, Khasais Kubra)

Narrated Ibn Abbas ﷺ: The Holy Quran's words: "The heart did not deny, what it saw " (Surah Najm 11) and" And indeed he did see the Spectacle again. (Surah Najm 13) imply that *the Holy Prophet* ﷺ *saw Allah twice with his heart.* (Muslim)

He could see & hear what others cannot.

Narrated Abu Zar Gifari 🙵: Holy Prophet ﷺ said, *"Indeed I see what you do not see, and I hear what you do not hear."* (Tirmizi, Ibn Majah, Mishkaat)

He saw what is in front and at the back.

Narrated Abu Hurairah 🙵: Allah's Apostle ﷺ said, "Do you consider or see that my face is towards the Qiblah? *By Allah, neither your submissiveness nor your bowing is hidden from me, surely I see you from my back.*" (Bukhari)

Narrated Anas bin Malik 🙵: The Holy Prophet ﷺ led us in a prayer and then got up on the pulpit and said, "In your prayer and bowing, *I certainly see you from my back as I see you (while looking at you.)*" (Bukhari)

Narrated Abu Hurairah 🙵: The Holy Prophet ﷺ said, *"Indeed I see towards my back in the same manner as I see towards the front."* (Abu Nuaim, Khasais Kubra, Zarkani)

The Holy Prophet could see Paradise, and Allah's great signs

[Surah b/Israel 17:1] Purity is to Him Who took His bondman in a part of the night from the Sacred Mosque to the Aqsa Mosque around which We have placed blessings, in order that We may show him Our great signs; indeed he is the listener, the beholder.

Narrated `Abdullah bin `Abbas 🙵: Once a solar eclipse occurred during the lifetime of Allah's Apostle ﷺ. He offered the eclipse prayer. His companions asked, "O Allah's Apostle ﷺ! We saw you trying to take something while standing at your place and then we saw you retreating." The Holy Prophet ﷺ said, *"I was shown Paradise and wanted to have a bunch of fruit from it. Had I taken it, you would have eaten from it as long as the world remains."* (Bukhari)

Narrated `Uqba bin Amir ﷺ: Allah's Apostle ﷺ offered the funeral prayers of the martyrs of Uhud eight years after (their death), as if bidding farewell to the living and the dead, then he ascended the pulpit and said, "I am your predecessor before you, and I am a witness on you, and your promised place to meet me will be Al-Haud (i.e. the Tank) (on the Day of Resurrection), and *I am (now) looking at it from this place of mine.* I am not afraid that you will worship others besides Allah, but I am afraid that worldly life will tempt you and cause you to compete with each other for it." That was the last look which I cast on Allah's Apostle. (Bukhari)

The Holy Prophet could see things far away from normal vision

Narrated Anas bin Malik ﷺ: The Holy Prophet ﷺ delivered a sermon and said, "*Zaid took the flag and was martyred, and then Ja`far took the flag and was martyred, and then `Abdullah bin Rawaha took the flag and was martyred too, and then Khalid bin Al-Walid took the flag though he was not appointed as a commander and Allah made him victorious.*" The Holy Prophet ﷺ further added, "It would not please us to have them with us." Ayyub, a sub-narrator, added, "Or the Holy Prophet ﷺ, shedding tears, said, 'It would not please them to be with us." (Bukhari, Mishkaat)

Narrated Al-Miswar bin Makhrama ﷺ and Marwan ﷺ, (whose narrations attest each other): Allah's Apostle ﷺ set out at the time of Al-Hudaibiya (treaty), and when they proceeded for a distance, he said, "*Khalid bin Al-Walid leading the cavalry of Quraish constituting the front of the army, is at a place called Al-Ghamim, so take the way on the right.*" By Allah, Khalid did not perceive the arrival of the Muslims till the dust arising from the march of the Muslim army reached him, and then he turned back hurriedly to inform

Quraish. The Holy Prophet ﷺ went on advancing till he reached the Thaniya (i.e. a mountainous way) through which one would go to them (i.e. people of Quraish). The she-camel of the Holy Prophet ﷺ sat down. The people tried their best to cause the she-camel to get up but in vain, so they said, "Al-Qaswa' (i.e. the she-camel's name) has become stubborn! Al-Qaswa' has become stubborn!" The Holy Prophet ﷺ said, "Al-Qaswa' has not become stubborn, for stubbornness is not her habit, but she was stopped by Him Who stopped the elephant." Then he said, "By the Name of Him in Whose Hands my soul is, if they (i.e. the Quraish infidels) ask me anything which will respect the ordinances of Allah, I will grant it to them." (Bukhari – part of a longer Hadeeth)

It is narrated on the authority of Jabir b. 'Abdullah that Allah's Apostle ﷺ said: *When the Quraish belied me, I was staying in Hatim and Allah lifted before me Bait-ul-Maqdis and I began to narrate to them (the Quraish of Mecca) its signs while I was in fact looking at it.* (Muslim)

The Holy Prophet could see the Angels, the Spirits of other Prophets & Martyrs

Narrated Abu Salama ﷺ: Syedah `Aisha ﷺ said that the Holy Prophet ﷺ said to her "O `Aisha' This is Gabriel and he sends his (greetings) salutations to you." `Aisha ﷺ said, "Salutations (Greetings) to him, and Allah's Mercy and Blessings be on him," and addressing the Holy Prophet ﷺ she said, "*You see what I don't see.*" (Bukhari)

Narrated 'Abdullah ibn 'Abbas ﷺ: He was sitting by Allah's Apostle ﷺ, and Asma' bint 'Umais was also present; Allah's Apostle ﷺ, after saying "Alaikum salam," declared: *'Oh Asma! Your husband Jafar came to me with Jibreel (ﷺ) and Mikaeel (ﷺ) just a moment ago.* They greeted me. I answered their greeting. He said, "I fought with disbelievers in the Battle of Muta for a few days. I got wounded on seventy-three points all over my body. I held the flag with my right hand. Then my right arm was cutoff. I held the flag with my left hand, them my left arm was cut off. *Allah ta'ala gave me two wings instead of my two arms: I fly with Jibreel and Mikaeel. I fly out from Paradise whenever I wish. And I go in and eat its fruits whenever I wish.*" ' Upon this, Asma' said, 'May Allah's favours do good to Jafar! But I am afraid people will not believe it when they hear it. Oh Allah's Apostle! Would you tell them on the minbar! They will believe you.' Allah's Apostle ﷺ honored the masjid and ascended the minbar. After praising and glorifying Allah ta'ala, he said, *'Jafar ibn Abi Talib came to me with Jibreel and Mikaeel. Allah ta'ala has granted him two wings. He greeted me.'* Then he repeated what he had told Asma' about her husband." (Hakim)

The Holy Prophet could see the matters of the grave

Anas b. Malik ﷺ reported: Allah's Apostle ﷺ said "I happened to pass by Moses on the occasion of the Night journey near the red mound (and found him) *saying his prayer in his grave.*" (Muslim)

Ibn Abbas ﷺ reported: Allah's Apostle ﷺ happened to pass by two graves and said: They (their occupants) are being tormented, but they are not tormented for a grievous sin. One of them carried tales and the other did not keep himself safe from being defiled by urine. He then called for a fresh twig and split it into two parts, and planted them on each grave and then said: Perhaps, their punishment will be mitigated as long as these twigs remain fresh. (Bukhari).

The vision given to Syedena Ibrahim

[Surah Ana`am 6:75] *And likewise We showed Ibrahim the entire kingdom of the heavens and the earth and so that he be of those who believe as eyewitnesses*

Syedena Umar could see Nahawand from Medina

Narrated Ibn Umar 🙼: Umar 🙼 sent an army (to Nahawand) and appointed a man named Sariyah as its commander. While Umar was delivering the (Friday) sermon (in Medina), he began to call aloud, *"O Sariyah! (Take recourse to) The mountain."* So a messenger came from the army and said, "O the Leader of the Faithful! *We have met our enemies and they were about to defeat us when suddenly an announcer proclaimed, 'O Sariyah! The mountain.' We inclined our backs to the mountain, so Allah the Supreme defeated them."* (Baihaqi, Mishkaat).

Chapter 5: Excellence of Seeing the Holy Prophet

Seeing the Holy Prophet in a state of Imaan

Narrated Jaber 🙼: The Holy Prophet 🙼 said, *"Fire will not touch the Muslim who saw me, and the Muslim who saw the Muslim who saw me."* (Tirmizi, Mishkaat).

Seeing the Holy Prophet in a dream

Narrated Abu Hurairah 🙼: The Holy Prophet 🙼 said, "Name yourselves with my name (use my name) but do not name yourselves with my Kunya name (i.e. Abul Qasim). *And whoever sees me in a dream then surely he has seen me for Satan cannot impersonate me.* And whoever tells a lie against me (intentionally), then (surely) let him occupy his seat in Hell-fire." (Bukhari).

Narrated Anas bin Malik 🙼: Allah's Apostle 🙼 said, *"A good dream (that comes true) of a righteous man is one of forty-six parts of prophet-hood."* (Bukhari, Muslim)

Narrated Abu Hurairah 🙼: I heard the Holy Prophet 🙼 saying, *"Whoever sees me in a dream will see me in his wakefulness,* and Satan cannot imitate me in shape." Abu `Abdullah said, "Ibn Seereen

said, 'Only if he sees the Holy Prophet ﷺ in his (real) shape.'"
(Bukhari)

Narrated Abu Sa'id Al-Khudri ﵁: The Holy Prophet ﷺ said,
"*Whoever sees me (in a dream) then he indeed has seen the truth*, as Satan
cannot appear in my shape." (Bukhari)

The eye-sight of Syedena Yaqub

[Surah Yusuf 12:93-96] "*Take along this shirt of mine and lay it on my
father's face, his vision will be restored*; and bring your entire household
to me." When the caravan left Egypt, their father *(Syedena Yaqub)*
said, "*Indeed I sense the fragrance of Yusuf, if you do not call me senile.*"
They said, "By Allah, you are still deeply engrossed in the same
old love of yours." Then when the bearer of glad tidings came, *he
laid the shirt on his face, he therefore immediately regained his eyesight*; he
said, "Was I not telling you? I know the great traits of Allah
which you do not know!"

The Sahaba seeing the spirits

Narrated Abu Hurairah ﵁: Allah's Apostle ﷺ deputized me to
keep Sadaqa *(al-Fitr)* of Ramadan. A comer came and started
taking handfuls of the foodstuff *(of the Sadaqa) (stealthily)*. *I took
hold of him and said, "By Allah, I will take you to Allah's Apostle.*" He
said, "I am needy and have many dependents, and I am in great
need." I released him, and in the morning Allah's Apostle ﷺ
asked me, "What did your prisoner do yesterday?" I said, "O
Allah's Apostle ﷺ! The person complained of being needy and
of having many dependents, so, I pitied him and let him go."
Allah's Apostle ﷺ said, "Indeed, he told you a lie and he will be
coming again." I believed that he would show up again as Allah's
Apostle ﷺ had told me that he would return. So, I waited for him
watchfully. *When he (showed up and) started stealing handfuls of foodstuff,
I caught hold of him again* and said, "I will definitely take you to
Allah's Apostle ﷺ" He said, "Leave me, for I am very needy and

have many dependents. I promise I will not come back again." I pitied him and let him go. In the morning Allah's Apostle ﷺ asked me, "What did your prisoner do?" I replied, "O Allah's Apostle ﷺ! He complained of his great need and of too many dependents, so I took pity on him and set him free." Allah's Apostle ﷺ said, "Verily, he told you a lie and he will return." I waited for him attentively for the third time, and when he (came and) started stealing handfuls of the foodstuff, *I caught hold of him* and said, "I will surely take you to Allah's Apostle ﷺ as it is the third time you promise not to return, yet you break your promise and come." He said, "(Forgive me and) I will teach you some words with which Allah will benefit you." I asked, "What are they?" He replied, "Whenever you go to bed, recite "Ayat-al-Kursi"-- 'Allah la ilaha illa huwa-l-Haiy-ul Qaiyum' till you finish the whole verse. (If you do so), Allah will appoint a guard for you who will stay with you and no satan will come near you till morning. "So, I released him. In the morning, Allah's Apostle ﷺ asked, "What did your prisoner do yesterday?" I replied, "He claimed that he would teach me some words by which Allah will benefit me, so I let him go." Allah's Apostle ﷺ asked, "What are they?" I replied, "He said to me, 'Whenever you go to bed, recite Ayat-al-Kursi from the beginning to the end ---- Allah la ilaha illa huwal-haiy-ul-Qaiyum----.' He further said to me, '(If you do so), Allah will appoint a guard for you who will stay with you, and no satan will come near you till morning.' (Abu Hurairah ﷺ or another sub-narrator) added that they (the companions) were very keen to do good deeds. The Holy Prophet ﷺ said, "He really spoke the truth, although he is an absolute liar. Do you know whom you were talking to, these three nights, O Abu Hurairah?" Abu Hurairah ﷺ said, "No." He said, "It was Satan." (Bukhari)

Section 9: The Excellent Speech

Chapter 1: What is the Best Sound for Allah?

Narrated Abu Hurairah ﷺ: Allah's Apostle ﷺ said, "*Allah never listens to anything as He listens to the Holy Prophet ﷺ reciting Qur'an in a pleasant sweet sounding voice.*" A companion of Abu Hurairah ﷺ said, "He means, reciting the Qur'an aloud." (Bukhari)

Abu Hurairah ﷺ reported Allah's Apostle ﷺ as saying: Allah has not heard anything (more pleasing) than listening to the Holy Prophet ﷺ reciting the Qur'an in a sweet loud voice. (Muslim, Bukhari)

Qatadah ﷺ narrated: Allah's Apostle ﷺ said: *Allah never sent a Prophet, except with a sweet voice.* (Tirmizi)

Narrated Al-Bara ﷺ: I heard the Holy Prophet ﷺ reciting "Wa t-teeni wa z-zaitun" (Surah 95) in the `Isha' prayer, and I never heard a sweeter voice or a better way of recitation than that of the Prophet ﷺ. (Bukhari, Muslim)

Chapter 2: The Speech of the Holy Prophet

[Surah Najm 53:3-4] *And he does not say anything by his own desire. It is but a divine revelation, which is revealed to him.*

Narrated Abdullah ibn Amr ibn al-'As ﷺ: I used to write everything which I heard from Allah's Apostle ﷺ. I intended (by it) to memorize it. The Quraish prohibited me saying: Do you write everything that you hear from him while Allah's Apostle ﷺ is a human being: he speaks in anger and pleasure? So I stopped writing, and mentioned it to Allah's Apostle ﷺ. *He signalled with his finger to his mouth and said: Write, by Him in Whose hand my soul lies, only right comes out from it.* [Abu Dawud]

Nothing brings My slave closer to Me, as does his performance of the obligations I placed upon him; and *he keeps coming closer to*

Me through performing Nawafil (praying or doing extra deeds besides what is obligatory) till I love him — so when I love him, I become his leg with which he walks, and his hand with which he grips, and his tongue with which he talks, and his heart (or mind) with which he reflects. If he asks Me, I give him, if he prays to Me, I accept his prayer. (Ibn Al-Saniyy)

Whoever hurts any of My friends has waged war against Me. And nothing brings My slave closer to Me, like his performance of the obligations; and *he keeps coming closer to Me through performing Nawafil (praying or doing extra deeds besides what is obligatory) till I love him — so when I love him, I become his eye with which he sees, and his ear with which he hears, and his leg with which he walks, and his heart (or mind) with which he reflects and his tongue with which he speaks. If he asks Me, I give him, if he prays to Me, I accept his prayer. I do not hesitate about anything I do — (however) I hesitate to take away his life, for he hates death and I dislike harming him.* (Ahmad bin Hambal)

Narrated Fazal bin Abbas ﷺ: When the Holy Prophet ﷺ was laid in his noble grave, I took a last glimpse at his face. *I noticed that his lips were moving, so I put my ear close to his lips to listen. He was saying, "O Allah, forgive my Ummah."* I related this to all those present, upon which they were all shocked at the compassion of the Holy Prophet ﷺ for his Ummah. (Kanzul-Ummaal, Hujjatullah Alalalameen, Madarij alNubuwaah)

Chapter 3: The Speech of Syedena Ibrahim & Syedena Omar

[Surah Baqarah 2:260] And when Ibrahim said, "My Lord! Show me how You will give life to the dead"; He said, "Are you not certain *(of it)*?" Ibrahim said, "Surely yes, why not? But because I wish to put my heart at ease"; He said, "Therefore take four birds *(as pets)* and cause them to become familiar to you, then place a part of each of them on separate hills*, then call them - they will come running towards you*; and know well that Allah is Almighty, Wise."

Narrated Ibn Omar 🌸: Allah's Apostle 🌸 said, "*Allah has indeed placed the truth upon the tongue of Umar, and upon his heart.*" (Tirmizi, Abu Dawud)

Narrated Ibn Umar 🌸: Umar 🌸 sent an army (to Nahawand) and appointed a man named Sariyah as its commander. While Umar was delivering the (Friday) sermon (in Medina), he began to call aloud, "*O Sariyah! (Take recourse to) The mountain.*" So an Apostle came from the army and said, "O the Leader of the Faithful! *We have met our enemies and they were about to defeat us when suddenly an announcer proclaimed, 'O Sariyah! The mountain.' We inclined our backs to the mountain, so Allah the Supreme defeated them.*" (Baihaqi, Mishkaat).

Chapter 4: The Prophets Speaking in Infancy

[Surah Maryam 19:30-31] The child proclaimed, "I am Allah's bondman; He has given me the Book and made me a Herald of the Hidden *(a Prophet)*." "And He has made me blessed wherever I be; and ordained upon me prayer and charity, as long as I live."

[Surah Maidah 5:110] When Allah will say, "O Eisa, the son of Maryam! Remember My favour upon you and your mother; when I supported you with the Holy Spirit; *you were speaking to people from the cradle* and in maturity; and when I taught you the Book and wisdom and the Taurat and the Injeel; and when you used to mould a birdlike sculpture from clay, by My command, and blow into it - so it *(the living bird)* used to fly by My command, and you used to cure him who was born blind and cure the leper, by My command; and when you used to raise up the dead, by My command; and when I restrained the Descendants of Israel against you when you came to them with clear proofs, and the disbelievers among them said, 'This is nothing but clear magic'."

[Surah Yusuf 12:26-27] Said Yusuf, "It was she who lured me, that I may not guard myself" - *and a witness from her own household testified*; "If his shirt is torn from the front, then the woman is truthful and he has spoken incorrectly. And if his shirt is torn from behind, then the woman is a liar and he is truthful."

Suhaib 🕮 reported that Allah's Apostle 🕮 thus said: ....The courtiers came to the king and it was said to him: Do you see that Allah has actually done what you aimed at averting. They (the people) have affirmed their faith in the Lord. He (the king) commanded ditches to be dug at important points in the path. When these ditches were dug, and the fire was lit in them it was said (to the people): He who would not turn back from his (boy's) religion would be thrown in the fire or it would be said to them to jump in that. (The people courted death but did not renounce religion) till a woman came with her child and she felt hesitant in jumping into the fire and the child said to her: O mother, endure (this ordeal) for it is the Truth. (Muslim - part of a longer Hadeeth)

Reported Abu Hurairah 🕮: He heard Allah's Apostle 🕮 saying, "While a lady was nursing her child, a rider passed by and she said, 'O Allah! Don't let my child die till he becomes like this (rider).' *The child said, 'O Allah! Don't make me like him,' and then returned to her breast* (sucking it). (After a while) they passed by a lady who was being pulled and teased (by the people). The child's mother said, 'O Allah! Do not make my child like her.' *The child said, 'O Allah! Make me like her.'* Then he said, 'As for the rider, he is an infidel, while the lady is accused of illegal sexual intercourse (falsely) and she (the lady) says: Allah is sufficient for me (He knows the truth). (Bukhari)

Narrated Saeed bin Abdul Azeez 🕮: No Azaan was given announced in the mosque (in Medina) of the Holy Prophet 🕮 during the days of the Harrah (when Yazeed's army took over). Saeed bin Musayyib 🕮 did not get up from or leave the mosque. *He did not recognize the time of the prayer except on account of the humming sound he heard from the Holy* Prophet's 🕮 *tomb.* (Darimi, Mishkaat).

Narrated Abu Hurairah 🕮 The Holy Prophet 🕮 said: "No one greets me except *Allah returns my soul to me* so that I can return his Salam" (Abu Dawud)

Narrated Abu Hurairah 🕮: The Holy prophet 🕮 said while standing near the graves of the martyrs of Uhud, "I bear witness that you are alive in the sight of Allah." Then turning towards those present he said, *"So visit them, and greet them – I swear by the One in whose power lies my life, they will answer back to whoever greets them until the Last Day."*(Hakim, Baihaqi)

Narrated 'Abdullah ibn 'Abbas 🕮: He was sitting by Allah's Apostle 🕮, and Asma' bint 'Umais was also present; Allah's Apostle 🕮, after saying "Alaikum salam," declared: *'Oh Asma! Your husband Jafar came to me with [Archangels] Jibreel and Mikaeel just a moment ago.* They greeted me. I answered their greeting. He said, "I fought with disbelievers in the Battle of Muta for a few days. I got wounded on seventy-three points all over my body. I held the flag with my right hand. Then my right arm was cutoff. I held the flag with my left hand, them my left arm was cut off. *Allah ta'ala gave me two wings instead of my two arms: I fly with Jibreel and Mikaeel. I fly out from Paradise whenever I wish. And I go in and eat its fruits whenever I wish."* 'Upon this, Asma' said, 'May Allah ta'ala's favours do good to Jafar! But I am afraid people will not believe it when they hear it. Oh Allah's Apostle! Would you tell them on the minbar! They will believe you.' Allah's Apostle 🕮 honoured the masjid and ascended the minbar. After praising and glorifying Allah ta'ala, he said, *'Jafar ibn Abi Talib ﷺ came to me with Jibreel (ﷺ) and Mikaeel (ﷺ). Allah ta'ala has granted him two wings. He greeted me.'* Then he repeated what he had told Asma' about her husband." (Hakim)

Narrated 'Abdullah ibn 'Abbas ﷺ: He was sitting by Allah's Apostle ﷺ, when suddenly Allah's Apostle ﷺ, raised his head and said "Wa alaykum as-salaamo wa rahmatu-Allah". Those present asked in surprise, "O Allah's Apostle ﷺ! What is this?" He said, *"Jafar bin Abi Talib (ﷺ) greeted me while passing by along with a group of angels, so I greeted him back."* (Khasais Kubra, Mustadrak)

Narrated Abu Dhar ﷺ: Allah's Apostle ﷺ said, "While I was at Mecca the roof of my house was opened and Gabriel descended, opened my chest, and washed it with Zam-zam water. Then he brought a golden tray full of wisdom and faith and having poured its contents into my chest, he closed it. Then he took my hand and ascended with me to the nearest heaven, when I reached the nearest heaven, Gabriel said to the gatekeeper of the heaven, 'Open (the gate).' The gatekeeper asked, 'Who is it?' Gabriel answered: 'Gabriel.' He asked, 'Is there anyone with you?' Gabriel replied, 'Yes, Muhammad I is with me.' He asked, 'Has he been called?' Gabriel said, 'Yes.' So the gate was opened and we went over the nearest heaven and there we saw a man sitting with some people on his right and some on his left. When he looked towards his right, he laughed and when he looked toward his left he wept. Then he said, 'Welcome! O pious Prophet and pious son.' I asked Gabriel, 'Who is he?' He replied, 'He is Adam and the people on his right and left are the souls of his offspring. Those on his right are the people of Paradise and those on his left are the people of Hell and when he looks towards his right he laughs and when he looks towards his left he weeps.'

Then he ascended with me till he reached the second heaven and he (Gabriel 🕊) said to its gatekeeper, 'Open (the gate).' The gatekeeper said to him the same as the gatekeeper of the first heaven had said and he opened the gate. Anas 🕊 said: "Abu Dhar 🕊 added that the Prophet 🕊 met Adam (🕊), Idris (🕊), Moses (🕊), Jesus (🕊) and Abraham (🕊), he (Abu Dhar 🕊) did not mention on which heaven they were but he mentioned that he (the Prophet 🕊) met Adarn 🕊 on the nearest heaven and Abraham (🕊) on the sixth heaven. Anas 🕊 said, "When Gabriel (🕊) along with the Prophet 🕊 passed by Idris (🕊), the latter said, 'Welcome! O pious Prophet 🕊 and pious brother.' The Prophet asked, 'Who is he?' Gabriel replied, 'He is Idris." The Prophet 🕊 added, "I passed by Moses (🕊) and he said, 'Welcome! O pious Prophet 🕊 and pious brother.' I asked Gabriel (🕊), 'Who is he?' Gabriel replied (🕊), 'He is Moses 🕊' Then I passed by Jesus (🕊) and he said, 'Welcome! O pious brother and pious Prophet 🕊 asked, 'Who is he?' Gabriel (🕊) replied, 'He is Jesus (🕊).

Then I passed by Abraham (🕊) and he said, 'Welcome! O pious Prophet 🕊 and pious son.' I asked Gabriel (🕊), 'Who is he?' Gabriel (🕊) replied, 'He is Abraham (🕊). The Prophet 🕊 added, 'Then Gabriel (🕊) ascended with me to a place where I heard the creaking of the pens." Ibn Hazm 🕊 and Anas bin Malik 🕊 said: The Prophet 🕊 said, "Then Allah enjoined fifty prayers on my followers when I returned with this order of Allah, I passed by Moses (🕊) who asked me, 'What has Allah enjoined on your followers?' I replied, 'He has enjoined fifty prayers on them.' Moses (🕊) said, 'Go back to your Lord (and appeal for reduction) for your followers will not be able to bear it.' (So I went back to Allah and requested for reduction) and He reduced it to half. When I passed by Moses (🕊) again and informed him about it, he said, 'Go back to your Lord as your followers will not be able to bear it.' So I returned to Allah and requested for further reduction and half of it was reduced. I again passed by Moses (﷽) and he said to me: 'Return to your Lord, for your followers will not be able to bear it. So I returned to Allah and He said, 'These are five prayers and they are all (equal to) fifty (in reward) for My Word does not change.' I returned to Moses (﷽) and he told me to go back once again. I replied, 'Now I feel shy of asking my Lord again.' Then Gabriel took me till we " reached Sidrat-il-Muntaha (Lote tree of; the utmost boundary) which was shrouded in colors, indescribable. Then I was admitted into Paradise where I found small (tents or) walls (made) of pearls and its earth was of musk." (Bukhari)

Chapter 6: The Speech of Inanimate Objects

[Surah Ambiya 21:79] And We explained the case to Sulaiman; and to both We gave the kingdom and knowledge; *and subjected the hills to proclaim the Purity along with Dawud, and (also subjected) the birds*; and these were Our works.

Narrated Abbas bin Abdul Muttalib ﷺ: I once humbly told the Holy Prophet ﷺ, "I had witnessed an event relating to you that evidenced your Prophethood, and which later became one of the main reasons of my accepting faith. The event is that I saw you talking to the moon while you were in the cradle, and the moon used to move at the command of your finger." The Holy Prophet ﷺ answered, "*I used to talk to him, and he used to talk to me. He used to prevent me from crying, and I could also hear it falling, when it used to prostrate below the throne.*"(Baihaqi, Ibn Asakir, Khasais Kubra).

Narrated `Abdullah ﷺ: We used to consider miracles as Allah's Blessings, but you people consider them to be a warning. Once we were with Allah's Apostle ﷺ on a journey, and we ran short of water. He said, "Bring the water remaining with you." The people brought a utensil containing a little water. *He placed his* hand in it and said, *"Come to the blessed water, and the Blessing is from Allah."* I saw the water flowing from among the fingers of Allah's Apostle ﷺ, and no doubt, we heard the meal glorifying Allah, when it was being eaten (by him). (Bukhari)

Narrated Jabir bin `Abdullah ﷺ: An Ansari woman said to Allah's Apostle ﷺ, "O Allah's Apostle ﷺ! Shall I make something for you to sit on, as I have a slave who is a carpenter?" He replied, "If you wish." So, she got a pulpit made for him. When it was Friday the Holy Prophet ﷺ sat on that pulpit. *The date-palm stem near which the Holy Prophet ﷺ used to deliver his sermons cried so much so that it was about to burst. The Holy Prophet ﷺ came down from the pulpit to the stem and embraced it and it started groaning like a child being persuaded to stop crying and then it stopped crying.* The Holy Prophet ﷺ said, "It has cried because of (missing) what it used to hear of the religions knowledge." (Bukhari)

Narrated Ibn `Umar ﷺ: The Holy Prophet ﷺ used to deliver his sermons while standing beside a trunk of a date-palm. When he had the pulpit made, he used it instead. *The trunk started crying and the Holy Prophet ﷺ went to it, rubbing his hand over it (to stop its crying).* (Bukhari)

Reported Syedena Ali ﷺ: We were with the Holy Prophet ﷺ in the suburbs of Mecca. *So whichever tree or rock we passed by, used to say, "As-Salaamo Alayka Yaa Rasulullah".* (Tirmizi, Darimi, Madarij un Nubuwwah)

Narrated Abdullah ibn Abbas ﷺ: The residents of Hadramaut came to meet the Holy Prophet ﷺ, and among them was also Ash'at bin Qais. They said, "We have hidden one matter in our hearts – so tell us what it is." The Holy Prophet ﷺ replied, "Purity is to Allah! This is the work of a soothsayer – and the soothsayer and his soothsaying, both are in hell." They said, "So how shall we come to know that you are indeed Allah's Apostle?" *He therefore picked up a handful of pebbles from the ground and said, "These pebbles bear witness that I am Allah's Apostle." So the pebbles in his hand began praising Allah, and said "We bear witness that you are indeed Allah's Apostle."* (Dalail Nubuwwah, Abu Nuaim, Khasais Kubra).

Section 10: The Sacred Breath

Chapter 1: The Breath of the Holy Prophet

Reported Syedah 'A'isha 🌺: When Allah's Apostle 🌸 fell ill, he recited over his body Mu'awwidhatan and blew over him and when his sickness was aggravated I used to recite over him and rub him with his hand with the hope that it was more blessed. (Muslim)

Narrated Syedah `Aisha 🌺: Whenever Allah's Apostle became ill, he used to recite Al-Mu'awwidhatan (i.e. the last two Surahs of the Qur'an) and then blow his breath and passed his hand over himself. When he had his fatal illness, *I started reciting Al-Muawidhatan and blowing my breath over him as he used to do,* and then I rubbed the hand of the Holy Prophet 🌸 over his body. (Bukhari)

Narrated Thabit ibn Qays ibn Shammas 🌸: Allah's Apostle 🌸 entered upon Thabit ibn Qays. The version of Ahmad (ibn Salih) has: When he was ill he said: Remove the harm, O Lord of men, from Thabit ibn Qays ibn Shammas. He then took some dust of Bathan, and put it in a bowl, and then mixed it with water and blew in it, and poured it on him. (Abu Dawud)

Chapter 2: The Breath of Prophet Eisa.

[Surah A/I`mran 3:49]: "And he will be a Noble Messenger towards the Descendants of Israel saying, 'I have come to you with a sign from your Lord, for *I mould a birdlike sculpture from clay for you, and I blow into it and it instantly becomes a (living) bird, by Allah's command;* and I heal him who was born blind, and the leper, and I revive the dead, by Allah's command; and I tell you what you eat and what you store in your houses; undoubtedly in these *(miracles)* is a great sign for you, if you are believers.'

[Surah Maidah 5:110] When Allah will say, "O Eisa, the son of Maryam! Remember My favour upon you and your mother; when

I supported you with the Holy Spirit; you were speaking to people from the cradle and in maturity; and when I taught you the Book and wisdom and the Taurat and the Injeel; *and when you used to mould a birdlike sculpture from clay, by My command, and blow into it - so it (the living bird) used to fly by My command,* and you used to cure him who was born blind and cure the leper, by My command; and when you used to raise up the dead, by My command; and when I restrained the Descendants of Israel against you when you came to them with clear proofs, and the disbelievers among them said, 'This is nothing but clear magic'."

Section 11: The Blessed Saliva

The Holy Prophet applied his saliva on the foot of Syedena Abu Bakr

Narrated Syedena Umar: There was mention of Syedena Abu Bakr near him and he wept and said, "I would like all my deeds to be like the deed of (just) one of his days and one of his nights. As for the night, it was the night in which he traveled along with Allah's Apostle to the cave. When they reached it, he said, "By Allah, don't enter it, till I enter before you. If there is anything, it will sting me, and not you!" So he entered it, and swept it, but found some holes in the corner. He tore his lower garments to pieces and blocked them with it. Two among the holes remained uncovered. Syedena Abu Bakr placed his feet upon them and then said to Allah's Apostle, "Enter". So Allah's Apostle entered the cave, and put his head in his lap and fell asleep. Abu Bakr was then bit in the foot (by a snake) from the hole, but he did not move fearing he would awaken Allah's Apostle. So when his tears fell on the face of Allah's Apostle. He said, "What is the matter with you, O Abu Bakr?" He said, "I have been bitten - may my father and mother be sacrificed for you!" So Allah's Apostle applied his saliva (on the bitten leg), therefore what he was experiencing vanished. It came back again for him later, and was the cause of his death. (Razeen, Mishkaat – part of a longer hadeeth).

The Companion's foot during the battle of Khaibar

Narrated Yazid bin Abi Ubaid: I saw the trace of a wound in Salama's leg. I said to him, "O Abu Muslim! What is this wound?" He said, "This was inflicted on me on the day of Khaibar and the people said, 'Salama (bin Akwa) has been wounded.' Then I went to the Holy Prophet and he puffed his saliva in it (i.e. the wound) thrice, and since then I have not had any pain in it till this hour." (Bukhari)

The Burnt Hand of a Child

Narrated Ibn Abbas ﷺ: The hand of Muhammad bin Hatib got burnt when a hot cooking pot fell on him. The Holy Prophet ﷺ stroked his hand over the child's arm, prayed and applied saliva on it. The child's arm was immediately cured. (Bukhari, Baihaqi, Zarqani)

The Devil is driven out

Hazrat Osama bin Zaid ﷺ narrates: We were with the Holy Prophet ﷺ on the Hajj journey. When we reached Batn Rauha, the Holy Prophet ﷺ saw a lady coming towards him. He stopped his mount. The lady came forward and said, "O Allah's Apostle! This is my child, who has been unconscious since he was born." The Holy Prophet ﷺ caught hold of the child and put his saliva into the child's mouth. He then said, "Get out, O the enemy of Allah! I am Allah's Apostle!" He then handed the child back to his mother and said, "He is now free from any evil effect." Hazrat Osama narrates that when the Holy Prophet ﷺ finished the Hajj and returned to the same place, the lady presented him with a roasted goat. The Holy Prophet ﷺ said, "Give me its shank." So I gave it to him. He again said, "Give me its shank." So I again gave it to him. Once again he said, "Give me its shank." I then submitted, "O Allah's Apostle ﷺ! There are only two shanks (in a goat), which I have already given you!" He said, "By the One in whose power rests my life, if you had kept silent, you would have kept on giving me (more) shanks as long as I would have kept on asking." (Baihaqi, Abu Yu'la, Khasais Kubra)

The Eyes of Syedena Ali Before Battle of Khyber

Narrated Sahl ﷺ: On the day (of the battle) of Khaibar the Holy Prophet ﷺ said, "Tomorrow I will give the flag to somebody who will be given victory (by Allah) and who loves Allah and His Apostle and is loved by Allah and His Apostle." So, the people wondered all that night as to who would receive the flag and in the morning everyone hoped that he would be that person. Allah's Apostle 🌸 asked, "Where is `Ali?" He was told that `Ali 🌸 was suffering from eye-trouble, so he applied saliva to his eyes and invoked Allah to cure him. He at once got cured as if he had no ailment. The Holy Prophet 🌸 gave him the flag. `Ali said, "Should I fight them till they become like us (i.e. Muslim)?" The Holy Prophet 🌸 said, "Go to them patiently and calmly till you enter the land. Then, invite them to Islam, and inform them what is enjoined upon them, for, by Allah, if Allah gives guidance to somebody through you, it is better for you than possessing red camels." (Bukhari)

Sahl bin Sa'd 🌸 reported: Allah's Apostle 🌸 said on the Day of Khaibar: I would certainly give this standard to a person at whose hand Allah would grant victory and who loves Allah and His Apostle and Allah and His Apostle love him also. The people spent the night thinking as to whom it would be given. When it was morning the people hastened to Allah's Apostle 🌸 all of them hoping that that it would be given to him. He (the Holy Prophet 🌸) said: Where is 'Ali bin Abi Talib? They said: Allah's Apostle 🌸, his eyes are sore. He then sent for him and he was brought and Allah's Apostle 🌸 applied saliva to his eyes and invoked blessings and he was all right, as if he had no ailment at all, and conferred upon him the standard. 'Ali said: Allah's Apostle 🌸, I will fight them until they are like us. Thereupon he (the Holy Prophet 🌸) said: Advance cautiously until you reach their open places, thereafter invite them to Islam and inform them what is obligatory for them from the rights of Allah, for, by Allah, if Allah guides aright even one person through you that is better for you than to possess the most valuable of the camels. (Muslim)

Chapter 2: The Companions' Wish to Have His Saliva.

The Companions Fought for His Saliva

Narrated Al-Miswar bin Makhrama 🙵 and Marwan 🙵: Before embracing Islam Al-Mughira was in the company of some people. He killed them and took their property and came (to Medina) to embrace Islam. The Holy Prophet 🙵 said (to him, "As regards your Islam, I accept it, but as for the property I do not take anything of it. (As it was taken through treason). `Urwa then started looking at the Companions of the Holy Prophet 🙵. By Allah, whenever Allah's Apostle 🙵 spat, the spittle would fall in the hand of one of them (i.e. the Holy Prophet's 🙵 companions) who would rub it on his face and skin; if he ordered them they would carry his orders immediately; if he performed ablution, they would struggle to take the remaining water; and when they spoke to him, they would lower their voices and would not look at his face constantly out of respect. `Urwa returned to his people and said, "O people! By Allah, I have been to the kings and to Caesar, Khosrau and An-Najashi, yet I have never seen any of them respected by his courtiers as much as Muhammad is respected by his companions.

By Allah, if he spat, the spittle would fall in the hand of one of them (i.e. the Holy Prophet's 🙵 companions) who would rub it on his face and skin; if he ordered them, they would carry out his order immediately; if he performed ablution, they would struggle to take the remaining water; and when they spoke, they would lower their voices and would not look at his face constantly out of respect." `Urwa added, "No doubt, he has presented to you a good reasonable offer, so please accept it." (Bukhari – part of a longer Hadeeth)

Narrated Sahl bin Sa`d 🙵: A tumbler (full of milk or water) was brought to the Holy Prophet 🙵 who drank from it, while on his

115

right side there was sitting a boy who was the youngest of those who were present and on his left side there were old men. The Holy Prophet ﷺ asked, "O boy, will you allow me to give it (i.e. the rest of the drink) to the old men?" The boy said, "O Allah's Apostle! I will not give preference to anyone over me to drink the rest of it from which you have drunk." So, the Holy Prophet ﷺ gave it to him. (Bukhari)

The Companions Cured Others with Saliva

Narrated Abu Sa'id Al-Khudri ؓ: Some of the companions of the Holy Prophet ﷺ came across a tribe amongst the tribes of the Arabs, and that tribe did not entertain them. While they were in that state, the chief of that tribe was bitten by a snake (or stung by a scorpion). They said, (to the companions of the Holy Prophet ﷺ), "Have you got any medicine with you or anybody who can treat with Ruqya?" The Holy Prophet's ﷺ companions said, "You refuse to entertain us, so we will not treat (your chief) unless you pay us for it." So they agreed to pay them a flock of sheep. One of them (the Holy Prophet's ﷺ companions) started reciting Surat-al-Fatiha and gathering his saliva and spitting it (at the snake-bite). The patient got cured and his people presented the sheep to them, but they said, "We will not take it unless we ask the Holy Prophet ﷺ (whether it is lawful)." When they asked him, he smiled and said, "How do you know that Surat-al-Fatiha is a Ruqya? Take it (flock of sheep) and assign a share for me." (Bukhari)

The Holy Prophet ﷺ once passed his hands over the head of Hazrat Hanzalah bin Huzaim ؓ, and said, "Blessings have been placed within you." Hazrat Zayaal ؓ relates that he witnessed that whenever any human or camel or goat had a sprain, people used to bring them to Hazrat Hanzalah ؓ. He used to put some saliva on his hand and rub it on his head, and supplicate thus, "With Allah's name upon the vestige of Allah's Apostle ﷺ" He then used to rub the hand on sprain, and the sprain used to disappear. (Bukhari in Tareekh, Ahmad, Khasais Kubra, Al-Tabarani)

Tahnik with Saliva

Narrated Asma' bint Abu Bakr ﷺ: I conceived `Abdullah bin AzZubair at Mecca and went out (of Mecca) while I was about to give birth. I came to Medina and encamped at Quba', and gave birth at Quba'. Then I brought the child to Allah's Apostle ﷺ and placed it (on his lap). He asked for a date, chewed it, and put his saliva in the mouth of the child. So the first thing to enter its stomach was the saliva of Allah's Apostle. Then he did its Tahnik with a date, and invoked Allah to bless him. It was the first child born in the Islamic era, therefore they (Muslims) were very happy with its birth, for it had been said to them that the Jews had bewitched them, and so they would not produce any offspring. (Bukhari, Muslim)

Anas ﷺ reported: When Umm Sulaim ﷺ gave birth to a child. She said to me: Anas, see that nothing is given to this child until he is brought to Allah's Apostle ﷺ in the morning, so that he should chew some dates and touch his palate with it. I went to him in the morning and he was in the garden at that time having the mantle of Jauiatiyah over him and he was busy in cauterizing (the camels) which had been brought to him (as spoils of war) in the Conquest (over the enemy) (Muslim)

His Saliva for Quenching Thirst

Narrated Abu Hurairah ﷺ: We were with the Holy Prophet ﷺ on a journey, when he heard Syedena Hasan ﷺ and Syedena Husain ﷺ crying. He therefore asked Syedah Fatima ﷺ as to why they were crying. She answered that it was because of thirst.

The Holy Prophet 🌸 then enquired if anyone had some water, but no one did. He said, "Give one of the children to me." He betook the child to his chest while it was crying. He then inserted his tongue into the child's mouth who began sucking it and then quietened. He then asked for the other child who had been crying all along. He repeated this with the other child. In this way, both the children quenched their thirst and did not cry again. (Tibrani, Ibn Asakir, Khasais Kubra).

Chapter 3: His Saliva Mixed with Food, Water & the Soil of Medina.

Water Mixed with His Saliva

Reported Abu Musa 🌸: I was in the company of Allah's Apostle🌸 as he had been sitting in Ji'ranah (a place) between Mecca and Medina and Bilal was also there, that there came to Allah's Apostle 🌸 a desert Arab, and he said: Muhammad, fulfill your promise that you made with me. Allah's Apostle 🌸 said to him: Accept glad tidings. Thereupon the desert Arab said: You shower glad tidings upon me very much; then Allah's Apostle 🌸 turned towards Abu Musa and Bilal seemingly in a state of annoyance and said: Verily he has rejected glad tidings but you two should accept them. We said: Allah's Apostle 🌸, we have readily accepted them. Then Allah's Apostle 🌸 called for a cup of water and washed his hands in that, and face too, and put the saliva in it and then said: Drink out of it and pour it over your faces and over your chest and gladden yourselves. They took hold of the cup and did as Allah's Apostle 🌸 had commanded them to do. Thereupon Umm Salamah 🌸 called from behind the veil: Spare some water in your vessel for your mother also, and they also gave some water which had been spared for her. (Muslim)

Narrated Abu Juhaifa 🌸: Allah's Apostle 🌸 came to us at noon and water for ablution was brought to him. After he had performed ablution, the remaining water was taken by the people and they started smearing their bodies with it (as a blessed thing). The Holy Prophet 🌼 offered two rak`at of the Zuhr prayer and then two rak`at of the `Asr prayer while a short spear (or stick) was there (as a Sutra) in front of him. Abu Musa 🌼 said: The Holy Prophet 🌼 asked for a tumbler containing water and washed both his hands and face in it and then threw a mouthful of water in the tumbler and said to both of us (Abu Musa and Bilal), "Drink from the tumbler and pour some of its water on your faces and chests." (Bukhari)

The Well Became Full Again

Narrated Al-Bara 🌼: We were one-thousand-and-four-hundred persons on the day of Al-Hudaibiya (Treaty), and (at) Al-Hudaibiya (there) was a well. We drew out its water not leaving even a single drop. The Holy Prophet 🌼 sat at the edge of the well and asked for some water with which he rinsed his mouth and then he threw it out into the well. We stayed for a short while and then drew water from the well and quenched our thirst, and even our riding animals drank water to their satisfaction. (Bukhari)

The Soil of Medina Mixed with Saliva

Syedah A'ishah 🌼 reported: When any person fell ill with a disease or he had any ailment or he had any injury, Allah's Apostle 🌼 placed his forefinger upon the ground (Sufian put his forefinger on the ground) and then lifted it by reciting the name of Allah (and said): The dust of our ground with the saliva of any one of us would serve as a means whereby our illness would be cured with the sanction of Allah. (Muslim)

Narrated Syedah `Aisha 🌼: The Holy Prophet 🌼 used to say to the patient, "In the Name of Allah The earth of our land and the saliva of some of us cure our patients." (Bukhari)

The Wells Mixed with His Saliva

Narrated Wael bin Hajar 🙵: Once the Holy Prophet 🙵 gargled into a well, due to which the entire well became fragrant like kasturi (perfume) and musk. (Qastallani, Madarij-un-Nubuwwah, Anwaarul Mohammadiyah)

The Food Did Not Diminish

Reported Jabir b. 'Abdullah 🙵: When the ditch was dug, I saw Allah's Apostle 🙵 feeling very hungry. I came to my wife and said to her: Is there anything with you? I have seen Allah's Apostle 🙵 feeling extremely hungry. She brought out a bag of provisions which contained a sa', (a measure of weight) of barley. We had also with us a lamb. I slaughtered it. She ground the flour. She finished (this work) along with me. I cut it into pieces and put it in the earthen pot and then returned to Allah's Apostle 🙵 (for inviting him). She said: Do not humiliate me in the presence of Allah's Apostle 🙵 and those who are with him. When I came to him I whispered to him saying: Allah's Apostle 🙵, we have slaughtered a lamb for you and she has ground a sa' of barley which we had with us. So you come along with a group of people with you. Thereupon Allah's Apostle 🙵 said loudly: O people of the ditch, Jabir has arranged a feast for you, so (come along). Allah's Apostle 🙵 said: Do not remove your earthen pot from the hearth and do not bake the bread from the kneaded flour until I come. So I came and Allah's Apostle 🙵 came and he was ahead of the people; and I came to my wife and she said (to me): You will be humbled. I said: I did what you had asked me to do. She (his wife) said: I brought out the kneaded flour and Allah's Apostle 🙵 put some saliva of his in that and blessed it. He then put saliva in the earthen pot and blessed it and then said. Call another baker who can bake with you and bring out the soup from it, but do not remove it from the hearth, and the guests were one thousand. (Jabir said): I take an oath by Allah that all of them ate (the food to their fill) until they left it and went away and our earthen pot was brimming over as before, and so was the case with our flour, or as Dahhak (another narrator) said: It (the flour) was in the same condition and loaves had been prepared from that. (Muslim)

Narrated Jabir bin `Abdullah ﷺ: When the Trench was dug, I saw the Holy Prophet ﷺ in the state of severe hunger. So I returned to my wife and said, "Have you got anything (to eat), for I have seen Allah's Apostle ﷺ in a state of severe hunger." She brought out for me, a bag containing one Sa of barley, and we had a domestic she-goat (i.e. a kid) which I slaughtered then, and my wife ground the barley and she finished at the time I finished my job (i.e. slaughtering the she-goat). Then I cut the meat into pieces and put it in an earthenware (cooking) pot, and returned to Allah's Apostle ﷺ. My wife said, "Do not disgrace me in front of Allah's Apostle ﷺ and those who are with him." So I went to him and said to him secretly, "O Allah's Apostle ﷺ! I have slaughtered a she-goat (i.e. kid) of ours, and we have ground a Sa of barley which was with us. So please come, you and another person along with you." The Holy Prophet ﷺ raised his voice and said, "O people of Trench! Jabir has prepared a meal so let us go." Allah's Apostle ﷺ said to me, "Don't put down your earthenware meat pot (from the fireplace) or bake your dough till I come." So I came (to my house) and Allah's Apostle ﷺ too, came, proceeding before the people. When I came to my wife, she said, "May Allah do so-and-so to you. "I said, "I have told the Holy Prophet ﷺ of what you said." Then she brought out to him (i.e. the Holy Prophet ﷺ the dough, and he spat in it and invoked for Allah's Blessings in it. Then he proceeded towards our earthenware meat-pot and spat in it and invoked for Allah's Blessings in it. Then he said (to my wife). Call a lady-baker to bake along with you and keep on taking out scoops from your earthenware meat-pot, and do not put it down from its fireplace." They were one-thousand (who took their meals), and by Allah they all ate, and when they left the food and went away, our earthenware pot was still bubbling (full of meat) as if it had not decreased, and our dough was still being baked as if nothing had been taken from it. (Bukhari, Muslim)

Further reported with variation, in other narrations: The Holy Prophet ﷺ ordered the bones of the kid to be gathered and put his hand over it, then recited some words over it (which Jabir did not hear). The she-goat got up shaking its head. The Holy Prophet ﷺ said (to Jabir) "Take away your she-goat". So I took the she-goat to my wife, who said, "What is this?" I replied "By Allah, this is the very she-goat of ours which we had slaughtered. Allah has resurrected it by the supplication of the Holy Prophet ﷺ." Upon hearing this, my wife said, "I bear witness that he is Allah's Apostle ﷺ." (Baihaqi, Abu Nuaim, Dalail-un-Nubuwwah, Khasais Kubra)

Section 12: The Excellent Ears & Hearing

Chapter 1: Says Allah - "I Become His Sense of Hearing"

Narrated Abu Hurairah ﷺ: Allah's Apostle ﷺ said, "Allah said, 'I will declare war against him who shows hostility to a pious worshipper of Mine. And the most beloved things with which My slave comes nearer to Me, is what I have enjoined upon him; and My slave keeps on coming closer to Me through performing Nawafil (praying or doing extra deeds besides what is obligatory) till I love him, so *I become his sense of hearing with which he hears,* and his sense of sight with which he sees, and his hand with which he grips, and his leg with which he walks; and if he asks Me, I will give him, and if he asks My protection (Refuge), I will protect him; (i.e. give him My Refuge) and I do not hesitate to do anything as I hesitate to take the soul of the believer, for he hates death, and I hate to disappoint him." (Bukhari)

Says Allah - "Indeed he (the Holy Prophet) is the listener"

[Surah b/Israel 17:1] Purity is to Him Who took His bondman in a part of the night from the Sacred Mosque to the Aqsa Mosque around which We have placed blessings, in order that We may show him Our great signs; *indeed he is the listener, the beholder. (This verse refers to the physical journey of Prophet Mohammed* ﷺ *)*

The Holy Prophet Proclaimed "I hear what you do not hear"

Narrated Abu Zar Gifari ﷺ: Holy Prophet said, *"Indeed I see what you do not see, and I hear what you do not hear."* (Tirmidhi, Ibn Majah, Mishkaat)

Narrated Abu Hurairah ﷺ: The Holy Prophet ﷺ said while standing near the graves of the martyrs of Uhud, "I bear witness that you are alive in the sight of Allah." Then turning towards those present he said, *"So visit them, and greet them – I swear by the One in whose power lies my life, they will answer back to whoever greets them until the Last Day."* (Hakim, Baihaqi)

Jews and polytheists being punished in their graves

Narrated Abi Ayyub ﷺ: Once the Holy Prophet ﷺ went out after sunset and heard a dreadful voice, and said, "*The Jews are being punished in their graves.*" (Bukhari)

Abu Sa'id al-Khudri ﷺ reported: I did not hear this hadith from Allah's Apostle ﷺ directly but it was Zaid b. Thibit ﷺ who narrated it from him. As Allah's Apostle ﷺ was going along with us towards the dwellings of Bani an-Najjar, riding upon his pony, it shied and he was about to fall. He found four, five or six graves there. He said: Who amongst you knows about those lying in the graves? A person said: It is I. Thereupon he (the Holy Prophet) said: In what state did they die? He said: They died as polytheists. He said: *These people are passing through the ordeal in the graves. If it were not the reason that you would stop burying (your dead) in the graves on listening to the torment in the grave which I am listening to, I would have certainly made you hear that.* Then turning his face towards us, he said: Seek refuge with Allah from the torment of Hell. They said: We seek refuge with Allah from the torment of Hell. He said: Seek refuge with Allah from the torment of the grave. They said: We seek refuge with Allah from the torment of the grave. He said: Seek refuge with Allah from turmoil, its visible and invisible (aspects), and they said: We seek refuge with Allah from turmoil and its visible and invisible aspects and he said: Seek refuge with

Allah from the turmoil of the Dajjal, and they said We seek refuge with Allah from the turmoil of the Dajjal. (Muslim)

Chapter 3: Hearing the Sounds from the Graves – by the Sahaba

Narrated Fazal bin Abbas ﷺ: When the Holy Prophet ﷺ was laid in his noble grave, I took a last glimpse at his face. *I noticed that his lips were moving, so I put my ear close to his lips to listen. He was saying, "O Allah, forgive my Ummah."* I related this to all those present, upon which they were all shocked at the compassion of the Holy Prophet ﷺ for his Ummah. (Kazul-Ummaal, Hujjatullah Alalalameen, Madarij alNubuwaah)

Narrated Saeed bin Abdul Azeez ﷺ: No Azaan was announced in the mosque (in Madinah) of the Holy Prophet ﷺ during the days of the Harrah (when Yazeed's army took over). Saeed bin Musayyib ﷺ did not get up from or leave the mosque. *He did not recognize the time of the prayer except on account of the humming sound he heard from the Holy* Prophet's ﷺ *tomb.* (Darimi, Mishkaat)

People praying in their graves

Said 'Abdullah ibn 'Abbas ﷺ: "Some Sahabis set up a tent at a place where there was a grave that could not be noticed. *They heard Surat al-Mulk being recited inside the tent.* Allah's Apostle ﷺ came in the tent after the recitation ended. When they told him what they had heard, he said, 'This honorable Surah protects men from the punishment in the grave.'" (Tirmizi, Hakim and Baihaqi)

Chapter 4: Hearing the Speech of Angels and the Souls.

The conversations during the Ascension (Me'raj)

Narrated Anas b. Malik ﷺ: Allah's Apostle ﷺ said: I was brought al-Buraq that is an animal white and long, larger than a donkey but smaller than a mule, *who would place his hoof a distance equal to the range of vision.* I mounted it and came to the Temple (Bait Maqdis in Jerusalem), then tethered it to the ring used by the Holy Prophet 🌸. I entered the mosque and prayed two rak'ahs in it, and then came out and Gabriel brought me a vessel of wine and a vessel of milk. I chose the milk, and Gabriel said: You have chosen the natural thing. Then he took me to heaven. Gabriel then asked the (gate of heaven) to be opened and he was asked who he was. He replied: Gabriel. He was again asked: Who is with you? He (Gabriel) said: Muhammad 🌸. It was said: Has he been sent for? Gabriel replied: He has indeed been sent for. And (the door of the heaven) was opened for us and lo! *we saw Adam (peace be upon him).* He welcomed me and prayed for my good.

Then we ascended to the second heaven. Gabriel (peace be upon him) (asked the door of heaven to be opened), and he was asked who he was. He answered: Gabriel; and was again asked: Who is with you? He replied: Muhammad 🌸. It was said: Has he been sent for? He replied: He has indeed been sent for. The gate was opened. *When I entered 'Isa b. Maryam and Yahya b. Zakariya (peace be upon both of them), cousins from the maternal side welcomed me and prayed for my good.* Then I was taken to the third heaven and Gabriel asked for the opening (of the door). He was asked: Who are you? He replied: Gabriel. He was (again) asked: Who is with you? He replied Muhammad 🌸. It was said: Has he been sent for? He replied He has indeed been sent for. *(The gate) was opened for us and I saw Yusuf (peace of Allah be upon him)* who had been given half of (world) beauty. He welcomed me prayed for my well-being. Then he ascended with us to the fourth heaven. Gabriel (peace be upon him) asked for the (gate) to be opened, and it was said: Who is he? He replied: Gabriel. It was (again) said: Who is with you? He said: Muhammad 🌸. It was said: Has he been sent for? He replied: He has indeed been sent for. *The (gate) was opened for us, and lo! Idris was there.* He welcomed me and prayed for my well-being (About him) Allah, the Exalted and the Glorious, has said:" We elevated him (Idris) to the exalted position" (Qur'an xix. 57).

Then he ascended with us to the fifth heaven and Gabriel asked for the (gate) to be opened. It was said: Who is he? He replied Gabriel. It was (again) said: Who is with you? He replied: Muhammad ﷺ. It was said Has he been sent for? He replied: He has indeed been sent for. *(The gate) was opened for us and then I was with Harun (Aaron-peace of Allah be upon him).* He welcomed me prayed for my well-being. Then I was taken to the sixth heaven. Gabriel (peace be upon him) asked for the door to be opened. It was said: Who is he? He replied: Gabriel. It was said: Who is with you? He replied: Muhammad ﷺ. It was said: Has he been sent for? He replied: He has indeed been sent for. *(The gate) was opened for us and there I was with Musa (Moses ﷺ).* He welcomed me and prayed for my well-being. Then I was taken up to the seventh heaven. Gabriel asked the (gate) to be opened. It was said: Who is he? He said: Gabriel It was said. Who is with you? He replied: Muhammad ﷺ. It was said: Has he been sent for? He replied: He has indeed been sent for. *(The gate) was opened for us and there I found Ibrahim (Abraham ﷺ)* reclining against the Bait-ul-Ma'mur and there enter into it seventy thousand angels every day, never to visit (this place) again. Then I was taken to Sidrat-ul-Muntaha whose leaves were like elephant ears and its fruit like big earthenware vessels. And when it was covered by the Command of Allah, it underwent such a change that none amongst the creation has the power to praise its beauty.

Then Allah revealed to me a revelation and He made obligatory for me fifty prayers every day and night. Then I went down to Moses ﷺ and he said: What has your Lord enjoined upon your Ummah? I said: Fifty prayers. He said: Return to thy Lord and beg for reduction (in the number of prayers), for your community will not be able to bear this burden as I have put to test the children of Isra'il and tried them (and found them too weak to bear such a heavy burden). He (the Holy Prophet ﷺ) said: I went back to my Lord and said: My Lord, make things lighter for my Ummah. (The Lord) reduced five prayers for me. I went down to Moses ﷺ and said. (The Lord) reduced five (prayers) for me, He said: Verily thy Ummah shall not be able to bear this burden; return to thy Lord and ask Him to make things lighter. *I then kept going back and forth between my Lord the Auspicious and Most High, and Moses,* till He said: There are five prayers every day and night. O Muhammad, each being credited as ten, so that makes fifty prayers. He who intends to do a good deed and does not do it will have a good deed recorded for him; and if he does it, it will be recorded for him as ten; whereas he who intends to do an evil deed and does not do, it will not be recorded for him; and if he does it, only one evil deed will be recorded. I then came down and when I came to Moses ﷺ and informed him, he said: Go back to thy Lord and ask Him to make things lighter. Upon this Allah's Apostle ﷺ remarked: I returned to my Lord until I felt ashamed before Him. (Muslim)

The conversation with Syedena Jaffer Tayyar.

Narrated 'Abdullah ibn 'Abbas ﷺ: He was sitting by Allah's Apostle ﷺ, and Asma' bint 'Umais was also present; Allah's Apostle ﷺ, after saying "Alaikum salam," declared: *'Oh Asma! Your husband Jafar came to me with [Archangels] Jibreel and Mikaeel just a moment ago.* They greeted me. I answered their greeting. He said, "I fought with disbelievers in the Battle of Muta for a few days. I got wounded on seventy-three points all over my body. I held the flag with my right hand. Then my right arm was cutoff. I held the flag with my left hand, them my left arm was cut off. *Allah ta'ala gave me two wings instead of my two arms: I fly with Jibreel and Mikaeel. I fly out from Paradise whenever I wish. And I go in and eat its fruits whenever I wish.*" ' Upon this, Asma' said, 'May Allah ta'ala's favors do good to Jafar! But I am afraid people will not believe it when they hear it. Oh Allah's Apostle! Would you tell them on the minbar! They will believe you.' Allah's Apostle 🌸 honoured the masjid and ascended the minbar. After praising and glorifying Allah ta'ala, he said, *'Jafar ibn Abi Talib came to me with Jibreel and Mikaeel. Allah ta'ala has granted him two wings. He greeted me.'* Then he repeated what he had told Asma' about her husband." (Hakim)

Narrated 'Abdullah ibn 'Abbas 🌸: He was sitting with Allah's Apostle 🌸, when suddenly Allah's Apostle🌸, raised his head and said "Wa alaykum as-salaamo wa rahmatu-Allah". Those present asked in surprise, "O Allah's Apostle🌸! What is this?" He said, *"Jafar bin Abi Talib greeted me while passing by along with a group of angels, so I greeted him back."* (Khasais Kubra, Mustadrak)

Chapter 5: Hearing Whilst Inside the Grave

Narrated Ibn Mas'ud 🌸: The Holy Prophet 🌸 said: "Allah has angels who travel about the earth; *they [do and will] convey to me the peace greeting from my ummah.*" (Abu Dawud)

Narrated Abu Hurairah 🌸: The Holy Prophet 🌸 said: "No one greets me except *Allah returns my soul to me* so that I can return his Salam" (Abu Dawud)

Narrated from Abu Hurairah 🌸: "*Whoever invokes blessings upon me at my grave I hear him, and whoever invokes blessings on me from afar, I am informed about it.*" (Baihaqi, Ibn Hajar in Fath al-Bari)

Narrated Abu Hurairah 🌸: The Holy Prophet 🌸 said while standing near the graves of the martyrs of Uhud, "I bear witness that you are alive in the sight of Allah." Then turning towards those present he said, *"So visit them, and greet them – I swear by the One in whose power lies my life, they will answer back to whoever greets them until the Last Day."* (Hakim, Baihaqi)

The Holy Prophet Heard the footsteps of Syedena Bilal in Paradise

Narrated Abu Hurairah 🙼: At the time of the Fajr prayer the Holy Prophet 🙼 asked Bilal, "Tell me of the best deed you did after embracing Islam, for *I heard your footsteps in front of me in Paradise.*" Bilal 🙼 replied, "I did not do anything worth mentioning except that whenever I performed ablution during the day or night, I prayed after that ablution as much as was written for me." (Bukhari, Muslim)

Talking to the Moon

Narrated Abbas bin Abdul Muttalib 🙼: I once humbly told the Holy Prophet 🙼, "I had witnessed an event relating to you that evidenced your Prophethood, and which later became one of the main reasons of my accepting faith. The event is that I saw you talking to the moon while you were in the cradle, and the moon used to move at the command of your finger." The Holy Prophet 🙼 answered, "*I used to talk to him, and he used to talk to me. He used to prevent me from crying, and I could also hear it falling, when it used to prostrate below the throne.*" (Baihaqi, Ibn Asakir, Khasais Kubra)

Abu Huraira 🙼 reported: We were in the company of Allah's Apostle 🙼 *when we heard a terrible sound.* Thereupon Allah's Apostle said: Do you know what this (sound) is? We said: Allah and His Apostle 🙼 know best. Thereupon he said: That is a stone which was thrown seventy years before in Hell and it has been constantly slipping down and now it has reached its base. (Muslim)

Chapter 7: Hearing Despite the Vast Distance – by the Sahaba

Hearing the Voice of Syedena Omar

Narrated Ibn Umar ؓ: Umar ؓ sent an army (to Nahawand) and appointed a man named Sariyah as its commander. While Umar was delivering the (Friday) sermon (in Medina), he began to call aloud, *"O Sariyah! (Take recourse to) The mountain."* So a messenger came from the army and said, "O the Leader of the Faithful! *We have met our enemies and they were about to defeat us when suddenly an announcer proclaimed, 'O Sariyah! The mountain.' We inclined our backs to the mountain, so Allah the Supreme defeated them."* (Baihaqi, Mishkaat)

Chapter 8: Hearing the Speech of Inanimate Objects

[Surah Ambiya 21:79] And We explained the case to Sulaiman; and to both We gave the kingdom and knowledge; *and subjected the hills to proclaim the Purity along with Dawud, and (also subjected) the birds;* and these were Our works.

The Case of the Tree in the Masjid Nabawi

Narrated Ibn `Umar ؓ: The Holy Prophet ﷺ used to deliver his sermons while standing beside a trunk of a date palm. When he had the pulpit made, he used it instead. *The trunk started crying and the Holy* Prophet ﷺ *went to it, rubbing his hand over it (to stop its crying).* (Bukhari)

Narrated Jabir bin `Abdullah ؓ: The Holy Prophet ﷺ used to stand by a tree or a date-palm on Friday. Then an Ansari woman or man said. "O Allah's Apostle! Shall we make a pulpit for you?" He replied, "If you wish." So they made a pulpit for him and when it was Friday, he proceeded towards the pulpit (for delivering the sermon). *The date-palm cried like a child! The Holy* Prophet ﷺ *descended (the pulpit) and embraced it while it continued moaning like a child being quietened.* The Holy Prophet ﷺ said, "It was crying for (missing) what it used to hear of religious knowledge given near to it." (Bukhari)

Narrated Anas bin Malik ﷺ: That he heard Jabir bin `Abdullah saying, "The roof of the Mosque was built over trunks of date-palms working as pillars. When the Holy Prophet ﷺ delivered a sermon, he used to stand by one of those trunks till the pulpit was made for him, and he used it instead. *Then we heard the trunk sending a sound like of a pregnant she-camel till the Holy Prophet ﷺ came to it, and put his hand over it, then it became quiet.*" (Bukhari)

Narrated Jabir bin `Abdullah ﷺ: An Ansari woman said to Allah's Apostle ﷺ, "O Allah's Apostle! Shall I make something for you to sit on, as I have a slave who is a carpenter?" He replied, "If you wish." So, she got a pulpit made for him. When it was Friday the Holy Prophet ﷺ sat on that pulpit. *The date-palm stem near which the Holy Prophet ﷺ used to deliver his sermons cried so much so that it was about to burst. The Holy Prophet ﷺ came down from the pulpit to the stem and embraced it and it started groaning like a child being persuaded to stop crying and then it stopped crying.* The Holy Prophet ﷺ said, "It has cried because of (missing) what it used to hear of the religious knowledge." (Bukhari)

The Stones Spoke in the Hands of Holy Prophet & the Sahaba

Narrated Abdullah ibn Abbas ﷺ: The residents of Hadramaut came to meet the Holy Prophet ﷺ, and among them was also Ash'at bin Qais. They said, "We have hidden one matter in our hearts – so tell us what it is." The Holy Prophet ﷺ replied, "Purity is to Allah! This is the work of a soothsayer – and the soothsayer and his soothsaying, both are in hell." They said, "So how shall we come to know that you are indeed Allah's Apostle ﷺ?" *He therefore picked up a handful of pebbles from the ground and said, "These pebbles bear witness that I am Allah's Apostle." So the pebbles in his hand began praising Allah, and said "We bear witness that you are indeed Allah's Apostle."* (Dalail Nubuwwah, Abu Nuaim, Khasais Kubra).

Reported Abu Zar Gifari ﷺ that once *he witnessed pebbles saying the Praise of Allah in the hands of the Holy* Prophet ﷺ, *Syedena Abu Bakr, Syedena Umar, Syedena Usman, and in the hands of Syedena Ali.* (Mawahib Ladunniyah, Shifa, Madarij)

The Poisoned Shank of the Lamb Spoke to the Holy Prophet

Narrated Abu Hurairah ﷺ: When Khaibar was conquered, a roasted poisoned sheep was presented to the Holy Prophet ﷺ as a gift (by the Jews). The Holy Prophet ﷺ ordered, "Let all the Jews who have been here, be assembled before me." The Jews were collected and the Holy Prophet ﷺ said (to them), "I am going to ask you a question. Will you tell the truth?" They said, "Yes.' The Holy Prophet ﷺ asked, "Who is your father?" They replied, "So-and-so." He said, "You have told a lie; your father is so-and-so." They said, "You are right." He said, "Will you now tell me the truth, if I ask you about something?" They replied, "Yes, O Abal-Qasim; and if we should tell a lie, you can realize our lie as you have done regarding our father." On that he asked, "Who are the people of the (Hell) Fire?" They said, "We shall remain in the (Hell) Fire for a short period, and after that you will replace us." The Holy Prophet ﷺ said, "You may be cursed and humiliated in it! By Allah, we shall never replace you in it." Then he asked, "Will you now tell me the truth if I ask you a question?" They said, "Yes, O Abal-Qasim." *He asked, "Have you poisoned this sheep?"* They said, "Yes." He asked, "What made you do so?" They said, "We wanted to know if you were a liar in which case we would get rid of you, and if you are a prophet then the poison would not harm you." (Bukhari)

Food Praised Allah in the Presence of the Holy Prophet

Narrated `Abdullah ﷺ: We used to consider miracles as Allah's Blessings, but you people consider them to be a warning. Once we were with Allah's Apostle ﷺ on a journey, and we ran short of water. He said, "Bring the water remaining with you." The people brought a utensil containing a little water. *He placed his hand in it and said, "Come to the blessed water, and the Blessing is from Allah."* I saw the water flowing from among the fingers of Allah's Apostle ﷺ, *and no doubt, we heard the meal glorifying Allah, when it was being eaten (by him).* (Bukhari)

Stones Used to Send Greetings to the Holy Prophet

Reported Syedena Ali ؓ: We were with the Holy Prophet ﷺ in the suburbs of Mecca. *So whichever tree or rock we passed by, used to say, "As-Salaamo Alayka Yaa Rasulullah".* (Tirmizi, Darimi, Madarij un Nubuwwah)

Jabir b. Samura ؓ reported Allah's Apostle ﷺ as saying: I recognise the stone in Mecca which used to pay me salutations before my advent as a Prophet and I recognise that even now. (Muslim)

Chapter 9: The Speech of Animals

Hearing the Speech of Animals

[Surah Ambiya 21:79] And We explained the case to Sulaiman; and to both We gave the kingdom and knowledge; *and subjected the hills to proclaim the Purity along with Dawud, and (also subjected) the birds*; and these were Our works.

[Surah Naml 27:17-19] And assembled together for Sulaiman were his armies of jinns and men, and of birds – so they had to be restricted. Until when they came to the valley of the ants, a she ant exclaimed, "O ants, enter your houses – may not Sulaiman and his armies crush you, unknowingly." He therefore smiled beamingly at her speech*, and submitted, "My Lord, bestow me guidance so that I thank you for the favour which You bestowed

135

upon me and my parents, and so that I may perform the good deeds which please You, and by Your mercy include me among Your bondmen who are worthy of Your proximity." *(*Prophet Sulaiman heard the voice of the she ant from far away.)*

[Surah Naml 27:20-22] And he surveyed the birds – he therefore said, "What is to me that I do not see the Hudhud *(hoopoe)*, or is he really absent?" "I will indeed punish him severely or slay him, or he must bring to me some clear evidence." So Hudhud did not stay absent for long, and presenting himself submitted, "I have witnessed a matter that your majesty has not seen, and I have brought definite information to you from the city of Saba." "I have seen a woman who rules over them, and she has been given from all things, and she has a mighty throne."

The Lesson by the Holy Prophet

Abu Hurairah reported Allah's Apostle ﷺ as saying: A person had been driving an ox loaded with luggage. The ox looked towards him and said: I have not been created for this but for lands (i.e. for ploughing the land and for drawing out water from the wells for the purpose of irrigating the lands). The people said with surprise and awe: Glory is for Allah, does the ox speak? Allah's Apostle ﷺ said: I believe it and so do Abu Bakr and 'Umar. Abu Hurairah reported Allah's Apostle ﷺ as saying: A shepherd was tendering the flock when a wolf came there and took away one goat. The shepherd pursued it (the wolf) and rescued it (the goat) from that (wolf). The wolf looked towards him and said: Who would save it on the day when there will be no shepherd except me? Thereupon people said: Glory is for Allah! Thereupon Allah's Apostle ﷺ said: I believe in it and so do Abu Bakr and Umar believe. (Muslim)

The Conversation with the Camel

Narrated Anas ﷺ: The families of Ansaar used to domesticate camels. Once an Ansaari came to the Holy Prophet ﷺ and said,

136

"O Allah's Apostle! We have a camel upon which we used to load water. That camel has now become rebellious and does not allow us to put any loads on him. Our fields and farms have turned dry." Upon this, the Holy Prophet ﷺ got up and went towards the camel. When he reached the farm, the camel was resting on the ground. The Ansaar said, "O Allah's Apostle! This is the camel – it tends to bite like a dog. We fear that it may bite you." The Holy Prophet ﷺ replied, "Do not fear for me." The Holy Prophet ﷺ went close to the camel and stood near him. *The camel lifted its head, and seeing the Holy Prophet ﷺ, put its head into prostration. Thereafter, the Holy Prophet ﷺ caught hold of the camel's forelock and put it to work.* The companions exclaimed, "O Allah's Apostle! This animal has no intellect, yet it prostrates to you! So we as humans have more right to prostrate to you." The Holy Prophet ﷺ replied, "It does not befit a human being to prostrate another human. Were I to command humans to prostrate each other, I would command women to prostrate to their husbands due to the great right the husbands have over them." (Imam Ahmad, Nasai) (In another narration, it is mentioned that the camel complained to the Holy Prophet ﷺ that the Ansaar wanted to slaughter it.)

Hearing the Deer's Complaint

Hazrat Zaid bin Arqam ☙ and Hazrat Anas ☙ narrated: We passed through one of the roads in Medina Munawarah along with the Holy Prophet ﷺ. On the way was a tent belonging to a villager, who was sleeping outside it in the sun. A female deer was tied next to the tent. *The deer called out to the Holy Prophet ﷺ three times thus, "O Allah's Apostle."* The Holy Prophet ﷺ said, "What is your problem?" The deer replied, "This villager has captured me whereas I have 2 very small kids who are in the jungle inside a mountain cave. Would you please release me so that I may suckle them and come back?" The Holy Prophet ﷺ said, "Will you really come back?" She answered, "If I do not come back, then may Allah give me a painful punishment." So the Holy Prophet ﷺ let her go. She therefore went, suckled her kids and came back. The Holy Prophet ﷺ tied her up, as she was before. Meanwhile, the villager woke up, and upon seeing the Holy Prophet ﷺ, said, "What brings you here?" The Holy Prophet ﷺ said, "Release this deer." He promptly released her. The deer began running speedily into the wild, jumping and dancing with joy while proclaiming, "I bear witness that none is worthy of worship except Allah, and that you (Prophet Mohammed ﷺ are Allah's Apostle." (Zarqani, Abu Nuaim)

Section 13: The Excellent Chests & Hearts

[Surah Ta-Ha 20:25] Said Moosa, "My Lord, open up my breast for me."

[Surah Zumar 39:23] Allah has sent down the best of Books *(the Holy Qur'an)*, which is consistent throughout, the one with paired statements; the hairs on the skins of those who fear their Lord, stand on end with it; then their skins and their hearts soften, inclined towards the remembrance of Allah; this is the guidance of Allah, He may guide whomever He wills with it; and whomever Allah sends astray, there is no guide for him.

[Surah Mujadilah 58:22] You will not find the people who believe in Allah and the Last Day, befriending those who oppose Allah and His Noble Messenger, even if they are their fathers or their sons or their brothers or their tribesmen; it is these upon whose hearts Allah has ingrained faith, and has aided them with a Spirit from Himself; and He will admit them into Gardens beneath which rivers flow, abiding in them forever; Allah is pleased with them, and they are pleased with Him; this is Allah's group; pay heed! Indeed it is Allah's group who are the successful.

[Surah Inshirah 94:1] Did We not widen your bosom for you?

Nothing brings My slave closer to Me, as does his performance of the obligations I placed upon him; and *he keeps coming closer to Me through performing Nawafil (praying or doing extra deeds besides what is obligatory) till I love him — so when I love him, I become his leg with which he walks, and his hand with which he grips, and his tongue with which he talks, and his heart (or mind) with which he reflects. If he asks Me, I give him, if he prays to Me, I accept his prayer.* (Ibn Al-Saniyy)

Whoever hurts any of My friends has waged war against Me. And nothing brings My slave closer to Me, like his performance of the obligations; and *he keeps coming closer to Me through performing Nawafil (praying or doing extra deeds besides what is obligatory) till I love him – so when I love him, I become his eye with which he sees, and his ear with which he hears, and his leg with which he walks, and his heart (or mind) with which he reflects and his tongue with which he speaks. If he asks Me, I give him, if he prays to Me, I accept his prayer. I do not hesitate about anything I do – (however) I hesitate to take away his life, for he hates death and I dislike harming him.* (Ahmad bin Hambal)

The Chest of the Holy Prophet

[Surah Noor 24:35] Allah is the Light of the heavens and the earth; the example of His light is like a niche in which is a lamp; the lamp is in a glass; the glass is as if it were a star shining like a pearl, kindled by the blessed olive tree, neither of the east nor of the west – it is close that the oil itself get ablaze although the fire does not touch it; light upon light; Allah guides towards His light whomever He wills; and Allah illustrates examples for mankind; and Allah knows everything. *(The Holy Prophet is a light from Allah)*

Says Hazrat Kaab ibn Ahbaar ﷺ: Here, in the words of Allah, *the second Noor means the Holy* Prophet ﷺ. (Shifa)

Says Hazrat Abdullah bin Umar ﷺ: The niche means the chest of the Holy Prophet ﷺ, the glass lamp means the heart of the Holy Prophet ﷺ, and the lamp means the light that Allah placed in it. The light is neither of the east nor of the west, neither Jewish nor Christian. The blessed tree is illuminated – i.e. there is light upon the light of Ibrahim ﷺ – i.e. *the light of Mohammed's ﷺ heart is upon the light of Ibrahim's ﷺ heart.* (Tafseer Khazin)

Narrated Hazrat Abdul Rehman bin Aaesh ﷺ: The Holy Prophet ﷺ said, "I saw my Lord in the best shape. He said, 'In what matter are the close angels disputing?' I said, 'It is You who know!'" The Holy Prophet ﷺ then said, "*He then placed His Hand of mercy between my shoulders and I felt its coolness at the centre of my chest – and I came to know all that is in the skies and in the earth.*" The Holy Prophet ﷺ then recited the following verse of the Holy Qur'an – "[Ana`am 6:75] And likewise We showed Ibrahim the entire kingdom of the heavens and the earth and so that he be of those who believe as eyewitnesses." (Mishkaat, Tirmidhi, Ahmad)

Seeing Allah with the Heart

Narrated Ibn Abbas ﷺ: The Holy Quran's words:" The heart did not deny, what it saw (Surah Najm 11) and" And indeed he did see the Spectacle again" (Surah Najm 13) imply that *the Holy Prophet* ﷺ *saw Allah twice with his heart.* (Muslim)

Said Abdullah ibn Abbas ﷺ: "Undoubtedly, the *Holy Prophet* ﷺ *saw his Lord (Allah) twice – once with the eyes of his head and once with the eyes of the heart.*" (Tibrani, Khasais Kubra)

The Opening of the Heart

Reported Anas b. Malik ﷺ: Gabriel came to Allah's Apostle ﷺ while he was playing with his playmates. He took hold of him and lay him prostrate on the ground and tore open his breast and took out the heart from it and then extracted a blood-clot out of it and said: That was the part of Satan in you. *And then he washed it with the water of Zamzam in a golden basin and then it was joined together and restored to its place.* The boys came running to his mother, i.e. his nurse, and said: Verily Muhammad has been murdered. They all rushed toward him (and found him all right) His color was changed, Anas said. *I myself saw the marks of needle on his breast.* (Muslim)

Narrated on the authority of Anas b. Malik 🙵: Allah's Apostle 🙵
said: *(Angels) came to me and took me to the Zamzam and my heart was
opened and washed with the water of Zamzam and then I was left (at my
place).* (Muslim)

Anas b. Malik reported 🙵: Abu Dharr used to relate that Allah's
Apostle 🙵 said: The roof of my house was cleft when I was in
Mecca and Gabriel descended and opened my heart and then
washed it with the water of Zamzam. He then brought a gold
basin full of wisdom and faith and after emptying it into my
breast, he closed it up. Then taking me by the hand, he ascended
with me to the heaven, and when we came to the lowest heaven,
Gabriel said to the guardian of the lowest heaven: Open. He
asked who was there? He replied. It is Gabriel. He again asked
whether there was someone with him. He replied: Yes, it is
Muhammad 🙵 with me. He was asked if he had been sent for,
He (Gabriel) said: Yes. Then he opened (the gate). (Muslim –
part of a longer Hadeeth)

Light in His Heart

Ibn 'Abbas 🙵 said: I spent the night in the house of my mother's
sister, Maimuna, and observed how Allah's Apostle 🙵 prayed (at
night). He got up and relieved himself. He then washed his face
and hands and then went to sleep. He again got up and went near
the water-skin and loosened its straps and then poured some
water in a bowl and inclined it with his hands (towards himself).
He then performed a good ablution between the two extremes
and then stood up to pray. I also came and stood by his left side.
He took hold of me and made me stand on his right side. It was
in thirteen rak'ahs that the (night) prayer of Allah's Apostle 🙵
was completed. He then slept till he began to snore, and we knew
that he had gone to sleep by his snoring. He then went out (for
the dawn prayer) and then again slept, and said while praying or
prostrating himself:" *O Allah! place light in my heart, light in my*

hearing, light in my sight, light on my right, light on my left, light in front of me, light behind me, light above me, light below me, make light for me," or he said:" Make me light." (Muslim)

The Heart Does Not Sleep

Ibn 'Abbas 🕮 reported that he spent a night in the house of his maternal aunt, Maimuna. Allah's Apostle 🕮 got up at night and performed short ablution (taking water) from the water-skin hanging there. (Giving a description of the ablution Ibn 'Abbas said: It was short and performed with a little water.) I also got up and did the same as Allah's Apostle 🕮 had done. I then came (to him) and stood on his left. He then made me go around to his right side. He then observed prayer and went to sleep till he began to snore. Bilal came to him and informed him about the prayer. *He (the Holy* Prophet 🕮 *) then went out and observed the dawn prayer without performing ablution. Sufyan said: It was a special (prerogative of the) Allah's* Apostle 🕮 *for it has been conveyed to us that the eyes of Allah's* Apostle 🕮 *sleep, but his heart does not sleep.* (Muslim)

I asked Syedah `Aisha 🕮, "How is the prayer of Allah's Apostle 🕮 during the month of Ramadan." She said, "Allah's Apostle 🕮 never exceeded eleven rak`at in Ramadan or in other months; he used to offer four rak`at-- do not ask me about their beauty and length, then four rak`at, do not ask me about their beauty and length, and then three rak`at." Aisha 🕮 further said, "I said, 'O Allah's Apostle 🕮! Do you sleep before offering the witr prayer?' He replied, *'O `Aisha! My eyes sleep but my heart remains awake'!*"(Bukhari)

Chapter 2: The Hearts & Chests of The Companions

Narrated by Syedena Ali 🕮: They are the fewest in number, but the greatest in rank before Allah. Through them Allah preserves His proofs until they bequeath it to those like them (before passing on) and *plant it firmly in their hearts.* By them knowledge has taken by assault the reality of things, so that they found easy what those given to comfort found hard, and found intimacy in what the ignorant found desolate. They accompanied the world with bodies whose spirits were attached to the highest regard *(al-mahall al-a`la)*. Ah, ah! how one yearns to see them! (Ibn al-Jawzi in Sifat al-safwa)

The Heart of Syedena Omar

Narrated Ibn Omar 🙏: Allah's Apostle 🌸 said, "*Allah has indeed placed the truth upon the tongue of Umar, and upon his heart.*" (Tirmizi, Abu Dawud)

The giving of knowledge to Abu Hurairah & others

Abu Hurairah 🙏 said: You are under the impression that Abu Hurairah 🙏 transmits so many hadiths from Allah's Apostle 🌸; (bear in mind) Allah is the great Reckoner. I was a poor man and I served Allah's Apostle 🌸 being satisfied with bare subsistence, whereas the Migrants remained busy with transactions in the bazaar; while the Ansar had been engaged in looking after their properties. (He further reported) that Allah's Apostle 🌸 said: He who spread the cloth would not forget anything that he would hear from me. *I spread my cloth until he narrated something. I then pressed it against my (chest), so I never forgot anything that I heard from him* (Muslim)

Narrated Ibn `Abbas 🙏: *Once the Holy* Prophet 🌸 *embraced me and said*, "O Allah! Bestow on him the knowledge of the Book (Qur'an). (Bukhari)

Narrated Hazrat Usman bin Abi AlAas 🙏: I once complained to the Holy Prophet 🌸 that I keep forgetting what I memorize from the Holy Quran. He answered that it is due to a Satan called "Khinzab". *He then asked me to come close to him, which I did. He placed his hand on my chest and I felt its coolness between my shoulders. He then said, "O Satan! Get out of the chest of Usman!"* From then on, I remembered each and everything that I ever listened to. (Baihaqi, Abu Nuaim, Khasais Kubra).

Narrated Abu Juhaifa ﷺ: Allah's Apostle ﷺ came to us at noon and water for ablution was brought to him. After he had performed ablution, the remaining water was taken by the people and they started smearing their bodies with it (as a blessed thing). The Holy Prophet ﷺ offered two rak`at of the Zuhr prayer and then two rak`at of the `Asr prayer while a short spear (or stick) was there (as a Sutra) in front of him. Abu Musa said: *The Holy Prophet ﷺ asked for a tumbler containing water and washed both his hands and face in it and then threw a mouthful of water in the tumbler and said to both of us (Abu Musa and Bilal), "Drink from the tumbler and pour some of its water on your faces and chests."* (Bukhari)

The Holy Prophet's hand over the Companions' chests.

Narrated Hazrat Ali bin Abi Talib ﷺ The Holy Prophet ﷺ wanted to appoint me as the governor of Yemen. I therefore submitted that I am inexperienced, so how shall I judge in cases referred to me? *Upon hearing this, the Holy* Prophet ﷺ *struck my chest with his blessed hand and supplicated thus, "O Allah! Guide his heart, and keep his tongue firm!"* By Allah, the Splitter of the Grain, I have never had any doubt in any judgment I gave between two parties." (Ibn Majah, Hakim, Khasais Kubra)

The Holy Prophet ﷺ once passed his hands over the head and chest of Usaid bin Abi Yaas ﷺ – so *whenever Usaid ﷺ used to enter a dark room, he used to illuminate it.* (Ibn Asakar, Kanz-ul-Ummal, Khasais Kubra)

Ubayy b. Ka'b ﷺ reported: I was in the mosque when a man entered and prayed and recited (the Qur'an) in a style to which I objected. Then another man entered (the mosque) and recited in a style different from that of his companion. When we had finished the prayer, we all went to Allah's Apostle ﷺ and said to him: This man recited in a style to which I objected, and the other entered and recited in a style different from that of his companion. Allah's Apostle ﷺ asked them to recite and so they recited, and Allah's Apostle ﷺ expressed approval of their affairs (their modes of recitation). And there occurred in my mind a sort of denial which did not occur even during the Days of Ignorance. When Allah's Apostle ﷺ saw how I was affected (by a wrong idea), *he struck my chest, whereupon I broke into sweating and felt as though I were looking at Allah with fear.* He (the Holy Prophet ﷺ) said to me: Ubayy, a message was sent to me to recite the Qur'an in one dialect, and I replied: Make (things) easy for my people. It was conveyed to me for the second time that it should be recited in two dialects. I again replied to him: Make affairs easy for my people. It was again conveyed to me for the third time to recite in seven dialects And (I was further told): You have got a seeking for every reply that I sent you, which you should seek from Me. I said: O Allah! Forgive my people, forgive my people, and I have deferred the third one for the day on which the entire creation will turn to me, including even Ibrahim (peace be upon him) (for intercession). (Muslim)

Section 14: The Excellent Hands

Narrated Abu Hurairah 🕮: Allah's Apostle 🕮 said, "Allah said, 'I will declare war against him who shows hostility to a pious worshipper of Mine. And the most beloved things with which My slave comes nearer to Me, is what I have enjoined upon him; and My slave keeps on coming closer to Me through performing Nawafil (praying or doing extra deeds besides what is obligatory) till I love him, so I become his sense of hearing with which he hears, and his sense of sight with which he sees, *and his hand with which he grips*, and his leg with which he walks; and if he asks Me, I will give him, and if he asks My protection (Refuge), I will protect him; (i.e. give him My Refuge) and I do not hesitate to do anything as I hesitate to take the soul of the believer, for he hates death, and I hate to disappoint him." (Bukhari)

Nothing brings My slave closer to Me, as does his performance of the obligations I placed upon him; and he keeps coming closer to Me through performing Nawafil (praying or doing extra deeds besides what is obligatory) till I love him – so when I love him, I become his leg with which he walks, *and his hand with which he grips*, and his tongue with which he talks, and his heart (or mind) with which he reflects. If he asks Me, I give him, if he prays to Me, I accept his prayer. (Ibn Al-Saniyy)

Allah is Pleased with Those Who Swore Allegiance on the Holy Prophets Hands

[Surah Fath 48:10] Those who swear allegiance to you *(O dear Prophet Mohammed 🕮 , do indeed in fact swear allegiance to Allah; Allah's Hand* of Power is above their hands*; so whoever breaches his oath, has breached his own greater promise; and whoever fulfills the covenant he has with Allah - so very soon Allah will bestow upon him a great reward. *(*Used as a metaphor.)*

[Surah Fath 48:18] *Indeed Allah was truly pleased with the believers when they swore allegiance to you* beneath the tree - so He knew what was in their hearts - He therefore sent down peace upon them, and rewarded them with an imminent victory.

Narrated Jabir bin `Abdullah 🙏: *On the day of Al-Hudaibiya, Allah's* Apostle 🙏 *said to us' "You are the best people on the earth!*" We were 1400 then. If I could see now, I would have shown you the place of the Tree (beneath which the Pledge of allegiance was given by us)," Salim said, "Our number was 1400." `Abdullah bin Abi `Aufa said, "The people (who gave the Pledge of allegiance) under the Tree numbered 1300 and the number of Bani Aslam was 1/8 of the Emigrants." (Bukhari, Muslim, Mishkaat).

Upon them is Allah's Hand of Power!

[Surah Fath 48:10] Those who swear allegiance to you *(O dear Prophet Mohammed 🙏 , do indeed in fact swear allegiance to Allah; Allah's Hand* of Power is above their hands*; so whoever breaches his oath, has breached his own greater promise; and whoever fulfills the covenant he has with Allah - so very soon Allah will bestow upon him a great reward. *(*Used as a metaphor.)*

Narrated `Uthman bin Mauhab 🙏: A man came to perform the Hajj to (Allah's) House. Seeing some people sitting, he said, "Who are these sitting people?" Somebody said, "They are the people of Quraish." He said, "Who is the old man?" They said, "Ibn `Umar (🙏)" He went to him and said, "I want to ask you about something; will you tell me about it? I ask you with the respect due to the sanctity of this (Sacred) House, do you know that `Uthman bin `Affan fled on the day of Uhud?" Ibn `Umar🙏 said, "Yes." He said, "Do you know that he (i.e. `Uthman 🙏) was absent from the Badr (battle) and did not join it?" Ibn `Umar🙏 said, "Yes." He said, "Do you know that he failed to be present at the Ridwan Pledge of allegiance (i.e. Pledge of allegiance at Hudaibiya) and did not witness it?" Ibn `Umar 🙏

151

replied, "Yes," He then said, "Allah-Akbar!" Ibn `Umar 🙵 said, "Come along; I will inform you and explain to you what you have asked. As for the flight (of `Uthman 🙵) on the day of Uhud, I testify that Allah forgave him. As regards his absence from the Badr (battle), he was married to the daughter of Allah's Apostle 🙵 and she was ill, so the Holy Prophet 🙵 said to him, 'You will have such reward as a man who has fought the Badr battle will get, and will also have the same share of the booty.' As for his absence from the Ridwan Pledge of allegiance if there had been anybody more respected by the Meccans than `Uthman bin `Affan 🙵, the Holy Prophet 🙵 would surely have sent that man instead of `Uthman 🙵. So the Holy Prophet 🙵 sent him (i.e. `Uthman 🙵 to Mecca) and the Ridwan Pledge of allegiance took place after `Uthman 🙵 had gone to Mecca. The Holy Prophet 🙵 raised his right hand saying. *'This is the hand of `Uthman,' and clasped it over his other hand* and said, "This is for `Uthman.'" Ibn `Umar 🙵 then said (to the man), "Go now, after taking this information."(Bukhari)

Allah Mentions It is He Who Threw the Sand!

[Surah Anfal 8:17] So you did not slay them, *but in fact Allah slew them*; and *(O dear Prophet Mohammed 🙵 you did not throw (the sand)* when you did throw, *but in fact Allah threw*; and in order to bestow an excellent reward upon the Muslims; indeed Allah is the All Hearing, the All Knowing.

Narrated on the authority of Salama 🙵 who said: We fought by the side of Allah's Apostle 🙵 at Hunain. When we encountered the enemy, I advanced and ascended a hillock. A man from the enemy side turned towards me and I shot him with an arrow. He (ducked and) hid himself from me. I could not understand what he did, but (all of a sudden) I saw that a group of people appeared from the other hillock. They and the Companions of the Holy Prophet 🙵 met in combat, but the Companions of the

Holy Prophet ﷺ turned back and I too turned back defeated. I had two mantles, one of which I was wrapping round the waist (covering the lower part of my body) and the other I was putting around my shoulders. My waist-wrapper got loose and I held the two mantles together. (In this downcast condition) I passed by Allah's Apostle ﷺ who was riding on his white mule. He said: The son of Akwa' finds himself to be utterly perplexed. *When the Companions gathered round him from all sides, Allah's Apostle ﷺ got down from his mule, picked up a handful of dust from the ground, threw it into their (enemy) faces and said: May these faces be deformed. There was no one among the enemy whose eyes were not filled with the dust from this handful.* So they turned back fleeing. And Allah the Exalted and Glorious defeated them, and Allah's Apostle ﷺ distributed their booty among the Muslims. (Muslim)

Narrated on the authority of 'Abbas ﷺ who said: I was in the company of Allah's Apostle ﷺ on the Day of Hunain. I and Abd Sufyan b. Harith b. 'Abd al-Muttalib stuck to Allah's Apostle ﷺ and we did not separate from him. And Allah's Apostle ﷺ was riding on his white mule which had been presented to him by Farwa b. Nufitha al-Judhami. When the Muslims had an encounter with the disbelievers, the Muslims fled, falling back, but Allah's Apostle ﷺ began to spur his mule towards the disbelievers. I was holding the bridle of the mule of Allah's Apostle ﷺ checking it from going very fast, and Abu Sufyan was holding the stirrup of the (mule of the) Allah's Apostle ﷺ, who said: Abbas, call out to the people of al-Samura. Abbas (who was a man with a loud voice) called out at the top of the voice: Where are the people of Samura? (Abbas said:) And by Allah, when they heard my voice, they came back (to us) as cows come back to their calves, and said: We are present, we are present! 'Abbas said: They began to fight the infidels. Then there was a call to The Ansar. Those (who called out to them) shouted: O ye party of the Ansar! O party of the Ansar! Banu al-Harith b. al-Khazraj were the last to be called. Those (who called out to them) shouted: O Banu Al-Harith b. al-Khazraj! O Banu Harith b. al-Khazraj! And Allah's Apostle ﷺ who was riding on his mule looked at their fight with his neck stretched forward and he said: This is the time when the fight is raging hot. *Then Allah's Apostle ﷺ took (some) pebbles and threw them in the face of the infidels.* Then he said: By the Lord of Muhammad, the infidels are defeated. 'Abbas said: I went round and saw that the battle was in the same condition in which I had seen it. By Allah, it remained in the same condition until he threw the pebbles. I continued to watch until I found that their force had been spent out and they began to retreat. (Muslim)

Chapter 2: The Blessed Touch of His Hands.

The Unique Softness and Fragrance of The Holy Prophet's Hands

Narrated Humaid ﷺ: I asked Anas about the fasting of the Holy Prophet ﷺ. He said "Whenever I liked to see the Holy Prophet ﷺ fasting in any month, I could see that, and whenever I liked to see him not fasting, I could see that too, and if I liked to see him praying in any night, I could see that, and if I liked to see him sleeping, I could see that too." Anas further said, "I never touched silk or velvet softer than the hand of Allah's Apostle ﷺ and never smelled musk or perfumed smoke more pleasant than the smell of Allah's Apostle ﷺ" (Bukhari)

Narrated Anas ﷺ: I have never touched silk or Dibaj (i.e. thick silk) softer than the palm of the Holy Prophet ﷺ nor have I smelt a perfume nicer than the sweat of the Holy Prophet ﷺ. (Bukhari)

The Companions Wished To Take Tabarruk through His Hands

Narrated Abu Juhaifa 🜚: I saw Allah's Apostle 🜚 in a red leather tent and I saw Bilal taking the remaining water with which the Holy Prophet 🜚 had performed ablution. *I saw the people taking the utilized water impatiently and whoever got some of it rubbed it on his body and those who could not get any took the moisture from the others' hands.* Then I saw Bilal carrying a short spear (or stick) which he planted in the ground. The Holy Prophet 🜚 came out tucking up his red cloak, and led the people in prayer and offered two rak`at (facing the Ka`ba) taking a short spear (or stick) as a Sutra for his prayer. I saw the people and animals passing in front of him beyond the stick. (Bukhari)

The People Whom the Holy Prophet Touched

Ubayy b. Ka'b 🜚 reported: I was in the mosque when a man entered and prayed and recited (the Qur'an) in a style to which I objected. Then another man entered (the mosque) and recited in a style different from that of his companion. When we had finished the prayer, we all went to Allah's Apostle 🜚 and said to him: This man recited in a style to which I objected, and the other entered and recited in a style different from that of his companion. Allah's Apostle 🜚 asked them to recite and so they recited, and Allah's Apostle 🜚 expressed approval of their affairs (their modes of recitation) and there occurred In my mind a sort of denial which did not occur even during the Days of Ignorance. When Allah's Apostle 🜚 saw how I was affected (by a wrong idea), *he struck my chest, whereupon I broke into sweating and felt as though I were looking at Allah with fear.* He (the Holy Prophet 🜚) said to me: Ubayy a message was sent to me to recite the Qur'an in one dialect, and I replied: Make (things) easy for my people. It was conveyed to me for the second time that it should be recited in two dialects. I again replied to him: Make affairs easy for my people. It was again conveyed to me for the third time to recite in seven dialects And (I was further told): You have got a seeking for every reply that I sent you, which you should seek from Me. I said: O Allah! Forgive my people, forgive my people, and I have deferred the third one for the day on which the entire creation will turn to me, including even Ibrahim (peace be upon him) (for intercession). (Muslim)

Narrated Hazrat Usman bin Abi AlAas ﷺ I once complained to the Holy Prophet ﷺ that I keep forgetting what I memorize from the Holy Quran. He answered that it is due to a Satan called "Khinzab". *He then asked me to come close to him, which I did. He placed his hand on my chest and I felt its coolness between my shoulders. He then said, "O Satan! Get out of the chest of Usman!"* From then on, I remembered each and everything that I ever listened to. (Baihaqi, Abu Nuaim, Khasais Kubra).

Jabir b. Samura ﷺ reported: I prayed along with Allah's Apostle ﷺ the first prayer. He then went to his family and I also went along with him when he met some children (on the way). He began to pat the cheeks of each one of them. *He also patted my cheek and I experienced a coolness or a fragrance of his hand as if it had been brought out from the scent bag of a perfumer.* (Muslim)

Narrated Zaid bin Aslam ﷺ: An arrow hit the eye of Hazrat Qatadah bin Noman in the battle of Uhud, causing the eye to fall down upon his cheek. He therefore came to the Holy Prophet ﷺ with it who said, "If you remain patient, Paradise is for you or if you wish I shall restore it and supplicate for you, so you will not find any defect in it." Hazrat Qatadah ﷺ submitted, "O Allah's Apostle! Indeed Paradise is a beautiful reward and a magnificent bestowal – but I have a wife whom I love dearly. I fear that she will not like me in this state, so please restore my eye, and also invoke Allah to grant me Paradise." He said, "Very well." *He then took Qatadah's eye in his hand and placed it back into its socket, and supplicated thus, "O Allah! Make it very beautiful." So that eye of*

Qatadah ﷺ *was more beautiful and better working than the other.* (Zarkani)

Usama ibn Sharik ﷺ narrates: "I came to see the Holy Prophet ﷺ while his Companions were with him, and they seemed as still as if birds had alighted on top of their heads. I gave him my salam and I sat down. [Then Bedouins came and asked questions which the Holy Prophet ﷺ answered.] ... The Holy Prophet ﷺ then stood up and the people stood up. *They began to kiss his hand, whereupon I took his hand and placed it on my face. I found it more fragrant than musk and cooler than sweet water."* (Abu Dawud, Tirmizi, Ibn Majah, Hakim, Ahmad, Baihaqi)

Narrated Hazrat Abu Zaid bin Amr bin Akhtab ﷺ: The Holy Prophet ﷺ *once passed his hands over my head and beard,* and supplicated thus, "O Allah, grant him beauty." The sub-narrator adds that Abu Zaid ﷺ lived for more than a hundred years but there was not a single white hair on his head or in his beard. *All his hair remained black, his face kept shining and there was not a single wrinkle on his face until he died.* (Tirmizi, Baihaqi, Khasais Kubra).

The Holy Prophet ﷺ once *passed his hands over the head and chest* of Usaid bin Abi Yaas ﷺ – so *whenever Usaid* ﷺ *used to enter a dark room, he used to illuminate it.* (Ibn Asakar, Kanz-ul-Ummal, Khasais Kubra)

Narrated Abu Hurairah ﷺ: The Holy Prophet ﷺ said, "A prophet amongst the Holy Prophet ﷺ carried out a holy military expedition, so he said to his followers, 'Anyone who has married a woman and wants to consummate the marriage, and has not done so yet, should not accompany me; nor should a man who has built a house but has not completed its roof; nor a man who has sheep or she-camels and is waiting for the birth of their young ones.' So, the Prophet carried out the expedition and when he reached that town at the time or nearly at the time of the `Asr prayer, he said to the sun, 'O sun! You are under Allah's order and I am under Allah's order. O Allah! Stop it (i.e. the sun) from setting.' It was stopped till Allah made him victorious. Then he collected the booty and the fire came to burn it, but it did not burn it. He said (to his men), 'Some of you have stolen something from the booty. So one man from every tribe should give me a pledge of allegiance by shaking hands with me.' *(They did so and) the hand of a man got stuck over the hand of their prophet.* Then that prophet said (to the man), 'The theft has been committed by your people. So all the persons of your tribe should give me the pledge of allegiance by shaking hands with me.' *The hands of two or three men got stuck over the hand of their prophet* and he said, "You have committed the theft.' Then they brought a head of gold like the head of a cow and put it there, and the fire came and consumed the booty. The Holy Prophet ﷺ added: Then Allah saw our weakness and disability, so he made booty legal for us." (Bukhari)

Narrated Abu Hurairah ﷺ: I said to Allah's Apostle ﷺ "I hear many narrations (Hadiths) from you but I forget them." Allah's Apostle ﷺ said, "Spread your Rida' (garment)." *I did accordingly and then he moved his hands as if filling them with something (and emptied them in my Rida') and then said, "Take and wrap this sheet over your body."* I did it and after that I never forgot anything. (Bukhari)

Narrated Al-Bara bin Azib ﷺ: Allah's Apostle ﷺ sent some men from the Ansar to (kill) Abu Rafi`, the Jew, and appointed `Abdullah bin Atik ﷺ as their leader. Abu Rafi` used to hurt Allah's Apostle ﷺ and help his enemies against him. He lived in his castle in the land of Hijaz. When those men approached (the castle) after the sun had set and the people had brought back their livestock to their homes. `Abdullah (bin Atik) ﷺ said to his companions, "Sit down at your places. I am going, and I will try to play a trick on the gate-keeper so that I may enter (the castle)."

So `Abdullah proceeded towards the castle, and when he approached the gate, he covered himself with his clothes, pretending to answer the call of nature. The people had gone in, and the gate-keeper (considered `Abdullah 🙵 as one of the castle's servants) addressing him saying, "O Allah's Servant! Enter if you wish, for I want to close the gate." `Abdullah added in his story, "So I went in (the castle) and hid myself. When the people got inside, the gate-keeper closed the gate and hung the keys on a fixed wooden peg. I got up and took the keys and opened the gate. Some people were staying late at night with Abu Rafi` for a pleasant night chat in a room of his. When his companions of nightly entertainment went away, I ascended to him, and whenever I opened a door, I closed it from inside. I said to myself, 'Should these people discover my presence, they will not be able to catch me till I have killed him.' So I reached him and found him sleeping in a dark house amidst his family, I could not recognize his location in the house. So I shouted, 'O Abu Rafi`!' Abu Rafi` said, 'Who is it?' I proceeded towards the source of the voice and hit him with the sword, and because of my perplexity, I could not kill him. He cried loudly, and I came out of the house and waited for a while, and then went to him again and said, 'What is this voice, O Abu Rafi`?' He said, 'Woe to your mother! A man in my house has hit me with a sword! I again hit him severely but I did not kill him. Then I drove the point of the sword into his belly (and pressed it through) till it touched his back, and I realized that I have killed him. I then opened the doors one by one till I reached the staircase, and thinking that I had reached the ground, I stepped out and fell down and got my leg broken in a moonlit night. I tied my leg with a turban and proceeded on till I sat at the gate, and said, 'I will not go out tonight till I know that I have killed him.' So, when (early in the morning) the cock crowed, the announcer of the casualty stood on the wall saying, 'I announce the death of Abu Rafi`, the merchant of Hijaz. Thereupon I went to my companions and said, 'Let us save ourselves, for Allah has killed Abu Rafi`,' So I (along with my companions proceeded and) went to the Holy Prophet ﷺ and described the whole story to him. *"He said, 'Stretch out your (broken) leg. I stretched it out and he rubbed it and it became all right as if I had never had any ailment whatsoever."* (Bukhari)

Abu Hurairah ﷺ said: You are under the impression that Abu Hurairah transmits so many hadiths from Allah's Apostle ﷺ; (bear in mind) Allah is the great Reckoner. I was a poor man and I served Allah's Apostle ﷺ being satisfied with bare subsistence, whereas the Migrants remained busy with transactions in the bazaar; while the Ansar had been engaged in looking after their properties. (He further reported) that Allah's Apostle ﷺ said: He who spread the cloth would not forget anything that he would hear from me. *I spread my cloth until he narrated something. I then pressed it against my (chest), so I never forgot anything that I heard from him* (Muslim)

The Holy Prophet ﷺ once passed his hands over the head of Hazrat Hanzalah bin Huzaim ﷺ, and said, "Blessings have been placed within you." Hazrat Zayaal relates that he witnessed that whenever any human or camel or goat had a sprain, people used to bring them to Hazrat Hanzalah. He used to put some saliva on his hand and rub it on his head, and supplicate thus, *'With Allah's name upon the vestige of Allah's* Apostle ﷺ *"* He then used to rub the *hand on sprain, and the sprain used to disappear.* (Bukhari in Tareekh, Ahmed, Khasais Kubra, Al-Tabarani)

The animals that the Holy Prophet touched

Narrated Abdullah bin Masood ﷺ: I used to shepherd the animals for Uqbah bin Abi Moheet. Once the Holy Prophet ﷺ came along with Syedena Abu Bakr Siddiq and asked me if I had some milk. I replied, "I certainly have some milk, but it is a trust and I cannot be unfaithful to the owner." The Holy Prophet ﷺ said, *"Bring a she-goat that has never mated."* Hazrat Abdullah bin

Masood further narrates that he brought such a she-goat. The Holy Prophet ﷺ passed his hand over the udder of the she-goat and supplicated to Allah, whilst Syedena Abu Bakr brought a large, wide pot. *The Holy* Prophet ﷺ *milked the she-goat till the pot was full* and then gave it to Abu Bakr, saying, "Drink it." He then commanded the udders to return to their original state, upon which the udders returned to their original state. This event was the reason why Abdullah bin Masood accepted faith.(Baihaqi, Shifa)

Hazrat Hazzaam bin Hashim ﷺ relates that when the Holy Prophet ﷺ was migrating from Mecca to Medina, he passed by the camp of Umme Ma'bad Atika bint Khalid Khuzaih. Umme Ma'bad's tribe was facing a severe drought. She used to sit outside her camp to give water and food to travellers. The Holy Prophet ﷺ wanted to buy some meat and dates from her, but she had neither of these. The Holy Prophet ﷺ saw a she-goat tied outside her tent, and asked her about it. She replied, "It is feeble and weak, and is therefore much behind the other animals." He then asked, "Does she give milk?" She replied, "No." He then said, "Do you permit me to milk it?" Umme Ma'bad replied, "My parents be sacrificed for you! If you see milk in her, then milk her!" The Holy Prophet ﷺ then passed his hands over the udders of the she-goat, proclaiming Allah's name and supplicated for her. The she-goat spread its legs for him, brought down its milk and began chewing its food. *The Holy* Prophet ﷺ *called for a vessel that would suffice all those present, and filled it with the milk extracted from it, until it began frothing.* He then gave it to Umme Ma'bad to drink, until she was full. He then gave it to his companions who also drank till they were full and lastly he drank from it himself. He then again began milking the she-goat, and filled the vessel – and as a token gave it to Umme Ma'bad. He then accepted Umme Ma'bad's allegiance to Islam, and left with his companions. (Sharhe Sunnah, Mishkaat)

Reported Syedah 'A'isha ﷺ: Allah's Apostle ﷺ commanded that a ram with black legs, black belly and black (circles) round the eyes should be brought to him, so that he should sacrifice it. He said to 'A'isha ﷺ: Give me the large knife, and then said: Sharpen it on a stone. She did that. He then took it (the knife) and then the ram; he placed it on the ground and then sacrificed it, saying: Bismillah, Allah-humma Taqabbal min Muhammadin wa Aal-i-Muhammadin, wa min Ummati Muhammadin (*In the name of Allah," O Allah, accept on behalf of Muhammad and the family of Muhammad and the Umma of Muhammad"*). (Muslim)

Narrated Abdullah ibn Qurt ﷺ: The Prophet ﷺ said: The greatest day in Allah's sight is the day of sacrifice and next the day of resting which Isa said on the authority of Thawr is the second day. Five or six sacrificial camels were brought to Allah's Apostle ﷺ and *they began to draw near to see which he would sacrifice first*. When they fell down dead, he said something in a low voice, which I could not catch. So I asked: What did he say? He was told that he had said: Anyone who wants can cut off a piece. (Abu Dawud)

The stones, pebbles and sticks touched by the Holy Prophet

Narrated Jabir bin `Abdullah ﷺ: *While Allah's Apostle ﷺ was carrying stones (along) with the people of Mecca for (the building of) the Ka`ba wearing an Izar (waist-sheet cover)*, his uncle Al-`Abbas said to him, "O my nephew! (It would be better) if you take off your Izar and put it over your shoulders underneath the stones." So he took off his Izar and put it over his shoulders, but he fell unconscious and since then he had never been seen uncovered. (Bukhari)

Narrated Abdullah ibn Abbas ﷺ: The residents of Hadramaut came to meet the Holy Prophet ﷺ, and among them was also

Ash'at bin Qais. They said, "We have hidden one matter in our hearts – so tell us what it is." The Holy Prophet ﷺ replied, "Purity is to Allah! This is the work of a soothsayer – and the soothsayer and his soothsaying, both are in hell." They said, "So how shall we come to know that you are indeed Allah's Apostle?" *He therefore picked up a handful of pebbles from the ground and said, "These pebbles bear witness that I am Allah's Apostle." So the pebbles in his hand began praising Allah, and said "We bear witness that you are indeed Allah's Apostle."* (Dalail Nubuwwah, Abu Nuaim, Khasais Kubra).

Reported Abu Zar Gifari ؓ that once *he witnessed pebbles saying the Praise of Allah in the hands of the Holy Prophet ﷺ, and in the hands of Syedena. Abu Bakr, Syedena Umar, Syedena Usman, and Syedena Ali.* (Mawahib Ladunniyah, Shifa, Madarij un-Nubuwwa)

The holy Kaaba had 360 idols placed in and around it by the polytheists. These were mostly made of stone and fixed on the ground, and it was extremely difficult to move them. They were also strong enough to withstand blows from pick-axes and hammers. When the Holy Prophet ﷺ entered Mecca in triumph, he went to the Holy Kaaba and had a stick in his hand. *He would simply touch each idol with the stick while reciting "Jaa-al-Haq wa zahaqa-al-Baatil" and the idol would come crashing down.* (Seerat Ibn Hishaam).

During the battle of Badr, the sword of Hazrat Okasha bin Mahsan ؓ broke. *He came to the Holy Prophet ﷺ, who gave him a dry stick and ordered him to fight with it. When Okasha took the stick in his and, it turned into a bright, long, solid and majestic sword.* He therefore fought in Badr using it. The sword remained with him after that, and he used it in all the battles he fought after that. Hazrat Okasha was martyred in the battle against the renegades. The sword became famous by the name of "Al Awn" (which means The Supporter). (Baihaqi, Ibn Asakir, Tabkaat ibn Saad, Shifa, Khasais Kubra).

The tree in Masjid Nabawi

Narrated Ibn `Umar ﷺ: The Holy Prophet ﷺ used to deliver his sermons while standing beside a trunk of a date palm. When he had the pulpit made, he used it instead. *The trunk started crying and the Holy* Prophet ﷺ *went to it, rubbing his hand over it (to stop its crying)*. (Bukhari)

Narrated Anas bin Malik ﷺ: That he heard Jabir bin `Abdullah ﷺ saying, "The roof of the Mosque was built over trunks of date-palms working as pillars. When the Holy Prophet ﷺ delivered a sermon, he used to stand by one of those trunks till the pulpit was made for him, and he used it instead. *Then we heard the trunk sending a sound like of a pregnant she-camel till the Holy* Prophet ﷺ *came to it, and put his hand over it, then it became quiet*." (Bukhari)

Food touched by the Holy Prophet

Narrated `Abdullah bin `Abbas ﷺ: Once a solar eclipse occurred during the lifetime of Allah's Apostle ﷺ. He offered the eclipse prayer. His companions asked, "O Allah's Apostle ﷺ! We saw you trying to take something while standing at your place and then we saw you retreating." The Holy Prophet ﷺ said, *"I was shown Paradise and wanted to have a bunch of fruit from it. Had I taken it, you would have eaten from it as long as the world remains."* (Bukhari)

Related by Abu Hurairah ﷺ: In one of the battle expeditions, the Muslim army had nothing to eat. Allah's Apostle ﷺ asked me if I had something. I told him that I had some dates in my pouch, upon which he ordered, "Bring them". I presented them to him and there were only 21 dates. *Allah's* Apostle ﷺ *placed his hand upon them and supplicated*. He then said, "Call ten men." So I called ten men. The ten men ate till they were full, and left. He then ordered to call another ten men. They too ate till they were full, and left. Similarly, groups of ten men came and left until the entire army had eaten. For the dates that were still remaining, Allah's Apostle ﷺ said, "*O Abu Hurairah* ﷺ, *keep them in your pouch, and eat as and when you wish by inserting your hand into the pouch. But do not overturn the pouch.*"Abu Hurairah ﷺ relates that he kept using and giving away the dates from the same pouch during the eras of the Holy Prophet ﷺ, Abu Bakr Siddiq ﷺ, Umar Farouk ﷺ and Usman ﷺ – and that he gave away at least 50 wasaqs in charity and himself ate about 20 wasaqs. The pouch was stolen on the day Syedena Usman ﷺ was martyred. (Tirmizi, Baihaqi, Abu Nuaim, Khasais Kubra)

Narrated `Abdullah ﷺ: We used to consider miracles as Allah's Blessings, but you people consider them to be a warning. Once we were with Allah's Apostle ﷺ on a journey, and we ran short of water. He said, "Bring the water remaining with you." The people brought a utensil containing a little water. *He placed his hand in it and said, "Come to the blessed water, and the Blessing is from Allah." I saw the water flowing from among the fingers of Allah's* Apostle ﷺ, *and no doubt, we heard the meal glorifying Allah, when it was being eaten (by him).* (Bukhari)

Narrated Jaber ﷺ: A man came to Allah's Apostle ﷺ, begging food from him. The Holy Prophet ﷺ gave him a half wasaq of wheat. *The man continued to eat from it, and also his wife and his guests until he once measured it, and it then came to an end.* He then came to the Holy Prophet ﷺ who said, "Had you not measured it, you would have kept eating from it, and it would have remained for you." (Muslim, Mishkaat).

Narrated Jabir ﷺ: We were digging (the trench) on the day of (Al-Khandaq (i.e. Trench)) and we came across a big solid rock. We went to the Holy Prophet ﷺ and said, "Here is a rock appearing across the trench." He said, "I am coming down." Then he got up, and a stone was tied to his belly for we had not eaten anything for three days. *So the Holy* Prophet ﷺ *took the spade and struck the big solid rock and it became like sand.* I said, "O Allah's Apostle ﷺ! Allow me to go home." (When the Holy Prophet ﷺ allowed me) I said to my wife, "I saw the Holy Prophet ﷺ in a state that I cannot treat lightly. Have you got something (for him to eat?" She replied, "I have barley and a she goat." So I slaughtered the she-kid and she ground the barley; then we put the meat in the earthenware cooking pot. Then I came to the Holy Prophet ﷺ when the dough had become soft and fermented and (the meat in) the pot over the stone trivet had nearly been well-cooked, and said, "I have got a little food prepared, so get up O Allah's Apostle, you and one or two men along with you (for the food)." The Holy Prophet ﷺ asked, "How much is that food?" I told him about it. He said, "It is abundant and good. Tell your wife not to remove the earthenware pot from the fire and not to take out any bread from the oven till I reach there." Then he said (to all his companions), "Get up." So the Muhajirin (i.e. Emigrants) and the Ansar got up. When I came to my wife, I said, "Allah's Mercy be upon you! The Holy Prophet ﷺ came along with the Muhajirin and the Ansar and those who were present with them." She said, "Did the Holy Prophet ﷺ ask you (how much food you had)?" I replied, "Yes." Then the Holy Prophet ﷺ said, "Enter and do not throng." The Holy Prophet ﷺ started cutting the bread (into pieces) and put the cooked meat over it. He covered the earthenware pot and the oven whenever he took something out of them. He would give the food to his companions and take the meat out of the pot. He went on cutting the bread and scooping the meat (for his companions) till they all ate their fill, and even then, some food remained. Then the Holy Prophet ﷺ said (to my wife), "Eat and present to others as the people are struck with hunger." (Bukhari, Mishkaat)

Narrated Abu Hurairahﷺ: By Allah except Whom none has the right to- be worshipped, (sometimes) I used to lay (sleep) on the ground on my liver (abdomen) because of hunger, and (sometimes) I used to bind a stone over my belly because of hunger. One day I sat by the way from where they (the Holy Prophet ﷺ and his companions) used to come out. When Abu Bakr passed by, I asked him about a Verse from Allah's Book and I asked him only that he might satisfy my hunger, but he passed by and did not do so. Then `Umar passed by me and I asked him about a Verse from Allah's Book, and I asked him only that he might satisfy my hunger, but he passed by without doing so. Finally AbulQasim (the Holy Prophet ﷺ) passed by me and he smiled when he saw me, for he knew what was in my heart and on my face. He said, "O Aba Hirr (Abu Hurairah)!" I replied, "Labbaik, O Allah's Apostle!" He said to me, "Follow me." He left and I followed him. Then he entered the house and I asked permission to enter and was admitted. He found milk in a bowl and said, "From where is this milk?" They said, "It has been presented to you by such-and-such man (or by such and such woman)." He said, "O Aba Hirr!" I said, "Labbaik, O Allah's Apostle!" He said, "Go and call the people of Suffah to me." These people of Suffah were the guests of Islam who had no families, nor money, nor anybody to depend upon, and whenever an object of charity was brought to the Holy Prophet ﷺ, he would send it to them and would not take anything from it, and whenever any present was given to him, he used to send some for them and take some of it for himself. The order of the Holy Prophet ﷺ upset me, and I said to myself, "How will this little milk be enough for the people of As-Suffah?" I thought I was more entitled to drink from that milk in order to strengthen myself, but behold! The Holy Prophet ﷺ came to order me to give that milk to them. I wondered what will remain of that milk for me, but anyway, I could not but obey Allah and His Apostleﷺ so I went to the people of As-Suffah and called them, and they came and asked the Holy Prophet's ﷺ permission to enter. They were admitted and took their seats in the house. The Holy Prophet ﷺ said, "O Aba-Hirr!" I said, "Labbaik, O Allah's Apostle!" He said, "Take it and give it to them." *So I took the bowl (of Milk) and started giving it to one man who would drink his fill and return it to me, whereupon I would give it to another man who, in his turn, would drink his fill and return it to me, and I would then offer it to another man who would drink his fill and return it to me. Finally, after the whole group had drunk their fill, I reached the Holy Prophet ﷺ who took the bowl and put it on his hand, looked at me and smiled and said. "O Aba Hirr!" I replied, "Labbaik, O Allah's Apostle!"* He said, "There remain you and I." I said, "You have said the truth, O Allah's Apostle!" He said, "Sit down and drink." I sat down and drank. He said, "Drink," and I drank. He kept on telling me repeatedly to drink, till I said, "No. by Allah Who sent you with the Truth, *I have no space for it (in my stomach).*" He said, "Hand it over to me." When I gave him the bowl, he praised Allah and pronounced Allah's Name on it and drank the remaining milk. (Bukhari)

Narrated Abu Hurairah ﷺ: Once while I was in a state of fatigue (because of severe hunger), I met `Umar bin Al-Khattab ﷺ, so I asked him to recite a verse from Allah's Book to me. He entered his house and interpreted it to me. (Then I went out and) after walking for a short distance, I fell on my face because of fatigue and severe hunger. Suddenly I saw Allah's Apostle ﷺ standing by my head. He said, "O Abu Hurairah!" I replied, "Labbaik, O Allah's Apostle, and Sadaik!" Then he held me by the hand, and made me get up. Then he came to know what I was suffering from. He took me to his house, and ordered a big bowl of milk for me. I drank thereof and he said, "Drink more, O Abu Hirr!" So I drank again, whereupon he again said, "Drink more." *So I drank more till my belly became full and looked like a bowl.* Afterwards I met `Umar and mentioned to him what had happened to me, and said to him, "Somebody, who had more right than you, O `Umar (ﷺ), took over the case. By Allah, I asked you to recite a Verse to me while I knew it better than you." On that `Umar ﷺ said to me, "By Allah, if I admitted and entertained you, it would have been dearer to me than having nice red camels." (Bukhari)

Chapter 3: Sahaba Kissed the Hands of the Holy Prophet

Narrated Hazrat Buraida ﷺ:- A villager once asked the Holy Prophet ﷺ to show him a miracle. The Holy Prophet ﷺ told the villager, "Tell that tree over there, that the Holy Prophet ﷺ has called you." When the villager did this, the tree shook and swayed to its right, left, front and back, thereby uprooting itself. It then moved forward, plowing the earth and raising dust behind it until it reached in front of the Holy Prophet ﷺ. It then said, "Peace be upon you, O Allah's Apostle!" The villager said, "Tell it to go back." Upon the command of the Holy Prophet ﷺ, the tree returned to its place and stood upright on its roots. The villager said, "Permit me to prostrate before you!" The Holy Prophet ﷺ said, "Would I command anyone to prostate to another, I would command the woman to prostate to her husband." The villager said, *"Then permit me to kiss your hands and feet!" So the Holy Prophet ﷺ permitted him.* (Shifa, Dalail Nubuwwa, Abu Nuaim).

Narrated Abdullah ibn Umar ﷺ: Ibn Umar was sent with a detachment of Allah's Apostle ﷺ. The people wheeled round in flight. He said: I was one of those who wheeled round in flight. When we stopped, we said (i.e. thought): How should we do? We have run away from the battlefield and deserve Allah's wrath. Then we said (thought): Let us enter Medina, stay there, and go there while no one sees us. So we entered (Medina) and thought: If we present ourselves before Allah's Apostle ﷺ, and if there is a change of repentance for us, we shall stay; if there is something else, we shall go away. So we sat down (waiting) for Allah's Apostle ﷺ before the dawn prayer. When he came out, we stood up to him and said: We are the ones who have fled. He turned to us and said: No, you are the ones who return to fight after wheeling away. *We then approached and kissed his hand, and he said; I am the main body of the Muslims.* (Abu Dawud)

Narrated Syedah Aisha 🌸, Ummul Mu'minin: I never saw anyone more like Allah's Apostle 🌸 in respect of gravity, calm deportment, pleasant disposition - according to al-Hasan's version: in respect of talk and speech. Al-Hasan did not mention gravity, calm deportment, pleasant disposition - than Fatimah (🌸), may Allah honour her face. *When she came to visit him (the Holy* Prophet 🌸 *he got up to (welcome) her, took her by the hand, kissed her and made her sit where he was sitting; and when he went to visit her, she got up to (welcome) him, took him by the hand, kissed him, and made him sit where she was sitting.* (Abu Dawud)

Narrated Safwan ibn `Asal al-Muradi 🌸: "One of two Jews said to his companion: Take us to this Prophet 🌸 so we can ask him about Musa's ten signs... [the Holy Prophet 🌸 replied in full and then] *they kissed his hands and feet and said: we witness that you are a Prophet...*" (Ibn Abi Shayba, Tirmizi, al-Nasa'i, Ibn Majah, and Hakim)

Narrated Anas ibn Malik 🌸: "*The whole Community of the people of Madina used to take the hand of the Holy* Prophet 🌸 *and rush to obtain their need with it.*" (Imam Ahmad)

Reported by Zare 🌸 when he was in the deputation of Abdel Qais 🌸: When we approached Medina, we began to hasten from our conveyances, and *then kiss the hand and foot of Allah's Apostle.*" (Abu Dawud, Bukhari in Mufrad, Mishkaat)

Sahaba & Tabeyeen Kissed the Hands That Touched the Holy Prophet

The Tabi`i Thabit al-Bunani 🌸 said : He used to go to Anas Ibn Malik, *kiss his hands, and say: "These are hands that touched the Holy*

170

Prophet ﷺ " He would kiss his eyes and say: "These are eyes that saw the Holy Prophet ﷺ " (Abu Ya`la, Ibn Hajar, al-Haythami, Bukhari in al-Adab al-mufrad)

Abd al-Rahman ibn Razin ؓ said: One of the Companions, Salama ibn al-Aku`, ؓ raised his hands before a group of people and said: "With these very hands I pledged allegiance (bay`a) to Allah's Apostle ﷺ ". *Upon hearing this, all who were present got up and went to kiss his hand.* (Bukhari in al-Adab al-mufrad, Ahmad.)

Abu Malik al-Ashja`i ؓ said: He once asked another Companion of the Tree, Ibn Abi Awfa ؓ, *"Give me the hand that swore bay`at to Allah's Apostle ﷺ, that I may kiss it."* (Ibn al-Muqri).

Narrated Hazrat Suhaib ؓ: I saw Hazrat Ali ؓ *kissing the hands and feet of Hazrat Abbas ؓ.* (Bukhari in Adab)

Narrated Qais ؓ: *I saw Talha's (ؓ) paralyzed hand with which he had protected the Holy* Prophet ﷺ *(from arrows) on the day of Uhud.* (Bukhari)

Chapter 4: The Treasures in Holy Prophet's Hands

Narrated `Uqba bin 'Amir ؓ: One day the Holy Prophet ﷺ went out and offered the funeral prayers of the martyrs of Uhud and then went up the pulpit and said, "I will pave the way for you as your predecessor and will be a witness on you. *By Allah! I see my Fount (Kauthar) just now and I have been given the keys of all the treasures of the earth* (or the keys of the earth). By Allah! I am not afraid that you will worship others along with Allah after my death, but I am afraid that you will fight with one another for the worldly things." (Bukhari)

Narrated Abu Hurairah ؓ: Allah's Apostle ﷺ said, "I have been sent with the shortest expressions bearing the widest meanings, and I have been made victorious with terror (cast in the hearts of the enemy), and while I was sleeping, *the keys of the treasures of the world were brought to me and put in my hand.*" (Bukhari) (Muslim with different version)

Narrated Abdullah ibn Umar ﷺ: The Holy Prophet ﷺ said, "*I have been given the keys of all things.*" (Tibrani, Musnad Ahmad, Khasais Kubra)

Thauban ﷺ reported: Allah's Apostle ﷺ said. *Verily, Allah drew the ends of the world near me until I saw its east and west and He bestowed upon me two treasures*, the red and the white. (Muslim)

Narrated from al-Bara' ibn `Azib ﷺ: At the time of the Battle of Ahzab or the battle of the Trench, the Holy Prophet ﷺ went down to hit a rock with his pick, whereupon he said: "Bismillah" and shattered one third of the rock. Then he exclaimed: "Allah Akbar! I have been given the keys of Syria. By Allah, verily I can see her red palaces right from where I stand." Then he said: "Bismillah," and shattered another third and exclaimed: "Allah Akbar! I have been given the keys of Persia. By Allah, I can see her cities and her white palace right from where I stand." Then he said: "Bismillah" and shattered the remainder of the rock and exclaimed: "Allah Akbar! I have been given the keys of Yemen. By Allah, I can see the gates of San`a' right from where I stand." (Ahmad)

Chapter 5: The Holy Prophet's Hands on the Day of Resurrection

[Surah b/Israel 17:78-79] Keep the prayer established, from the declining of the sun until darkness of the night, and the Qur'an at dawn; indeed the angels witness the reading of the Qur'an at dawn. And forego sleep in some part of the night - an increase for you; it is likely *your Lord will set you on a place where everyone will praise you.*

Narrated ibn 'Abbas ﷺ: A group of the Sahaba of the Holy Prophet ﷺ was sitting together and the Holy Prophet ﷺ came and approached them and he heard them talking to each other. some of them said that Allah subhanahu wa ta'la took Ibrahim ﷺ as His friend, and others said that Allah subhanahu wa ta'la took Musa ﷺ as His kaleem [the one who spoke directly with Allah], and others said Allah subhanahu wa ta'la took 'Isa ﷺ as a word of Allah, and others said that Allah subhanahu wa ta'la chose Adam ﷺ. The holy Prophet ﷺ said to them, 'I heard your conversation and you are wondering at Ibrahim ﷺ being the friend of Allah, and it is true, and Musa ﷺ being Najeeullah [the saved one of Allah], and 'Isa ﷺ being Rawhullah, and it is true, and Adam ﷺ being chosen by Allah and it is true, but, I am the Beloved of Allah and I say it without pride [Habeebullah wa laa fakhr], and *I am the bearer of the flag of praise on the judgment day*, and Adam ﷺ and everyone descended from him are under my flag on judgment day and I say it without pride. I am the first intercessor and the first to intercede on the judgment day and I say it without pride. *And I am the first to move the handles of the door of paradise* and Allah will open paradise for me and I am the first to enter it and with me will be the poor and humble of the believers, and I say it without pride, and I am the first to be honoured among the first and last of creation and I say it without pride." (Tirmizi, Darmi, ibn Kathir, Imam Suyuti and others.)

Reported Anas b. Malik ﷺ: Allah's Apostle ﷺ said: Amongst the Apostles I would have the largest following on the Day of Resurrection, and *I would be the first to knock at the door of Paradise.* (Muslim)

On the day of Qiyamah, when people will despair, *the keys of honour will be in my hands and the flag of praise will also be in my hands.* (Darmi, Mishkaat)

Jabir bin 'Abdullah 🕮 reported: I fell sick and there came to me on foot Allah's Apostle 🕮 and Abu Bakr for inquiring after my health. *I fainted. He (the Holy Prophet 🕮) performed ablution and then sprinkled over me the water of his ablution.* I felt some relief and said: Allah's Apostle 🕮, how should I decide about my property? He said nothing to me in response until this verse pertaining to the law of inheritance was revealed: O dear Prophet *(Mohammed 🕮)*, they ask you for a decree; say, "Allah decrees you concerning the solitary person *(without parents or children)(4:176)*; (Muslim)

Reported Anas b. Malik 🕮: When Allah's Apostle 🕮 used to completed his dawn prayer, the servants of Medina came to him with utensils containing water, *and no utensil was brought in which he did not dip his hand*; and sometime they came in the cold dawn (and he did not feel reluctant in acceding to their request even in the cold weather) and dipped his hand in them. (Muslim)

(The water was then used by the people of Medinah to treat their sick ones.)

Syedah 'A'isha 🕮 reported: When any person amongst us fell ill, Allah's Apostle 🕮 *used to rub him with his right hand and then say*: O Lord of the people, grant him health, heal him, for You are the Great Healer. There is no healing, but with Your healing power one is healed and illness is removed. (Muslim)

Syedah 'A'isha 🕮 reported that when any of the members of the household fell ill Allah's Apostle 🕮 used to blow over him by reciting Mu'awwidhatan, and when he suffered from illness of which he died I used to blow over him and rubbed his body with his hand for his hand had greater healing power than my hand. (Muslim)

Syedah 'A'isha ﷺ reported that when Allah's Apostle ﷺ fell ill, he recited over his body Mu'awwidhatan and blew over him and when his sickness was aggravated I used to recite over him and rub him with his hand with the hope that it was more blessed. (Muslim)

Narrated Yazid ibn Sa'id al-Kindi ﷺ: When the Holy Prophet ﷺ made supplication (to Allah) he would raise his hands and wipe his face with his hands. (Abu Dawud)

Chapter 7: The Hands of Other Prophets

[Surah Ta-Ha 20:17-22] "And what is this in your right hand, O Moosa?" He said, "This is my staff; I support myself on it, and I knock down leaves for my sheep with it, and there are other uses for me in it." He said, "Put it down, O Moosa!" So Moosa put it down - thereupon it became a fast moving serpent. He said, "Pick it up and do not fear; We shall restore it to its former state." "And put your hand inside your armpit - it will come out shining white, not due to any illness - one more sign."

[Surah Kahf 18:77] So they both set out again; until they came to the people of a dwelling – they asked its people for food - they refused to invite them – then in the village *they both found a wall about to collapse, and the chosen bondman straightened it*; said Moosa, "If you wished, you could have taken some wages for it!"

[Surah Saba 34:10-11] And indeed We gave Dawud the utmost excellence from Us; "O the hills and birds, repent towards Allah along with him"; *and We made iron soft for him*. "Make large coats of armour and keep proper measure while making; and all of you perform good deeds; I am indeed seeing your deeds."

Section 15: The Excellent Fingers & Finger Nails

Chapter 1: The Splitting of the Moon

[Surah Qamar 54:1-2] The Last Day came near, and the moon split apart. And when they see a sign, they turn away and say, "Just a customary magic!"

Narrated Abdullah ﷺ: The moon was cleft asunder while we were in the company of the Holy Prophet ﷺ, and it became two parts. The Holy Prophet ﷺ said, Witness, witness (this miracle)."(Bukhari)

Narrated Anas ﷺ: The people of Mecca asked the Holy Prophet ﷺ to show them a sign (miracle). So he showed them (the miracle) of the cleaving of the moon. (Bukhari)

Chapter 2: Water from the Holy Prophet's Fingers

Narrated Salim ﷺ: Jabir said "On the day of Al-Hudaibiya, the people felt thirsty and Allah's Apostle ﷺ had a utensil containing water. He performed ablution from it and then the people came towards him. Allah's Apostle ﷺ said, 'What is wrong with you?' The people said, 'O Allah's Apostle! We haven't got any water to perform ablution with or to drink, except what you have in your utensil.' *So the Holy Prophet ﷺ put his hand in the utensil and the water started spouting out between his fingers like springs. So we drank and performed ablution.*" I said to Jabir, "What was your number on that day?" He replied, "Even if we had been one hundred thousand, that water would have been sufficient for us. *Anyhow, we were 1500.*' (Bukhari)

Narrated Anas bin Malik ﷺ: I saw Allah's Apostle ﷺ when the `Asr prayer was due and the people searched for water to perform ablution but they could not find it. Later on (a pot full of) water for ablution was brought to Allah's Apostle ﷺ. *He put his hand in that pot and ordered the people to perform ablution from it. I saw the water springing out from underneath his fingers till all of them performed the ablution (it was one of the miracles of the Holy* Prophet ﷺ. (Bukhari)

Reported Hazrat Anas ﷺ: Allah's Apostle ﷺ called for water and *he was given a vessel and the people began to perform ablution in that and I counted (the persons) and they were between fifty and eighty and I saw water which was spouting from his fingers.* (Muslim)

Narrated Anas ﷺ: A bowl of water was brought to the Holy Prophet ﷺ while he was at Az-Zawra. *He placed his hand in it and the water started flowing among his fingers. All the people performed ablution (with that water).* Qatada asked Anas, "How many people were you?" Anas replied, "Three hundred or nearly three-hundred." (Bukhari)

Narrated Anas bin Malik ﷺ: I saw Allah's Apostle ﷺ at the time when the `Asr prayer was due. Then the people were searching for water for ablution but they could not find any. Then some water was brought to Allah's Apostle ﷺ and he placed his hand in the pot and ordered the people to perform the ablution with the water. *I saw water flowing from underneath his fingers and the people started performing the ablution till all of them did it.* (Bukhari)

Narrated Anas bin Malik ﷺ: The Holy Prophet ﷺ went out on one of his journeys with some of his companions. They went on walking till the time of the prayer became due. They could not find water to perform the ablution. *One of them went away and brought a little amount of water in a pot. The Holy* Prophet ﷺ *took it and performed the ablution, and then stretched his four fingers on to the pot and said (to the people), "Get up to perform the ablution." They started performing the ablution till all of them did it, and they were seventy or so persons.* (Bukhari)

Narrated Humaid ﷺ: Anas bin Malik said, "Once the time of the prayer became due and the people whose houses were close to the Mosque went to their houses to perform ablution, while the others remained (sitting there). *A stone pot containing water was brought to the Holy* Prophet ﷺ, *who wanted to put his hand in it, but it was too small for him to spread his hand in it, and so he had to bring his fingers together before putting his hand in the pot. Then all the people performed the ablution (with that water).*" I asked Anas, "How many persons were they." He replied, "There were eighty men." (Bukhari)

Narrated Salim bin Abi Aj-Jad ﷺ: Jabir bin `Abdullah said, "The people became very thirsty on the day of Al-Hudaibiya (Treaty). A small pot containing some water was in front of the Holy Prophet ﷺ and when he had finished the ablution, the people rushed towards him. He asked, 'What is wrong with you?' They replied, 'We have no water either for performing ablution or for drinking except what is present in front of you.' *So he placed his hand in that pot and the water started flowing among his fingers like springs. We all drank and performed ablution (from it).*" I asked Jabir, "How many were you?" he replied, "Even if we had been one-hundred-thousand, it would have been sufficient for us, but we were fifteen-hundred." (Bukhari)

Chapter 3: The Holy Prophet Distributed His Finger Nails

Narrated Hazrat Anas bin Malik ﷺ: *The Holy* Prophet ﷺ *clipped his nails, and distributed them among the people.* (Musnad Imam Ahmad)

Chapter 4: The Holy Prophet Commanded the Moon, Whilst in His Cradle

Narrated Abbas bin Abdul Muttalib ﷺ: I once humbly told the Holy Prophet ﷺ, "I had witnessed an event relating to you that evidenced your Prophethood, and which later became one of the main reasons of my accepting faith. *The event is that I saw you talking to the moon while you were in the cradle, and the moon used to move at the command of your finger.*" The Holy Prophet ﷺ answered, "I used to talk to him, and he used to talk to me. He used to prevent me from crying, and I could also hear it falling, when it used to prostrate below the throne." (Baihaqi, Ibn Asakir, Khasais Kubra)

Section 16: The Excellent Feet

[Surah Balad 90:1-2] I swear by this city *(Mecca)*. For you *(O dear Prophet Mohammed)* are in this city.

Allah's Command Regarding the Standing Place of Ibrahim

[Surah Baqarah 2:125] And remember when We made this House *(at Mecca)* a recourse for mankind and a sanctuary; and take the place where Ibrahim stood, as your place of prayer; and We imposed a duty upon Ibrahim and Ismail *(Ishmael)*, to fully purify My house for those who go around it, and those who stay in it *(for worship)*, and those who bow down and prostrate themselves.

[Surah A/I`mran 3:97] In it are clear signs - the place where Ibrahim stood *(is one of them)*; and whoever enters it shall be safe; and performing the Hajj *(pilgrimage)* of this house, for the sake of Allah, is a duty upon mankind, for those who can reach it; and whoever disbelieves - then Allah is Independent *(Unwanting)* of the entire creation!

Narrated Ibn `Abbas ﷺ: Ibraham ﷺ came to Ismael's ﷺ house and asked. "Where is Ismael?" Ismael's wife replied, "He has gone out hunting," and added, "Will you stay (for some time) and have something to eat and drink?' Ibraham ﷺ asked, 'What is your food and what is your drink?' She replied, 'Our food is meat and our drink is water.' He said, 'O Allah! Bless their meals and their drink." Abu Al-Qa-sim (i.e. Prophet ﷺ) said, "Because of Ibraham's invocation there are blessings (in Mecca)." Once more Ibraham thought of visiting his family he had left (at Mecca), so he told his wife (Sarah ﷺ) of his decision. He went and found Ismael behind the Zamzam well, mending his arrows. He said, "O Ismail, Your Lord has ordered me to build a house for Him." Ismael said, "Obey (the order of) your Lord." Ibraham said, "Allah has also ordered me that you should help me therein." Ismael said, "Then I will do." So, both of them rose and

Abraham started building (the Ka`ba) while Ismael went on handing him the stones, and both of them were saying, "O our Lord! Accept (this service) from us, Verily, You are the All-Hearing, the All-Knowing." (2.127). *When the building became high and the old man (i.e. Ibraham) could no longer lift the stones (to such a high position), he stood over the stone of Al-Maqam and Ismael carried on handing him the stones,* and both of them were saying, "'Our Lord! Accept it from us; indeed You only are the All Hearing, the All Knowing.'".(2.127) (Bukhari – part of a longer Hadeeth)

Chapter 2: Stones Became Soft for the Footprint of the Holy Prophet

Narrated Abu Hurairah ﷺ and Abu Amamah ﷺ: *When the Holy Prophet ﷺ used to walk upon stones, his footprints used to get imprinted upon them.* (Baihaqi, Ibn Asakir, Zarkani)

A stone with the footprints of the Holy Prophet ﷺ is displayed in the Topkapi Palace Museum, in Istanbul, Turkey.

The foot-print of Syedena Ibrahim ﷺ, lies in the Holy Haram of Mecca.

Chapter 3: Kissing the Feet

Narrated Hazrat Zara'a ﷺ: They once came as a deputation to Medinah, *and they kissed the hands and feet of the Holy* Prophet ﷺ. (Abu Dawud, Mishkaat)

Narrated Hazrat Suhaib ﷺ: I saw Syedena Ali ﷺ *kissing the hands and feet of Hazrat Abbas ﷺ.* (Bukhari in al-Adab al-mufrad)

Narrated Hazrat Buraida ﷺ: A villager once asked the Holy Prophet ﷺ to show him a miracle. The Holy Prophet ﷺ told the villager, "Tell that tree over there, that the Holy Prophet has called you." When the villager did this, the tree shook and swayed to its right, left, front and back, thereby uprooting itself. It then moved forward, plowing the earth and raising dust behind it until it reached in front of the Holy Prophet ﷺ. It then said, "Peace be upon you, O Allah's Apostle!" The villager said, "Tell it to go back." Upon the command of the Holy Prophet ﷺ, the tree returned to its place and stood upright on its roots. The villager said, "Permit me to prostrate before you!" The Holy Prophet ﷺ said, "Would I command anyone to prostate to another, I would command the woman to prostate to her husband." The villager said, *"Then permit me to kiss your hands and feet!" So the Holy Prophet* ﷺ *permitted him.* (Shifa, Dalail Nubuwwa, Abu Nuaim).

Narrated Safwan ibn `Asal al-Muradi ﷺ: "One of two Jews said to his companion: Take us to this Prophet so we can ask him about Musa's ﷺ ten signs... [the Holy Prophet ﷺ replied in full and then] *they kissed his hands and feet and said: we witness that you are a Prophet...*" (Ibn Abi Shayba, Tirmizi, al-Nasa'i, Ibn Maja, and al-Hakim)

The pulpit of the Holy Prophet ﷺ had three steps. The Holy Prophet ﷺ used to sit on the topmost step and rest his legs on the middle step. *When Syedena Abu Bakr Siddiq* ﷺ *became the Khalifa, he used to sit on the middle step out of reverence to the Holy Prophet* ﷺ, and place his legs on the lower most step. When Syedena Umar Farouq ﷺ became the Khalifa, he used to sit on lower most step and place his legs on the ground. When Syedena Usman Ghani ﷺ became the Khalifa, he increased the number of steps of the pulpit (from under), and leaving the top three steps, he used to stand on the lower most step. (Wafa Al Wafa, Kash-ul-Ghumma)

Chapter 4: When the Holy Prophet Struck His Foot

Narrated Syedena Anas ﷺ: Allah's Apostle ﷺ ascended the mountain of Uhud with Abu Bakr, `Umar and `Uthman and it shook. Allah's Apostle ﷺ said, "*Be calm, O Uhud!*" *I think he stroked it with his foot and added, "There is none on you but a Prophet, a Siddiq and two martyrs.*" (The two martyrs were `Umar and `Uthman) (Bukhari)

Syedena Ali ﷺ reported: Once Allah's Apostle ﷺ passed by near me, and I was ill and I was saying, "O Allah! If my death has come, then give me rest. If it is late, cure me. If it is a trial, give me patience." Allah's Apostle ﷺ said, "How did you pray?" I repeated to him what I had said. *He struck him (Ali) with his foot and said, "O Allah! Pardon him (or he said Cure him). Said Ali, "So I never complained about the pain again.*" (Tirmizi, Mishkaat)

Prophet Ayyub struck his foot on the ground for water

[Surah Saad 38:42] We said to him, "Strike the earth with your foot; this cool spring is for bathing and drinking." *(A spring gushed forth when he struck the earth with his foot)*

Chapter 5: Mankind At His Feet, on the Day of Resurrection

[Surah b/Israel 17:79] And forego sleep* in some part of the night - an increase for you**; *it is likely your Lord will set you on a place where everyone will praise you***. (*For worship. **Obligatory only upon the Holy* Prophet ﷺ ****On the Day of Resurrection.)*

Reported Jubair bin Mut'im ﷺ: Allah's Apostle ﷺ said: I am Muhammad and I am Ahmad, and I am Al-Mahi (the obliterator) by whom unbelief would be obliterated, and I am Hashir (the gatherer) *at whose feet mankind will be gathered*, and I am 'Aqib (the last to come) after whom ('Aqib) there will be no Prophet (Muslim, Bukhari)

Section 17: The Excellent Skin, Sweat &
Blood

Narrated As-Sa'ib bin Yazid 🙴: My aunt took me to the Prophet🙴 and said, "O Allah's Apostle 🙴! This son of my sister has got a disease in his legs." So he passed his hands on my head and prayed for Allah's blessings for me; then he performed ablution and I drank from the remaining water. *I stood behind him and saw the seal of Prophet-hood* between his shoulders, and it was like the "Zir-al-Hijla" (means the button of a small tent, but some said 'egg of a partridge.' etc.) (Bukhari)

Narrated Buraidah 🙴, regarding Salman Farsi 🙴: Syedena Rasulullah 🙴 did not partake any of it (Sadaqah). I said to myself that one sign has been fulfilled and I returned to Madinah and collected a few things. In the meantime Syedena Rasulullah 🙴 came to live in Madinah. I presented some things (dates, food etc) and said: "This a gift." The Holy Prophet 🙴 accepted the gift, I said to myself that the second sign has also been fulfilled. Thereafter I attended his noble assembly. Syedena Rasulullah 🙴 was at the Baqi (attending a Sahabi's funeral). I greeted him and made an attempt to look at his back. Syedena Rasulullah 🙴 understood what I was doing and lifted his sheet. I saw the Seal of the Holy Prophet 🙴 and in zeal bowed towards it. *I kissed it and cried.* Syedena Rasulullah 🙴 said: "Come in front of me." I came before him and related the whole story. (Tirmizi)

Narrated Usayd ibn Hudayr 🙴: Abdur Rahman ibn Abu Layla🙴, quoting Usayd ibn Hudayr 🙴, a man of the Ansar, said that while he was given to jesting and was talking to the people and making them laugh, the Holy Prophet 🙴 poked him under the ribs with a stick. He said: Let me take retaliation. He said: Take retaliation. He said: You are wearing a shirt but I am not. *The Holy Prophet 🙴 then raised his shirt and the man embraced him and began to kiss his side. Then he said: This is what I wanted, Allah's* Apostle 🙴! (Abu Dawud)

Narrated Buhaysah al-Fazariyyah ﷺ: My father sought permission from the Holy Prophet ﷺ. *Then he came near him, lifted his shirt, and began to kiss him and embrace him out of love for him.* (Abu Dawud)

Reported Anas ﷺ: that Allah's Apostle ﷺ had a very fair complexion and (the drops) of his perspiration shone like pearls. (Muslim, Bukhari)

Chapter 2: The Excellent Blood

Sahaba Drinking the Blood of the Holy Prophet

The Holy Prophet ﷺ got himself cupped (to drain out blood). He gave the blood to Abdullah bin Zubair ﷺ ordering him to hide it where no one would be able to see it. He went out (of the room) and drank the blood. When he came back the Holy Prophet ﷺ said, "What have you done?" He submitted, "I have hidden it in such a place where no one would be able to see it." The Holy Prophet ﷺ then said "Perhaps you drank it." He submitted, "Yes, I have, for I know that the fire of hell will not touch the one in whom your blood is!" Upon this, the Holy Prophet ﷺ said, "*Go! You too have been saved from the fire of hell. Woe upon the people who will martyr you and regrettably, you will not be able to escape from them.*" (Mustadrak, Kanz-ul-Ummal, Shifa, Baihaqi, Bazzar, Abu Yula, Khasais Kubra, Zarqani)

Narrated Ibn Abbas ﷺ: The Holy Prophet ﷺ once got himself cupped (to drain out excess blood). A Quraishi slave drank the Holy Prophet's ﷺ blood, upon which the Holy Prophet ﷺ said, "*Go! You have saved yourself from the fire (of hell).*" (Khasais Kubra, Zarqani)

Smell of musk from martyrs blood

Narrated Abu Hurairah ﷺ: The Holy Prophet ﷺ said, "A wound which a Muslim receives in Allah's cause will appear on the Day of Resurrection as it was at the time of infliction; blood will be flowing from the wound and its color will be that of the blood *but will smell like musk*." (Bukhari)

Chapter 3: The Excellent Sweat

Narrated Wael bin Hajar ﷺ: Whenever I used to grasp the hand of the Holy Prophet ﷺ or touch my skin with his, I used to find its effects upon my hands, that they used to be *more fragrant & better than musk.* (Tibrani, Baihaqi)

Narrated Thumama ﷺ: Anas said, "Um Sulaim used to spread a leather sheet for the Holy Prophet ﷺ and he used to take a midday nap on that leather sheet at her home." *Anas added, "When the Holy Prophet ﷺ had slept, she would take some of his sweat and hair and collect it (the sweat) in a bottle and then mix it with Suk (a kind of perfume) while he was still sleeping. "When the death of Anas bin Malik ﷺ approached, he advised that some of that Suk be mixed with his Hanut (perfume for embalming the dead body), and it was mixed with his Hanut.* (Bukhari)

Jabir b. Samura ﷺ reported: I prayed along with Allah's Apostle ﷺ the first prayer. He then went to his family and I also went along with him when he met some children (on the way). He began to pat the cheeks of each one of them. *He also patted my cheek and I experienced a coolness or a fragrance of his hand as if it had been brought out from the scent bag of a perfumer.* (Muslim)

Usama ibn Sharik ﷺ narrates: "I came to see the Holy Prophet ﷺ while his Companions were with him, and they seemed as still as if birds had alighted on top of their heads. I gave him my salam and I sat down. Then Bedouins came and asked questions which the Holy Prophet ﷺ answered. The Holy Prophet ﷺ then stood up and the people stood up. *They began to kiss his hand, whereupon I took his hand and placed it on my face. I found it more fragrant than musk and cooler than sweet water.*" (Abu Dawud, Tirmizi, Ibn Majah, al-Hakim, and Ahmad, al-Hafiz Imam Baihaqi)

Reported Anas ﷺ: that Allah's Apostle ﷺ had a very fair complexion and (the drops) of his perspiration shone like pearls. (Muslim, Bukhari)

Anas b. Malik ﷺ reported that Allah's Apostle ﷺ used to come to our house and there was perspiration upon his body. My mother brought a bottle and began to pour the sweat in that. When Allah's Apostle ﷺ got up he said: Umm Sulaim, what is this that you are doing? Thereupon she said: *That is your sweat which we mix in our perfume and it becomes the most fragrant perfume.* (Muslim)

Anas b. Malik ﷺ reported that Allah's Apostle ﷺ came to the house of Umm Sulaim and slept in her bed while she was away from her house. On the other day too he slept in her bed. She came and it was said to her: It is Allah's Apostle ﷺ who is having siesta in your house, lying in your bed. *She came and found him sweating and his sweat falling on the leather cloth spread on her bed. She opened her scent-bag and began to fill the bottles with it.* Allah's Apostle ﷺ was startled and woke up and said: Umm Sulaim, what are you doing? She said: Allah's Apostle ﷺ, we seek blessings for our children through it. *Thereupon he said: You have done something right.* (Muslim)

Narrated Anas ﷺ: I have never touched silk or Dibaj (i.e. thick silk) softer than the palm of the Holy Prophet ﷺ *nor have I smelt a perfume nicer than the sweat of the Holy* Prophet ﷺ. (Bukhari, Muslim)

Narrated Hazarat Jabir and Hazrat Anas ﷺ: When the Holy Prophet ﷺ used to pass through the street of Medinah, the people used to find them fragrant and conclude that he must have passed through this way. (Darimi, Baihaqi, Abu Nuaim, Bazaar, and others)

Narrated Hazrat Abu Hurairah ﷺ: A man came to the Holy Prophet ﷺ and said that he had a daughter whose marriage he had arranged, but did not have any perfume to give her. So he asked the Holy Prophet ﷺ for some perfume. The Holy Prophet ﷺ ordered him to bring a bottle the next day. When he did, the Holy Prophet ﷺ slowly began collecting sweat from his own arms into the bottle until it was full and then said, "Give this to your daughter, and tell her to apply this as perfume." So whenever the girl used to apply it, the entire town of Medinah used to become fragrant to the extent that the people of Medinah named their house "The house of the fragrant ones". (Tibrani, Zarqani, Khasais Kubra)

Chapter 4: The Holy Prophet's Urine

Narrated Hazrat Umme Ayman ﷺ: The Holy Prophet ﷺ once urinated into a pot during the night. I got up during the night and thinking that it was water, drank it as I was thirsty. At morning, when the Holy Prophet ﷺ asked me about the pot, I told him, "By Allah, I drank it!' So he laughed and then said, *"From this day, you will never ever suffer from any gastric disease."* (Mustadrak Hakim, Abu Nuaim, Khasais Kubra, others)

Section 18: Tabarruk From Things Used By The Holy Prophet And Pious Bondmen

[Surah Hajj 22:32] So it is; and whoever reveres the symbols of Allah – this is then part of the piety of the hearts.

[Surah Baqarah 2:248] And their Prophet said to them, "Indeed the sign of his kingdom will be the coming of a *(wooden)* box to you, *in which from your Lord is the contentment of hearts and containing some souvenirs (remnants)* left behind by the honourable Moosa and the honourable Haroon *(Aaron)*, borne by the angels; indeed in it is a great sign for you if you are believers."

The wooden box was three yards long and two yards wide. It was bestowed by Allah to Prophet Adam 🕮. It contained the natural photographs of several prophets and it had been passed on from one Prophet to another until it reached Prophet Moses 🕮. It remained with Bani Israel at which time it also contained the staff and sandals of Prophet Moses 🕮, the staff and turban of Prophet Haroon 🕮, and some pieces of the Tablet (of Torah). *At the time of battle, the Bani Israel used to place this wooden box in front and by its blessings Allah used to grant them victory. And whenever Bani Israel had some need, they used to place it in front of them and supplicate to Allah, and their need used to be fulfilled.* Later on when Bani Israel fell into sin, Allah imposed upon them another nation called Amalikah, who abused them and took the wooden box away from them. The Amalikah placed this sacred box in a filthy place. This defilement brought Allah's wrath upon them, destroying several of their towns. An old woman from Bani Israel who was with them, advised them to banish the wooden box. The Amalikah tied two rowdy bullocks to a cart and placing the wooden box on it released it into the open country. The angels brought the bullock cart to the new king of Bani Israel (Talut). When the box reached them, Allah granted them victory. This had been foretold to them by their Prophet Samuel 🕮, according to the above verse. (Tafseer Khazin, Madarik)

[Surah Yusuf 12:93-96] *"Take along this shirt of mine and lay it on my father's face, his vision will be restored*; and bring your entire household to me." When the caravan left Egypt, their father said, *"Indeed I sense the fragrance of Yusuf, if you do not call me senile."* They said, "By Allah, you are still deeply engrossed in the same old love of yours." Then when the bearer of glad tidings came, *he laid the shirt on his face, he therefore immediately regained his eyesight*; he said, "Was I not telling you? I know the great traits of Allah which you do not know!"

Chapter 2: The Things Used by the Holy Prophet

The Staff used by the Holy Prophet

Narrated Abdullah bin Anees ﷺ: The Holy Prophet ﷺ sent me to kill Khalid bin Sufyan bin Baleekh Hazli. When I returned after killing him, the Holy Prophet ﷺ gifted me his staff and said, "Come along with this to Paradise." *At the time of his death Abdullah bin Anees willed that the staff be buried along with him, which was duly done.* (Baihaqi, Abu Nuaim, Zarqani)

The Holy Prophet's Staff in the Hands of Syedena Usman

When Syedena Usman Ghani ﷺ was martyred, he had the staff of the Holy Prophet ﷺ in his hands. Jahjah (his murderer) took it from his hand, in order to snap it into two using his knee. People tried to prevent him, but he did not listen and broke it. *Soon, a lesion developed on his knee, which became gangrenous causing his leg to be cut off.* He later died because of the same. (Kitaabus-Shifa)

The Staves Touched by the Holy Prophet.

Narrated Abu Said Khudri ﷺ: Hazrat Qatadah bin Noman ﷺ once remained in the company of the Holy Prophet ﷺ, while it was a dark and stormy night. When he was about to leave, the Holy Prophet ﷺ gave him a stick of date palm, and said, "Take this with you – it shall illuminate the space around you by ten yards in front and ten yards behind. When you reach home, you will see a dark object there – so beat it with this stick until it goes away from there, for that dark object is the Satan." *So when Hazrat Qatadah left, the stick turned bright and he reached home. Entering his home, he found the dark object and he beat it so much that it ran away.* (Kitabus-Shifa, Zarqani)

During the battle of Badr, the sword of Hazrat Okasha bin Mahsan ﷺ broke. *He came to the Holy* Prophet ﷺ, *who gave him a dry stick and ordered him to fight with it. When Okasha took the stick in his hand, it turned into a bright, long, solid and majestic sword.* He therefore fought in Badr using it. The sword remained with him after that, and he used it in all the battles he fought after that. Hazrat Okasha ﷺ was martyred in the battle against the renegades. The sword became famous by the name of "Al Awn" (which means The Supporter). (Baihaqi, Ibn Asakir, Tabkaat ibn Saad, Shifa, Khasais Kubra)

Narrated Anas bin Malik ﷺ: Two of the companions of the Holy Prophet ﷺ departed from him on a dark night and were led by two lights like lamps (going in front of them) lighting the way in front of them, and when they parted, each of them was accompanied by one of these lights till they reached their homes. (Bukhari)

The Sword of the Holy Prophet

Narrated `Ali bin Al-Husain ﷺ: That when they reached Medina after returning from Yazid bin Mu'awaiya after the martyrdom of Husain bin `Ali ﷺ, Al-Miswar bin Makhrama met him and said to him, "Do you have any need you may order me to satisfy?" `Ali said, "No." Al-Miswar said, Will you give me the sword of Allah's Apostle ﷺ for I am afraid that people may take it from you by force? *By Allah, if you give it to me, they will never be able to take it till I die.*" (Bukhari)

The Blanket Used by the Holy Prophet

Narrated Sahl 🕮: A woman brought a woven Burda (sheet) having edging (border) to the Holy Prophet 🌸, Then Sahl 🕮 asked them whether they knew what is Burda, they said that Burda is a cloak and Sahl confirmed their reply. Then the woman said, "I have woven it with my own hands and I have brought it so that you may wear it." The Holy Prophet 🌸 accepted it, and at that time he was in need of it. So he came out wearing it as his waist-sheet. A man praised it and said, "Will you give it to me? How nice it is!" The other people said, "You have not done the right thing as the Holy Prophet 🌸 is in need of it and you have asked for it when you know that he never turns down anybody's request." *The man replied, "By Allah, I have not asked for it to wear it but to make it my shroud." Later it was his shroud.* (Bukhari)

Narrated Um 'Atiyya 🕮: One of the daughters of the Holy Prophet 🌸 passed away and he came to us and said, "Wash her with Sidr (water) for odd number of times, i.e. three, five or more, if you think it necessary, and in the last, put camphor or (some camphor on her), and when you finish, notify me." So when we finished we informed him. *He gave his waist-sheet to us (to shroud her).* We entwined the hair (of the deceased girl) in three braids and made them fall at her back. (Bukhari)

Narrated Abu Burda 🕮: Syedah `Aisha 🕮 brought out to us a patched woolen garment, and she said, "(It chanced that) the soul of Allah's Apostle 🌸 was taken away while he was wearing this." Abu-Burda added, "Aisha 🕮 brought out to us a thick waist sheet like the ones made by the Yemenites, and also a garment of the type called Al-Mulabbada. (Bukhari)

Narrated Abu Abdullah 🕮: My grandfather had the blanket of the Holy Prophet 🌸. When Hazrat Umar bin Abdul Azeez 🕮 became the Khalifah, he summoned my grandfather. My grandfather went to him with the blanket, wrapped in leather. *Hazrat Umar bin Abdul Azeez ﷺ rubbed the blanket over his face.* (Bukhari in Tareekh)

The bow touched by the Holy Prophet

Narrated Hazrat Abu Abdul Rehman Aslami ﷺ: Ahmed bin Fazlvia was a great warrior and extremely pious person. He had a bow with him, which had been touched by the Holy Prophet ﷺ. He used to say, *"I have never laid my hand on this bow except with ablution, ever since I learnt that the Holy* Prophet ﷺ *had held it in his hand."* (Shifa)

The pulpit used by the Holy Prophet

The pulpit of the Holy Prophet ﷺ had three steps. The Holy Prophet ﷺ used to sit on the top most step and rest his legs on the middle step. *When Syedena Abu Bakr Siddiq ﷺ became the Caliph, he used to sit on the middle step out of reverence to the Holy Prophet*ﷺ and place his legs on the lower most step. When Syedena Umar Farouq ﷺ became the Caliph, he used to sit on lower most step and place his legs on the ground. When Syedena Usman Ghani ﷺ became the Caliph, he increased the number of steps of the pulpit (from under), and leaving the top three steps, he used to stand on the lower most step. (Wafa Al Wafa, Kash-ul-Ghumma)

Hazrat Abdullah Ibn `Umar ﷺ used to touch the seat of the Holy Prophet's ﷺ *minbar and then wipe his hands on his face for blessing.* (al-Mughni, Shifa', Tabaqat Ibn Saad)

Yazid ibn `Abd al-Malik ibn Qusayt ﷺ and al-`Utbi ﷺ narrated that it was the practice of the Companions in the mosque of the Holy Prophet ﷺ to place their hands on the pommel of the hand rail (rummana) of the pulpit (minbar) where the Holy Prophet ﷺ used to place his hand. *There they would face the qibla and supplicate* *(make du`a) to Allah hoping He would answer their supplication because they were placing their hands where the Holy Prophet ﷺ placed his while making their supplication.* Abu Mawduda ؓ said: "And I saw Yazid ibn `Abd al-Malik ؓ do the same. (Ibn Abi Shayba, Musannaf)

The turban used by the Holy Prophet

Narrated Ibn Saad ؓ: During the battle of Khandak (Ditch), Amroo bin Abd Vud from the disbelievers' camp challenged the Muslims to fight him. Upon this, Hazrat Ali ؓ stood up and sought permission from the Holy Prophet ﷺ. The Holy Prophet ﷺ asked him to come near. *When he came near, the Holy Prophet ﷺ bestowed his sword to Ali, and tied his turban on the head of Ali, and supplicated, "O Allah! Bestow victory to Ali, over Amroo bin Abd Vud!"* Although the disbeliever was a strong warrior, he was no challenge for Syedena Ali ؓ. With a single strike, Ali cut of the head of Amroo, by which frightened the disbelievers and they ran away. The Muslims were thus victorious. (Tabkaat Ibn Saad).

The Shirt Worn by the Holy Prophet

When Fatimah ؓ the mother of Syedena Ali ؓ died, the Holy Prophet ﷺ at first lay down in her grave and prayed for her, and then she was buried wrapped in the shirt of the Holy Prophet ﷺ. Hazrat Umar ؓ expressed his surprise as to why the Holy Prophet ﷺ did what he did for this lady. Upon this the Holy Prophet ﷺ replied, "O Umar! The lady was like my real mother, and Abu Talib used to express his favours upon me, while she used to teach him better behavior. Indeed Jibreel (علیہ السلام) has informed me from my Lord, that she is of the women of Paradise and that Allah had ordered seventy thousand angels to offer funeral prayers for her." (Al Hakim)

Narrated Ibn `Umar ؓ: When `Abdullah bin Ubai (the chief of hypocrites) died, his son came to the Holy Prophet ﷺ and said, "O Allah's Apostle ﷺ! *Please give me your shirt to shroud him in it, offer his funeral prayer and ask for Allah's forgiveness for him*." So Allah's Apostle ﷺ gave his shirt to him and said, "Inform me (When the funeral is ready) so that I may offer the funeral prayer." So, he informed him and when the Holy Prophet ﷺ intended to offer the funeral prayer, `Umar took hold of his hand and said, "Has Allah not forbidden you to offer the funeral prayer for the hypocrites? The Holy Prophet ﷺ said, "I have been given the choice for Allah says: '(It does not avail) Whether you (O Muhammad) ask forgiveness for them (hypocrites), or do not ask for forgiveness for them. Even though you ask for their forgiveness seventy times, Allah will not forgive them. (9.80)" So the Holy Prophet ﷺ offered the funeral prayer and on that the revelation came: "And never (O Muhammad) pray (funeral prayer) for any of them (i.e. hypocrites) that dies." (9. 84) (Bukhari)

Narrated Jabir bin `Abdullah ﷺ: When it was the day (of the battle) of Badr, prisoners of war were brought including Al-Abbas who was undressed. *The Holy Prophet ﷺ looked for a shirt for him. It was found that the shirt of `Abdullah bin Ubai would do, so the Holy Prophet ﷺ let him wear it. That was the reason why the Holy Prophet ﷺ took off and gave his own shirt to `Abdullah.* (The narrator adds, "He had done the Holy Prophet ﷺ some favour for which the Holy Prophet ﷺ liked to reward him.") (Bukhari)

It is reported that Abdullah bin Ubai's son had become a Muslim, and had requested the Holy Prophet ﷺ to grant his shirt to his father.

Abdullah ﷺ, the freed slave of Asma' (the daughter of Abu Bakr ﷺ), the maternal uncle of the son of 'Ata ﷺ, reported: Asma' sent me to 'Abdullah b. 'Umar ﷺ saying: The news has reached me that you prohibit the use of three things: the striped robe, saddle cloth made of red silk and the fasting in the holy month of Rajab. 'Abdullah said to me: So far as what you say about fasting in the month of Rajab, how about one who observes continuous fasting? - and so far as what you say about the striped garment, I heard Umar b. Khatab ﷺ say that he had heard from Allah's Apostle ﷺ: He who wears silk garment has no share for him (in the Hereafter), and I am afraid it may not be that striped garment; and so far as the red saddle cloth is concerned that is the saddle cloth of Abdullah ﷺ and it is red. I went back to Asma' and informed her, whereupon she said: Here is the cloak of Allah's Apostle ﷺ and she brought out to me that cloak made of Persian cloth with a hem of brocade, and its sleeves bordered with brocade and said: This was Allah's Apostle's ﷺ cloak with 'A'isha ﷺ until she died, and when she died, I got possession of it. *Allah's Apostle ﷺ used to wear that, and we washed it for the sick and sought cure thereby.* (Muslim)

The Sandals Used by the Holy Prophet

Narrated by Abu Qatada ﷺ: I asked Anas to describe the sandals of Allah's Apostle ﷺ and he replied: "Each sandal had two straps" (Bukhari and Tirmidhi)

Narrated `Isa bin Tahman ﷺ: Anas brought out to us two worn out leather shoes without hair and with pieces of leather straps. Later on Thabit Al-Banani told me that Anas said that they were the shoes of the Prophet ﷺ. (Bukhari)

Ubayd ibn Jarih ﷺ said to `Abd Allah ibn `Umar ﷺ: "I saw you wear tanned sandals." He replied: *"I saw the Holy Prophet ﷺ wearing sandals with no hair on them and perform ablution in them, and so I like to wear them."* (Bukhari, Abu Dawud, Malik)

Abdullah Ibn Mas`ud ﷺ was one of the Holy Prophet's ﷺ servants and that he used to bring for the Holy Prophet ﷺ his cushion (wisada), his tooth-stick (siwak), his two sandals (na`layn), and the water for his ablution. *When the Holy Prophet ﷺ*

rose he would put his sandals on him; when he sat he would carry his sandals in his arms until he rose. (Qastallani in Mawahib al-laduniyya)

The handkerchief used by the Holy Prophet

Narrated Ibaad bin Abdul Samad 🙛: We once went to the house of Anas bin Malik 🙛. He ordered his maid-servant, "Serve food, we shall eat." She brought the food. He then said, "Bring the handkerchief too." She brought the handkerchief which was soiled. He then said, "Put it in the oven." She inserted the handkerchief into the oven that was burning fiercely. After a while when it was removed, the handkerchief was white like milk. Astonished, we asked him what was the secret of this. He answered, *"This was the handkerchief of the Holy* Prophet 🙛*, which he used for cleaning his holy face. Whenever it gets soiled, we clean it by inserting it into the burning oven, like we did now — because fire does not destroy any thing that has touched the face of any Prophet."* (Abu Nuaim, Khasais Kubra).

The Place of Prayer of the Holy Prophet

Narrated Yazid bin Al `Ubaid 🙛: I used to accompany Salama bin Al-Akwa` 🙛 and he used to pray behind the pillar which was near the place where the Qur'ans were kept. I said, "O Abu Muslim! I see you always seeking to pray behind this pillar." He replied, "*I saw Allah's* Apostle 🙛 *always seeking to pray near that pillar.*" (Bukhari)

Narrated Fudail bin Sulaiman 🙛: Musa bin `Uqba 🙛 said, "I saw Salim bin `Abdullah looking for some places on the way and prayed there. *He narrated that his father used to pray there, and had seen the Holy* Prophet 🙛 *praying at those very places.*" (Bukhari)

Narrated Nafi` 🙛: Whenever Ibn `Umar 🙛 entered the Ka`ba he used to walk straight keeping the door at his back on entering, and used to proceed on till about three cubits from the wall in front of him, and *then he would offer the prayer there aiming at the place where Allah's* Apostle ﷺ *prayed*, as Bilal ؓ had told him. There is no harm for any person to offer the prayer at any place inside the Ka`ba. (Bukhari)

Narrated Mahmud bin Rabi` Al-Ansari ؓ: `Itban bin Malik ؓ used to lead his people (tribe) in prayer and was a blind man, he said to Allah's Apostle ﷺ, "O Allah's Apostle! At times it is dark and flood water is flowing (in the valley) and I am blind man, *so please pray at a place in my house so that I can take it as a Musalla (praying place)*." So Allah's Apostle ﷺ went to his house and said, "*Where do you like me to pray?*" 'Itban ؓ pointed to a place in his house and Allah's Apostle ﷺ, offered the prayer there. (Bukhari)

The House Visited by the Holy Prophet

Narrated Abu Burda ؓ: When I came to Medina, I met Abdullah bin Salam. He said, "Will you come to me so that I may serve you with Sawiq and dates, and *let you enter a (blessed) house in which the Holy* Prophet ﷺ *entered?*" (Bukhari)

The Ring Worn by the Holy Prophet

Narrated Anas bin Malik ؓ: When the Prophet ﷺ intended to write to the Byzantines, the people said, "They do not read a letter unless it is sealed (stamped)." Therefore the Prophet ﷺ took a silver ring----as if I am looking at its glitter now----and its engraving was: 'Muhammad, Allah's Apostle'. (Bukhari)

Narrated Ibn `Umar ؓ: Allah's Apostle ﷺ had a silver ring made for himself and it was worn by him on his hand. *Afterwards it was worn by Abu Bakr ؓ, and then by `Umar ؓ, and then by `Uthman ؓ* till it fell in the Aris well. (On that ring) was engraved: 'Muhammad, Allah's Apostle." (Bukhari)

The Cup Used by the Holy Prophet

Narrated Anas bin Malik 🌸: When the cup of Allah's Apostle 🌸 got broken, he fixed it with a silver wire at the crack. (The sub-narrator, `Asim 🌸 said, "*I saw the cup and drank (water) in it.*" (Bukhari)

Hajjaj ibn Hassan 🌸 said: "We were at Anas's 🌸 house and he brought up the Holy Prophet's 🌸 cup from a black pouch. He ordered that it be filled with water and we drank from it and poured some of it on our heads and faces and sent blessings on the Holy Prophet 🌸". (Ahmad, Ibn Kathir).

The bathing water used by the Holy Prophet

Narrated Hazrat Salma 🌸 w/o Abi Rafey 🌸: The Holy Prophet 🌸 once took a bath, so I drank the bath water and then informed him. Thereupon the Holy Prophet 🌸 said, "*Go! Allah has forbidden the fire of hell upon your body!.*" (Tibrani, Khasais Kubra)

The Ablution Water of the Holy Prophet

Al-Sa'ib bin Yazid 🌸 reported: My aunt took me to Allah's Apostle 🌸 and said: Allah's Apostle 🌸, here is the son of my sister and he is ailing. *He touched my head and invoked blessings upon me. He then performed ablution and I drank the water left from his ablution*; then I stood behind him and I saw the seal between his shoulders (Muslim)

Abû Juhayfa 🌸 said, "Allah's Apostle 🌸, came out in mid-morning. Water for ablution was brought to him and he performed his ablution, then the people took what remained and rubbed it on themselves. Those who could not reach any took the water that dripped from their companions' hands." (Bukhari)

Reported Abu Musa 🌸: I was in the company of Allah's Apostle 🌸 as he had been sitting in Ji'ranah (a place) between

Mecca and Medina and Bilal 🏵 was also there, that there came to Allah's Apostle 🏵 a desert Arab, and he said: Muhammad, fulfill your promise that you made with me. Allah's Apostle 🏵 said to him: Accept glad tidings. Thereupon the desert Arab said: You shower glad tidings upon me very much; then Allah's Apostle 🏵 turned towards Abu Musa and Bilal seemingly in a state of annoyance and said: Verily he has rejected glad tidings but you two should accept them. We said: Allah's Apostle 🏵, we have readily accepted them. Then Allah's Apostle 🏵 called for a cup of water and washed his hands in that, and face too, and put the saliva in it and then said: Drink out of it and pour it over your faces and over your chest and gladden yourselves. They took hold of the cup and did as Allah's Apostle 🏵 had commanded them to do. Thereupon Umm Salamah called from behind the veil: Spare some water in your vessel for your mother also, and they also gave some water which had been spared for her. (Muslim)

Section 19: The Holy Places Built &
Touched By Allah's Beloved Slaves

[Surah Hajj 22:32] So it is; and whoever reveres the symbols of Allah – this is then part of the piety of the hearts.

The Holy Kaa'ba, Built by the Hands of the Prophets

[Surah A/I`mran 3:96 - 97] Indeed the first house that was appointed as a place of worship for mankind, is the one at Mecca *(the Holy Ka'aba)*, blessed and a guidance to the whole world; In it are clear signs - the place where Ibrahim stood *(is one of them)*; and whoever enters it shall be safe; and performing the Hajj *(pilgrimage)* of this house, for the sake of Allah, is a duty upon mankind, for those who can reach it; and whoever disbelieves - then Allah is Independent *(Unwanting)* of the entire creation!

'Abdullah b. Zaid b. 'Asim 🕮 reported: Allah's Apostle 🕮 said: Verily Ibrahim declared Mecca sacred and supplicated (for blessings to be showered) upon its inhabitants, *and I declare Medina to be sacred as Ibrahim had declared Mecca to be sacred.* I have supplicated (Allah for His blessings to be showered) in its sa' and its mudd (two standards of weight and measurement) twice as did Ibrahim for the inhabitants of Mecca. (Muslim)

Narrated Ibn Abbas 🕮: Then Abraham stayed away from them for a period as long as Allah wished, and called on them afterwards. He saw Ismail under a tree near Zamzam, sharpening his arrows. When he saw Abraham, he rose up to welcome him (and they greeted each other as a father does with his son or a son does with his father). Abraham said, 'O Ismail! Allah has given me an order.' Ismail said, 'Do what your Lord has ordered you to do.' Abraham asked, 'Will you help me?' Ismail said, 'I will help you.' Abraham said, Allah has ordered me to build a house here,' pointing to a hillock higher than the land surrounding it." The Holy Prophet 🕮 added, "Then they raised the foundations of the House (i.e. the Ka`ba). *Ismail brought the stones and Abraham was*

210

building, and when the walls became high, Ismail brought this stone and put it for Abraham who stood over it and carried on building, while Ismail was handing him the stones, and both of them were saying, 'O our Lord! Accept (this service) from us, Verily, You are the All-Hearing, the All-Knowing.' The Holy Prophet ﷺ added, "Then both of them went on building and going round the Ka`ba saying: O our Lord ! Accept (this service) from us, Verily, You are the All-Hearing, the All-Knowing." (2.127) (Bukhari – part of a longer Hadeeth)

The Importance of Syedena Ibrahim's Laid Foundations

'A'isha ﷺ, the wife of Allah's Apostle ﷺ, reported Allah's Apostle ﷺ as having said this: Didn't you see that when your people built the Ka'ba, they reduced (its area with the result that it no longer remains) on the foundations (laid) by Ibrahim (ﷺ)? I said: Allah's Apostle why don't you rebuild it on the foundations (laid by) Ibrahim (ﷺ)? Thereupon Allah's Apostle ﷺ said: Had your people not been new converts to Islam, I would have done that. 'Abdullah b. 'Umar ﷺ said: If 'A'isha had heard it from Allah's Apostle ﷺ, I would not have seen Allah's Apostle ﷺ abandoning the touching of the two corners situated near al-Hijr, but (for the fact) that it was not completed on the foundations (laid) by Ibrahim. (Muslim)

The Excellence of Prayers in Masjid Al-Haram

Narrated Abu Hurairah ﷺ: Allah's Apostle ﷺ said, *"One prayer in my Mosque is better than one thousand prayers in any other mosque excepting Al-Masjid-Al-Haram."* (Bukhari)

Abu Haraira ﷺ reported Allah's Apostle ﷺ as saying: One should undertake journey to three mosques: the mosque of the Ka'ba, my mosque, and the mosque of Elia (Bait al-Maqdis). (Muslim)

The Holy Prophet ﷺ said: A prayer in Al-Masjid Al-Haraam is better than a prayer in any other mosque with one hundred thousand prayers and a prayer in the mosque of Al-Madeenah is better than one thousand prayers in any other mosque and a prayer in Al-Masjid Al-Aqsa is better than five hundred prayers in any other mosque." [At-Tabaraani and Ibn Khuzaymah]

The Footprints of Syedena Ibrahim - As Place of Prayer

[Surah Baqarah 2:125] And remember when We made this House *(at Mecca)* a recourse for mankind and a sanctuary; and take the place where Ibrahim stood, as your place of prayer; and We imposed a duty upon Ibrahim and Ismail *(Ishmael)*, to fully purify My house for those who go around it, and those who stay in it *(for worship),* and those who bow down and prostrate themselves.

[Surah A/I`mran 3:97] In it are clear signs - the place where Ibrahim stood *(is one of them)*; and whoever enters it shall be safe; and performing the Hajj *(pilgrimage)* of this house, for the sake of Allah, is a duty upon mankind, for those who can reach it; and whoever disbelieves - then Allah is Independent *(Unwanting)* of the entire creation!

Abdullah b. 'Umar ﷺ reported: Allah's Apostle ﷺ observed Tamattu' in Hajjat-ul-Wada'. He first put on Ihram for 'Umra and then for Hajj, and then offered the animal sacrifice. So he drove the sacrificial animals with him from Dhu'l-Hulaifa. Allah's Apostle ﷺ commenced Ihram of Umra and thus pronounced Talbiya for 'Umra. And then (put on Ihram for Hajj) and pronounced Talbiya for Hajj. And the people performed Tamattu' in the company of Allah's Apostle ﷺ. They put on Ihram for Umra (first) and then for Hajj. Some of them had sacrificial animals which they had brought with them, whereas some of them had none to sacrifice. So when Allah's Apostle ﷺ came to Mecca, he said to the people: He who amongst you has brought sacrificial animals along with him must not treat as lawful anything which has become unlawful for him till he has completed the Hajj; and he, who amongst you has not brought the sacrificial animals should circumambulate the House, and run between al-Safa' and al-Marwa and clip (his hair) and put off the Ihram, and then again put on the Ihram for Hajj and offer sacrifice of animals. But he who does not find the sacrificial animal, he should observe fast for three days during the Hajj and for seven days when he returns to his family. Allah's Apostle ﷺ circumambulated (the House) when he came to Mecca: he first kissed the corner (of the Ka'ba containing the Black Stone), then ran in three circuits out of seven and walked in four circuits. *And then when he had finished the circumambulation of the House he observed two rak'ahs of prayer at the Station (of Ibrahim), and then pronounced Salaam (for concluding the rak'ahs), and departed and came to al-Safa' and ran seven times between al-Safa' and al-Marwa.* (Muslim – part of a longer Hadeeth).

The Holy Prophet Himself Installed the Black Stone on the Kaaba

Narrated Jabir bin `Abdullah ﷺ: *While Allah's* Apostle ﷺ *was carrying stones (along) with the people of Mecca for (the building of) the Ka`ba wearing an Izar (waist-sheet cover),* his uncle Al-`Abbas said to him, "O my nephew! (It would be better) if you take off your Izar and put it over your shoulders underneath the stones." So he took off his Izar and put it over his shoulders, but he fell unconscious and since then he had never been seen uncovered. (Bukhari)

Narrated `Abis bin Rabi`a ﷺ: `*Umar came near the Black Stone and kissed it* and said "No doubt, I know that you are a stone and can neither benefit anyone nor harm anyone. *Had I not seen Allah's* Apostle ﷺ *kissing you I would not have kissed you.*" (Bukhari)

Suwayd ibn Ghafalah ﷺ reported: *I saw `Umar kissing the Stone and clinging to it and saying: "I saw Allah's Apostle ﷺ bearing great love for* *you."* This hadith has been narrated on the authority of Sufyan with the same chain of transmitters (and the words are): "He (`Umar) said: "I know that you are a stone, nor would I consider you of any worth, except that I saw Abu al-Qasim bearing great love for you." And he did not mention about clinging to it. (Muslim)

The Mounts of Safa & Marwa are the Symbols of Allah

[Surah Baqarah 2:158] *Undoubtedly Safa and Marwah are among the symbols of Allah;* so there is no sin on him, for whoever performs the Hajj (pilgrimage) of this House (of Allah) or the Umrah (lesser pilgrimage), to go back and forth between them; and whoever does good of his own accord, then (know that) indeed Allah is Most Appreciative (rewards virtue), the All Knowing.

Hisham b. 'Urwa ﷺ narrated on the authority of his father who reported: I said to Syedah 'A'isha ﷺ: I do not see any harm to me if I do not circumambulate betweez al-Safa' and al-Marwa. She said: On what ground do you say so? (I said:) Since Allah, the Exalted and Majestic, says: "Verily al-Safa' and al-Marwa are among the Signs of Allah." If it (your assertion) were (correct), it would have been said like this: "There is no harm for him, that he should not circumambulate between them." It (this verse) has been revealed about the people of Ansar. Whenever they pronounced the Talbiya, they pronounced it in the name of al-Manat during the Days of Ignorance; so they (thought) that it was not permissible for them (for the Muslims) to circumambulate between Safa and al-Marwa. When they (the Muslims) came with Allah's Apostle ﷺ for Hajj, they mentioned it to him. So Allah, the Exalted and Majestic, revealed this verse. *By my life, Allah will not complete the Hajj of one who has not circumambulated between al-Safa and al-Marwa.* (Muslim)

Narrated Ibn `Abbas ﷺ: When the water in the water-skin had all been used up, she (Hajra) became thirsty and her child also became thirsty. She started looking at him (i.e. Ismael) tossing in agony; She left him, for she could not endure looking at him, and found that the mountain of Safa was the nearest mountain to her on that land. She stood on it and started looking at the valley keenly so that she might see somebody, but she could not see anybody. Then she descended from Safa and when she reached the valley, she tucked up her robe and ran in the valley like a person in distress and trouble, till she crossed the valley and reached the Marwa mountain where she stood and started looking, expecting to see somebody, but she could not see anybody. She repeated that (running between Safa and Marwa) seven times." *The Holy* Prophet 🕮 *said, "This is the source of the tradition of the walking of people between them (i.e. Safa and Marwa).* (Bukhari - part of longer Hadeeth).

Qaza'ah 🕮 reported: I heard a hadith from Abu Sa'id 🕮 and it impressed me (very much), so I said to him: Did you hear it (yourself) from Allah's Apostle 🕮? Thereupon he said: (Can) I speak of anything about Allah's Apostle 🕮 which I did not hear? He said: I heard Allah's Apostle 🕮 saying: *Do not set out on a journey (for praying in a mosque) but for the three mosques-for this mosque of mine (at Medina) the Sacred Mosque (at Mecca), and the Mosque al-Aqsa (Bait al-Maqdis),* and I heard him saying also: A woman should not travel for two days duration, but only when there is a Mahram with her or her husband. (Muslim)

Chapter 2: The Holy City of Makkah

Allah swears by the holy city of Mecca

[Surah Balad 90:1-2] I swear by this city *(Mecca) - For you (O dear Prophet Mohammed 🕮 are in this city.*

[Surah Naml 27:91] "I *(Prophet Mohammed 🕮 have been* commanded to worship the Lord of this city, *Who has deemed it sacred,* and everything belongs to Him; and I have been commanded to be among the obedient."

Syedena Ibrahim Declared Mecca as Sacred

'Abdullah b. Zaid b. 'Asim ﷺ reported: Allah's Apostle ﷺ said: Verily Ibrahim declared Mecca sacred and supplicated (for blessings to be showered) upon its inhabitants, *and I declare Medina to be sacred as Ibrahim had declared Mecca to be sacred.* I have supplicated (Allah for His blessings to be showered) in its sa' and its mudd (two standards of weight and measurement) twice as did Ibrahim for the inhabitants of Mecca. (Muslim)

Narrated Anas bin Malik ﷺ: When the mountain of Uhud came in the sight of Allah's Apostle ﷺ he said. "This is a mountain that loves us and is loved by us. *O Allah! Ibraham made Mecca a sanctuary, and I make (the area) in between these two mountains (of Medina) a sanctuary.*" (Bukhari)

Narrated Syedena Anas bin Malik ﷺ: The Holy Prophet ﷺ said, "There will be no town which Ad-Dajjal will not enter except Mecca and Medina, and there will be no entrance (road) (of both Mecca and Medina) but the angels will be standing in rows guarding it against him, and then Medina will shake with its inhabitants thrice (i.e. three earthquakes will take place) and Allah will expel all the non-believers and the hypocrites from it." (Bukhari)

Chapter 3: Medina – The Holy Prophet's City

The Holy Prophet Declared Medina as Sacred

'Abdullah b. Zaid b. 'Asim ﷺ reported: Allah's Apostle ﷺ said: Verily Ibrahim declared Mecca sacred and supplicated (for blessings to be showered) upon its inhabitants, *and I declare Medina to be sacred as Ibrahim had declared Mecca to be sacred.* I have supplicated (to Allah) in its sa' and its mudd (two standards of weight and measurement) twice as did Ibrahim for the inhabitants of Mecca. (Muslim)

Nafi' b. Jubair reported ﷺ that Marwan b. al-Hakam addressed people and made mention of Mecca and its inhabitants and its sacredness, but he made no mention of Medina, its inhabitants and its sacredness. Rafi' b. Khadij called to him and said: *What is this that I hear you making mention of Mecca and its inhabitants and its sacredness, but you did not make mention of Medina and its inhabitants and its sacredness, while Allah's* Apostle ﷺ *has also declared sacred (the area) between its two lava lands (Medina)?* And (we have record of this) with us written on Khaulani parchment. If you like, I can read it out to you. Thereupon Marwan became silent, and then Said: I too have heard some part of it. (Muslim)

Jabir ﷺ reported Allah's Apostle ﷺ as saying: *Ibrahim ﷺ declared Mecca as sacred; I declare Medina, that between the two mountains, as inviolable.* No tree should be lopped and no game is to be molested. (Muslim)

Amir b. Sa'd ﷺ reported on the authority of his father ﷺ: Allah's Apostle ﷺ said: *I have declared sacred the territory between the two lava plains of Medina,* so its trees should not be cut down, or its game killed; and he also said: Medina is best for them if they knew. No one leaves it through dislike of it without Allah putting in it someone better than he in place of him; and no one will stay there in spite of its hardships and distress without my being an intercessor or witness on behalf of him on the Day of Resurrection. (Muslim)

Narrated Anas bin Malik ﷺ: When the mountain of Uhud came in the sight of Allah's Apostle ﷺ he said. "This is a mountain that loves us and is loved by us. *O Allah! Abraham made Mecca a sanctuary, and I make (the area) in between these two mountains (of Medina) a sanctuary.*" (Bukhari)

Medina is pure and removes the impure

Narrated Syedena Abu Hurairah 🕮: Allah's Apostle 🕮 said, "I was ordered to migrate to a town which will swallow (conquer) other towns and is called Yathrib and that is Medina, and it turns out (bad) persons as a furnace removes the impurities of iron." (Bukhari)

Narrated Syedena Abu Humaid 🕮: We came with the Holy Prophet 🕮 from Tabuk, and when we reached near Medina, the Holy Prophet 🕮 said, "This is Tabah." (Bukhari)

Medina is protected from evil of Dajjal

Narrated Syedena Abu Hurairah 🕮: Allah's Apostle 🕮 said, "There are angels guarding the entrances (or roads) of Medina, neither plague nor Ad-Dajjal will be able to enter it." (Bukhari)

Narrated Syedena Anas bin Malik 🕮: The Holy Prophet 🕮 said, "There will be no town which Ad-Dajjal will not enter except Mecca and Medina, and there will be no entrance (road) (of both Mecca and Medina) but the angels will be standing in rows guarding it against him, and then Medina will shake with its inhabitants thrice (i.e. three earthquakes will take place) and Allah will expel all the non-believers and the hypocrites from it." (Bukhari)

Medina has double the blessings

Narrated Syedena Anas 🕮: The Holy Prophet 🕮 said, "O Allah Bestow on Medina twice the blessings You bestowed on Mecca." (Bukhari, Muslim)

The Holy Prophet's love for Medina

Narrated Syedena Anas ﷺ: Whenever the Holy Prophet ﷺ returned from a journey and observed the walls of Medina, he would make his Mount go fast, and if he was on an animal (i.e. a horse), he would make it gallop because of his love for Medina. (Bukhari)

Narrated Anas bin Malik ﷺ: When the mountain of Uhud appeared before Allah's Apostle ﷺ he said, "*This is a mountain that loves us and is loved by us.* O, Allah! Abraham made Mecca a Sanctuary, and I have made Medina (i.e. the area between its two mountains) a Sanctuary as well." (Bukhari)

Sahaba wished to die in Medina

Narrated Zaid bin Aslam ﷺ from his father ﷺ: `Umar ﷺ said, O Allah! Grant me martyrdom in Your cause, and *let my death be in the city of Your Apostle* ﷺ." (Bukhari)

Chapter 4: The Holy Prophet's Mosque

Abu Hurairah ﷺ reported Allah's Apostle ﷺ as saying: One should undertake journey to three mosques: the mosque of the Ka'ba, my mosque, and the mosque of Elia (Bait al-Maqdis). (Muslim)

Narrated Abu Hurairah ﷺ: Allah's Apostle ﷺ said, "One prayer in my Mosque is better than one thousand prayers in any other mosque excepting Al-Masjid-Al-Haram." (Bukhari)

Narrated Anas ﷺ: When the Prophet ﷺ arrived Medina he dismounted at `Awali-i-Medina amongst a tribe called Banu `Amr bin `Auf. He stayed there for fourteen nights. Then he sent for Bani An-Najjar and they came armed with their swords. As if I am looking (just now) as the Prophet ﷺ was sitting over his Rahila (Mount) with Abu Bakr ﷺ riding behind him and all Banu

An-Najjar around him till he dismounted at the courtyard of Abu Aiyub's house. The Prophet ﷺ loved to pray wherever the time for the prayer was due even at sheep-folds. *Later on he ordered that a mosque should be built* and sent for some people of Banu-An-Najjar and said, "O Banu An-Najjar! Suggest to me the price of this (walled) piece of land of yours." They replied, "No! By Allah! We do not demand its price except from Allah." Anas ﷺ added: There were graves of pagans in it and some of it was unleveled and there were some date-palm trees in it. The Prophet ﷺ ordered that the graves of the pagans be dug out and the unleveled land be leveled and the date-palm trees be cut down . (So all that was done). *They aligned these cut date-palm trees towards the Qibla of the mosque (as a wall) and they also built two stone side-walls (of the mosque).* His companions brought the stones while reciting some poetic verses. The Prophet ﷺ was with them and he kept on saying, "There is no goodness except that of the Hereafter, O Allah! So please forgive the Ansars and the emigrants. (Bukhari)

Narrated `Abdullah bin Zaid Al-Mazini: Allah's Apostle ﷺ said, "Between my house and the pulpit there is a garden of the gardens of Paradise."(Bukhari)

Narrated Abu Hurairah ﷺ: The Holy Prophet ﷺ said, "*Between my house and my pulpit there is a garden of the gardens of Paradise, and my pulpit is on my fountain tank* (i.e. Al-Kauthar)." (Bukhari)

Chapter 5: The Mosque At Quba (In Medina)

[Surah Taubah 9:108] Never stand *(for worship)* in that mosque *; indeed the mosque ** that has been founded on piety from the very first day deserves that you should stand in it; in it are the people who wish to thoroughly cleanse themselves; and Allah loves the clean. *(*The mosque built by the hypocrites. ** The mosque at Quba)*

Narrated Ibn 'Umar ﷺ: The Holy Prophet ﷺ used to go to the Mosque of Quba (sometimes) walking and sometimes riding. Added Nafi` (in another narration), "He then would offer two rak`at (in the Mosque of Quba)." (Bukhari)

Narrated 'Abdullah bin Dinar ﷺ: Ibn 'Umar ﷺ said, "The Prophet ﷺ used to go to the Mosque of Quba every Saturday (sometimes) walking and (sometimes) riding." 'Abdullah (Ibn 'Umar) used to do the same.

The Quba mosque was built by the Holy Prophet ﷺ and his companions. The merit of praying 2 Raka' Nawafil in it is equal to the reward of an Umrah.

Chapter 6: The Prayer At Baitul Maqdis

[Surah b/Israel 17:1] Purity is to Him Who took His bondman in a part of the night from the Sacred Mosque to the Aqsa Mosque around which We have placed blessings, in order that We may show him Our great signs; indeed he is the listener, the beholder. *(This verse refers to the physical journey of Prophet Mohammed ﷺ to Al Aqsa Mosque & and beyond.)*

[Surah Saba 34:13-14] They made for him whatever he wished - synagogues and statues, basins like ponds, and large pots built into the ground; "Be thankful, O the people of Dawud!" And few among My bondmen are grateful. So when We sent the command of death towards him, no one revealed his death to the jinns except the termite of the earth which ate his staff; and when he came to the ground, the truth about the jinns was exposed - if they had known the hidden, they would not have remained in the disgraceful toil.

Narrated Abu Hurairah ﷺ: The angel of death was sent to Moses and when he went to him, Moses slapped him severely, spoiling one of his eyes. The angel went back to his Lord, and said, "You sent me to a slave who does not want to die." Allah restored his eye and said, "Go back and tell him (i.e. Moses) to place his hand over the back of an ox, for he will be allowed to live for a number of years equal to the number of hairs coming under his hand." (So the angel came to him and told him the same). Then Moses asked, "O my Lord! What will be then?" He said, "Death will be then." He said, "(Let it be) now." *He asked Allah that He bring him near the Sacred Land at a distance of a stone's throw.* Allah's Apostle ﷺ said, "Were I there I would show you the grave of Moses by the way near the red sand hill." (Bukhari)

Jibreel ﷺ said: "Alight and pray here." The Holy Prophet ﷺ did so then remounted. Jibreel said: "Do you know where you prayed?" He said no. Jibreel said: "*You prayed in Madyan at the tree of Musa.*" The Burâq continued his lightning flight, then Jibreel said: "Alight and pray here." He did so then remounted, then Jibreel said: "Do you know where you prayed?" He said no. Jibreel said: "*You prayed at the mountain of Sînâ' where Allah addressed Musa.*" Then he reached a land where the palaces of al-Shâm became visible to him. Jibreel said to him: "Alight and pray." He did so and remounted, then the Burâq continued his lightning flight and Jibreel said: "Do you know where you prayed?" He said no. Jibreel said: "*You prayed in Bayt Laham, where `Isa ibn Maryam was born.*"... He continued travelling until he reached the city of the Hallowed House and he entered it by its Southern gate. He dismounted the Burâq and tied it at the gate of the mosque, using the ring by which the Holy Prophet tied it before him. "We entered the mosque from a gate through which the sun and the moon could be seen when they set. I prayed in the mosque for as long as Allah wished." – (Nasai, Baihaqi)

Syedena Zakaria Prayed At the Mehrab of Syedah Maryam

[Surah A/I`mran 3:37-39] So her Lord fully accepted her *(Maryam)*, and gave her an excellent development; and gave her in Zakaria's guardianship; *whenever Zakaria visited her at her place of prayer, he found new food with her*; he said, "O Maryam! From where did this come to you?" She answered, "It is from Allah; indeed Allah gives to whomever He wills, without limit account." *It is here that Zakaria prayed to his Lord*; he said, "My Lord! Give me from Yourself a righteous child; indeed You only are the Listener Of Prayer." And the angels called out to him while he was standing, offering prayer at his place of worship, "Indeed Allah gives you glad tidings of Yahya *(John)*, who will confirm a Word *(or sign)* from Allah, - a leader, always refraining from women, a Prophet from one of Our devoted ones."

The Sahabah prayed where the Holy Prophet prayed

Narrated Yazid bin Al `Ubaid ﷺ: I used to accompany Salama bin Al-Akwa` ﷺ and he used to pray behind the pillar which was near the place where the Qur'ans were kept. I said, "O Abu Muslim! I see you always seeking to pray behind this pillar." He replied, "*I saw Allah's Apostle ﷺ always seeking to pray near that pillar.*" (Bukhari)

Narrated Fudail bin Sulaiman ﷺ: Musa bin `Uqba ﷺ said, "I saw Salim bin `Abdullah looking for some places on the way and prayed there. *He narrated that his father used to pray there, and had seen the Holy Prophet ﷺ praying at those very places.*" (Bukhari)

Narrated Nafi` ﷺ: Whenever Ibn `Umar ﷺ entered the Ka`ba he used to walk straight keeping the door at his back on entering, and used to proceed on till about three cubits from the wall in front of him, and *then he would offer the prayer there aiming at the place where Allah's* Apostle 🌸 *prayed*, as Bilal 🌸 had told him. There is no harm for any person to offer the prayer at any place inside the Ka`ba. (Bukhari)

Narrated Mahmud bin Rabi` Al-Ansari 🌸: `Itban bin Malik 🌸 used to lead his people (tribe) in prayer and was a blind man, he said to Allah's Apostle 🌸, "O Allah's Apostle 🌸! At times it is dark and flood water is flowing (in the valley) and I am blind man, *so please pray at a place in my house so that I can take it as a Musalla (praying place)*." So Allah's Apostle 🌸 went to his house and said, "*Where do you like me to pray?*" 'Itban pointed to a place in his house and Allah's Apostle 🌸, offered the prayer there. (Bukhari)

The Holy Prophet's Prayers during Me'raaj

Angel Jibreel 🌸 said: "Alight and pray here." The Holy Prophet 🌸 did so then remounted. Jibreel 🌸 said: "Do you know where you prayed?" He said no. Jibreel 🌸 said: "*You prayed in Madyan at the tree of Musa*." The Burâq continued his lightning flight, then Jibreel 🌸 said: "Alight and pray here." He did so then remounted, then Jibreel 🌸 said: "Do you know where you prayed?" He said no. Jibreel 🌸 said: "*You prayed at the mountain of Sînâ' where Allah addressed Musa*." Then he reached a land where the palaces of al-Shâm became visible to him. Jibreel 🌸 said to him: "Alight and pray." He did so and remounted, then the Burâq continued his lightning flight and Jibreel 🌸 said: "Do you know where you prayed?" He said no. Jibreel 🌸 said: "*You prayed in Bayt Laham, where `Isa ibn Maryam was born*."... He continued travelling until he reached the city of the Hallowed House and he entered it by its Southern gate. He dismounted the Burâq and tied it at the gate of the mosque, using the ring by which the Holy Prophet 🌸 tied it before him. "We entered the mosque from a gate through which the sun and the moon could be seen when they set. I prayed in the mosque for as long as Allah wished." (Narrated with various chains in Nasai, Baihaqi)

Tabarruk with places the Holy Prophet visited

Narrated Abu Burda 🙵: When I came to Medina, I met Abdullah bin Salam 🙵. He said, "Will you come to me so that I may serve you with Sawiq and dates, and *let you enter a (blessed) house in which the Holy Prophet* 🕊 *entered?*" (Bukhari)

Chapter 8: The Exalted Position of His Grave

Al-`Utbi 🙵, a Sahabi, said: "As I was sitting by the grave of the Holy Prophet 🕊, a Bedouin Arab came and said: "Peace be upon you, O Allah's Apostle! I have heard Allah saying: "and if they, when they have wronged their own souls, come humbly to you *(O dear Prophet Mohammed - peace and blessings be upon him)* and seek forgiveness from Allah, and the Noble Messenger intercedes for them, they will certainly find Allah as the Most Acceptor Of Repentance, the Most Merciful. (4:64)", SO I HAVE COME TO YOU ASKING FORGIVENESS FOR MY SIN, SEEKING YOUR INTERCESSION with my Lord." Then he began to recite poetry: *'O best of those whose bones are buried in the deep earth, And from whose fragrance the depth and the height have become sweet, May I be the ransom for a grave which you inhabit, And in which are found purity, bounty and munificence!'* Then he left, and *I dozed and saw the Holy Prophet in my sleep.* He said to me: "O `Utbi, run after the Bedouin and give him glad tidings that Allah has forgiven him."" (Nawawi, al-Qurtubi, Ibn Kathir, Ibn al-Jawzi)

The Place Touching the Body of the Holy Prophet

It is the consensus of all Ulema that the portion of earth upon which rests the body of the Holy Prophet 🕊 *, is the most superior of all places – better that any place on earth, in the skies or in heaven.*

Angels Beat their Wings on the Holy Prophet's Tomb

Narrated Nubaihah bin Wahab ﷺ: Hazrat Kaab ﷺ went to Syedah Aisha ﷺ and they remembered Allah's Apostle ﷺ. Ka'ab ﷺ said, 'No day dawns but that 70,000 angels descend, *till they go around the tomb of the Allah's Apostle ﷺ striking their wings on it, and sending blessings upon Allah's* Apostle ﷺ; till it is evening and they go up and another like number come down. They will keep on doing this till he comes out of the earth, and he will come out among the 70,000 angels who will be guarding him. (Darimi, Mishkaat).

Narrated Aws ibn Aws ﷺ: The Holy Prophet ﷺ said: Among the most excellent of your days is Friday; on it Adam ﷺ was created, on it he died, on it the last trumpet will be blown, and on it the shout will be made, so invoke more blessings on me that day, for your blessings will be submitted to me. The people asked: Allah's Apostle ﷺ how can it be that our blessings will be submitted to you while your body is decayed? He replied: *Allah, the Exalted, has prohibited the earth from consuming the bodies of Prophets.* (Abu Dawud)

"*The Prophets are alive in their graves. They perform salat.*" (Baihaqi, Ibn 'Asakir, Ibn Hajar)

Narrated `Amr bin Maimun Al-Audi ﷺ: I saw `Umar bin Al-Khattab ﷺ (when he was stabbed) saying, "O `Abdullah bin `Umar! Go to the mother of the believers Aisha and say, `*Umar bin Al-Khattab sends his greetings to you,*' and request her to allow me to be buried with my companions.*" (So, Ibn `Umar conveyed the message to `Aisha ﷺ) She said, "I had the idea of having this place for myself but today I prefer him (`Umar) to myself (and allow him to be buried there)." When `Abdullah bin `Umar returned, `Umar asked him, "What (news) do you have?" He replied, "O chief of the believers! She has allowed you (to be buried there)." *On that `Umar said, "Nothing was more important to me than to be buried in that (sacred) place.* So, when I expire, carry me there and pay my greetings to her (`Aisha) and say, `Umar bin Al-Khattab asks permission; and if she gives permission, then bury me (there) and if she does not, then take me to the graveyard of the Muslims. I do not think any person has more right for the caliphate than those with whom Allah's Apostle ﷺ was always pleased till his death. And whoever is chosen by the people after me will be the caliph, and you people must listen to him and obey him," and then he mentioned the name of `Uthman ؓ, `Ali ؓ, Talha ؓ, Az-Zubair ؓ, `Abdur-Rahman bin `Auf ؓ and Sa`d bin Abi Waqqas ؓ. (Bukhari – part of a longer Hadeeth)

When Syedena Abu Bakr ؓ was nearing his death, he wished to be buried next to the Holy Prophet ﷺ. As per his wishes, his bier was carried to the Holy Prophet's tomb, and the Sahaba ؓ sought permission from the Holy Prophet ﷺ to enter. The lock of the room dropped and the door opened. A voice was heard from inside, proclaiming "Let the beloved one enter – indeed whom he loves, is waiting for him!" The great Caliph ؓ and beloved of the Holy Prophet ﷺ was then buried near him. (Tafseer Kabeer, Khasais Kubra)

Tabarruk with the Tomb of the Holy Prophet

Dawud ibn Salih ؓ says: "Marwan [ibn al-Hakam] one day saw a man placing his face on top of the grave of the Holy Prophet ﷺ. He said: "Do you know what you are doing?" When he came near him, he realized it was Abu Ayyub al-Ansari ؓ. The latter said: *"Yes; I came to the Holy Prophet ﷺ, not to a stone."* (Ibn Hibban, Ahmad, Tabarani, Haythami, al-Hakim)

Mu`adh ibn Jabal ؓ and Bilal ؓ also *came to the grave of the Holy Prophe t ﷺ and sat weeping, and the latter rubbed his face against it.* (Ibn Majah, Ahmad, Tabarani, Subki, Ibn `Asakir.)

The Famine and the Advice of Syedah Aisha

Narrated Abul Jauza ⚜: The people of Medina were once faced by a severe famine. So they complained to Syedah Aisha ⚜, and she said, *"Look towards the grave of the Holy* Prophet ⚜ *and make a ladder towards the sky from there, until there remains no canopy between the grave and the sky."* So they did likewise, and it rained so much that the grass sprouted, and the animals became fat. That year was therefore named as the year of Fateq. (Darimi, Mishkaat).

All Praise is to Allah – and countless blessings & peace be upon his beloved apostle Mohammed – and peace be upon all the noble Prophets – and all his Companions and those who righteously follow him in faith, until the last day.

Suffah Foundation Publications

The Blessed Touch

Who Are Deaf & Blind

Parents – An Islamic Perspective

The Parents of the Prophet ﷺ were Muslim

The Prophet's Ramadhaan

Respect of the Prophet ﷺ

Dhikr in a Raised Voice

Rules of Islamic Law (Qanoon-e-Shariat)

Coming Soon.....

Allah - Lord of All the Worlds

Muhammad ﷺ - Prophet of all Prophets

Ramadhan - The Month of Blessings

101 Islamic Terms

Traditional Scholarship & Modern Misunderstandings

Erasing the Accusation of Shirk

Personal Involvement & Donations

Suffah Foundation is a non-profit making organisation. If you wish to contribute or be part of and further advance the work of Suffah Foundation you can do so by depositing your donations in the accounts below:

Suffah Foundation UK Account

Name: HSBC
Account Number: 74092694
Sort Code: 40-25-10

International Account

Name: HSBC
Account Number (IBAN):   GB36MIDL40251074092694
Branch Identifier Code: MIDLGB2104U

Suffah Foundation wishes to thank you in advance for any donation or involvement. If you would like to contact Suffah Foundation directly you can do so using the following details:

www.suffahfoundation.com

info@suffahfoundation.com

Many Thanks & Jazak'Allah Khair